"What I'm wond[...] "is why someb[...] should have an[...] interest in comets at all."

The defector, Laine Tammsalu, looked seriously at him. "It was not so long ago," she reminded him, "that even sub-orbital rocketry was believed to have little military application."

"Even so, this comet business seems a little far-fetched. What's your guess?"

She was uncomfortable with the question. She was trained in rigid scientific disciplines and found premature extrapolation on insufficient data distasteful. "Are you asking me for—what is the expression I have heard since coming here—a stomach feeling?"

"Gut feeling. Yes, I guess that's what I'm asking for."

"Very well. My gut feeling, for what it is worth, is that Sergei Nekrasov has seen in Project Peter the Great some implication that has escaped other people. It must be something that will give the Soviet Union some kind of advantage, either in space or on the Earth. The advantage will be of a military nature; otherwise a man like Nekrasov would not be interested. Whatever it is, it is something important enough to warrant the personal intervention of the Deputy Premier of the Politboro."

ACT OF GOD

**ERIC KOTANI
AND
JOHN MADDOX
ROBERTS**

BAEN
science fiction
BOOKS

ACT OF GOD

Copyright © 1985 by Eric Kotani and John Maddox Roberts

A Baen Book

Baen Enterprises
8-10 W. 36th Street
New York, N.Y. 10018

First printing, September 1985

ISBN: 0-671-55978-6

Cover art by David Egge

Printed in the United States of America

Distributed by
SIMON & SCHUSTER
MASS MERCHANDISE SALES COMPANY
1230 Avenue of the Americas
New York, N.Y. 10020

To Robert A. Heinlein

PROLOGUE

TUNGUSKA REGION, SIBERIA

June 30, 1908

The Podkamennaya Tunguska River lies in the Central Siberian Upland, a vast region of low mountains covered by pine forest, inhabited largely by reindeer and a few nomadic tribes of hunters and herdsmen. It is one of the remotest, least-inhabited places on Earth. On this June morning of 1908, it is a part of the vast domain of Tsar Nicholas II, although he has little use for it, nor has anybody else, save those who hunt and trap and follow the reindeer. To the south lies the Verkhnaya Tunguska River, which flows from Lake Baikal. To the north is the Nizhnyaya Tunguska River, which throws a loop to the south completely around the valley of the Podkamennaya Tunguska. All three rivers flow into the Yenisey River, which flows north into the Kara Sea, far north of the Arctic Circle. The land is vast and unchanging. But on this June morning, something extraordinary happens, and it happens with extraordinary suddenness.

Reindeer start in panic and primitive men gaze up in fear and wonder as the clear vault of the sky is bisected by the searing path of an immense fireball. Moments later the sky is lit up by an enormous flash. The fireball is visible hundreds of kilometers away, though it endures only a few seconds, to be followed by a titanic shock wave.

Hundreds of kilometers to the south, a driver on the Trans-Siberian Railway thinks his boilers have exploded. When he stops the train passengers tell him of the flash they saw many seconds before from the windows. For hundreds of kilometers around the blast site, houses are shaken, windows are broken and people are knocked off their feet. The blast is registered in London, thousands of kilometers away.

Within hours, news of the mysterious event is telegraphed around the world. A meteorite fall is assumed and expeditions to the site are proposed. But mounting an expedition is no small endeavor; the Tsar is preoccupied with more important matters, and to the rest of the world central Siberia is less accessible than the remotest parts of Africa. Most of the year it is locked in winter of Arctic severity and accessible only briefly in spring and summer. Besides, there are many other matters of great scientific interest afoot in 1908, and while a large meteorite strike is interesting, it is hardly unique.

Gradually, Siberian nomads emerge from the area, with strange tales of forests laid flat and herds of reindeer slain. Miraculously, it seems that not a single human being has been killed or even injured by the blast. Much is made of this in later years. There are very few places on land where a blast of such magnitude could have taken place without the loss of a single human life.

Over the years, proposals for expeditions to find the Tunguska meteorite are proposed, but Russia is involved first in revolution, then in civil war.

Not until 1927, nineteen years after the event, does an expedition penetrate into the remote region. What they find is unbelievable. Even after nearly two decades the forests remain flattened, the trunks of the trees radiating from the center of the blast like spokes of a wheel. The magnitude of the blast that caused such destruction staggers the imagination. At the center of this devastation must lie a giant crater.

There is no crater. Instead, at the very center, trees still stand. They are stripped of branches and foliage and much of their bark, but they still stand. Perhaps the giant meteor broke up just before striking; a search is made for smaller craters. Many small depressions are found but they turn out to be a natural phenomenon of the region, unrelated to the blast. Later expeditions find tiny meteoric particles, nothing more. All of them together could not mass enough to account for more than the tiniest fraction of the colossal blast of 1908. The mystery seems unsolvable.

Over the years the Tunguska event becomes a favorite with the wilder fringes of science. With each discovery of physics, with each new fad of pseudo-science the event is reexamined, often with more enthusiasm than precision, and applied to the new sensation. At last A-bomb and H-bomb testing reveals the torus or "donut" effect of aerial nuclear blasts and it is recalled that the trees were still standing at the center of the Tunguska blast. The torus effect would cause just such a phenomenon. A natural H-bomb from space is speculated, although how such a natural bomb could be constituted is never satisfactorily explained.

The great UFO fad brings the suggestion that the engines of a damaged spaceship had exploded. Perhaps the controllers of the craft, knowing that it was doomed, steered it to a spot where it was unlikely humans would be harmed. The Arctic or an ocean seems an even better choice for a harmless blast, but the idea remains attractive to enthusiasts.

Next, it is pointed out that the collision of a small particle of antimatter with the Earth's atmosphere might cause something resembling the Tunguska event. Where it came from, or how it survived the trip (the vacuum of space isn't quite a vacuum) is not explained.

Then the media are full of the black hole concept. The Tunguska event is unearthed again. Maybe the Earth collided with a black hole, a very small one. The superdense object went right through the planet, in at Siberia, making a hole too small to detect, out through the ocean on the other side. Why this would generate an aerial blast effect is not explained.

Except when under the influence of alchohol or whatever, responsible scientists refrain from such speculations. That the event occurred is beyond dispute, but scientists require reliable data in order to draw conclusions. The event is too long past, the recording instruments of the period too few, too primitive and too far away from the event. The eyewitness accounts differ radically, and every policeman knows how unreliable eyewitness accounts are even minutes after an event occurs. When the event witnessed is something outside human experience, eyewitness accounts are little better than useless. Until a similar event can be observed and properly quantified the Tunguska event will remain a mystery.

And so, until the final decade of the Twentieth Century, the Tunguska event remained.

CHAPTER ONE

TSIOLKOVSKY SPACE CENTER

KAZAKH REPUBLIC, U.S.S.R.

The automobile stopped before the administration building, its tires raising a small cloud of dust from the dirt road. A young man emerged from the vehicle and climbed the steps which still smelled of new-cut pine. At the top of the steps he turned and admired the view. The administration building stood on high ground, and below him stretched the still-growing expanse of roads and buildings that was the world's newest space center. Beyond the center was the Aral Sea, but the facility did not end at the shore. Gigantic piers crowned with gantries and spidery structures of steel and glass linked water and land. The sight filled him with awe. Something unprecedented was being done here. That was why the project was being carried out here, instead of at the old space center. He was proud to be a part of all this.

The young man turned and went inside. He had to walk carefully over the wrinkled cloths that covered the floor, littered with brushes and empty paint cans. The workmen who desultorily stroked the walls were short slit-eyed Uzbeks, brought across the Aral by boat. Like most of the laborers here, they had been chosen because they spoke no Russian and were illiterate in their own tongue. He walked to the desk that guarded the Director's door, where a strikingly handsome young woman sat. She looked up at his approach.

"Is the Director in?" he asked.

"Yes. What is your name and your business with the Director, please?" She had a lovely smile and a voice that took the edge off the dry, bureaucratic demands. He could not quite place her accent. Finnish? Lithuanian? From that area, he was sure. That fitted with her blonde good looks.

"Alexei Ilyich Kamarovsky. I'm here to take him to the air strip. There's a visitor arriving, you know."

"Ah," she said, "*that* visitor." She pushed a button on an intercom.

"Comrade Tarkovsky, a Comrade Kamarovsky to see you."

"Just a moment." The rumbling voice had a trace of the power that had made hundreds of students and subordinates quake.

"I haven't seen you here before," Alexei Ilyich said. "Are you the Director's new secretary?"

"No," she said, again with the dazzling smile. He noted that her teeth were rather large, but at least none of them were steel. None of the visible ones, in any case. He wasn't so sure about the molars. "I'm an astronomer. His usual secretary lives in my dorm. She's been sick all week and the rest of us have been standing in for her. Mostly, it's been me. I got here last month and found that the bureau where I'm supposed to work won't be ready to operate until October. Until then, I'm everybody's stand-in."

"Typical," Alexei said. Then he caught himself

and looked about guiltily. Had anyone noticed his disloyal acknowledgement of official inefficiency? Probably not. It was the kind of thing everyone joked about, but not in front of strangers. He glanced at the Uzbeks. You never know.

"Where did you come in from?" he asked, to change the subject. "Lithuania?"

"Close," she said. "I'm from Mustvee, on Lake Peipus in Estonia." He tried to bring up a mental picture of the place, but all he could remember was something about Alexander Nevsky fighting the Teutonic Knights on the frozen lake. There had been a movie about it, once. He'd seen it on television. The music had been by Prokofiev.

"Send him in," said the rumbling voice.

"I'll see you later," Alexei said. He hoped that he would. She was the first remotely attractive woman he had seen since moving to this wilderness of Asiatics. He went through the still-unpainted door.

Even in this short time, the old man had managed to turn his office into a total wreck. The floor was littered with paper; books were stacked everywhere. Food scraps littered the desk and dishes and teacups overflowed with cigarette butts. In a corner stood an old-fashioned samovar. The massive man behind the desk wore an ill-fitting suit that was years out of date. His shaggy hair was still mostly black, white about the ears. The face was that of a bulldog who has been bashed across the nose with a hockey stick. He looked up from his slide rule. Despite the availability of Japanese calculators, Tarkovsky still preferred the slide rule. He had been known to win hundreds of rubles in bets with mathematicians who thought they could work out problems faster with one of the little Japanese miracles.

"Come in, Alyosha," Tarkovsky said. He had

known Alexei's father for many years and could use the familiar form. "What do you want?"

"I think you know, Comrade Tarkovsky," Ivan said. Had the matter not been so serious, he would have addressed the director as "Pyotr Maximovich".

"Oh, sit down, Alyosha," Tarkovsky said. He opened a drawer and rummaged around until he found a bottle of vodka. "Here, have a drink." He poured a generous dollop into a none-too-clean teacup.

"Pyotr Maximovich," Alexei fumed impatiently, "I'm to take you to the air strip. We can't let our visitor land and wait for you."

"That's better," Tarkovsky said. The younger man refused to touch the cup so Tarkovsky drank it himself. "Visitor," he said, turning the innocent word into an obscenity appreciable only to another Russian. "Another damned politician down from Moscow. Do they think I have nothing better to do? Do they think my space city is—" he waved his hands expressively, searching for the word, "—what's that place in Caifornia, where Khrushchev wanted to go? Disneyland? Yes, do they think this is Disneyland and I am some kind of tour guide?"

Alexei winced slightly. He hoped there were no listening devices in the room. "This is a fairly high-powered politician we're to meet, Comrade Tarkovsky," Alexei reminded him.

Tarkovsky snorted. "Deputy Premier. How many of those have come and gone in my time? I can't keep count. How many men in the Soviet Union could hold that job? You could, Alyosha. One of those Tartars out there painting could. How many men could direct this project?"

Alexei sighed. "Only you, Pyotr Maximovich."

"Remember it. He'd better remember it, too." He tossed off the last of the vodka in the glass, dropped the bottle back in the drawer, shut the drawer. "Let's go meet this big shot," he said.

The automobile drove out the bumpy road past the docks, past the workers' housing, to the airstrip. There was a small airport building standing beneath the control tower. Most of what came here arrived by rail.

Tarkovsky got out of the car and stood with head hunched between his shoulders, hands in pockets. Both airstrip and sky were innocent of aircraft. "Damned Moscow pimp," he muttered, "I knew he'd be late."

"Here it comes," Alexei said, hearing the engines of the Ilyushin. Tarkovsky's look brightened as the aircraft came into view, but not for the passenger. He admired the sleek lines of the new aircraft, an outrageously expensive supersonic transport designed to fly better, higher, faster than anything the Americans had.

"That's beautiful," he said. "That's worth the trip out here." The aircraft landed, tiny puffs of smoke rising from its tires. It braked, turned, and taxied to the building where Tarkovsky and Alexei waited. By now, a number of other scientists and administrators had arrived to greet the great man. First to emerge from the Ilyushin was a tall, thin, bespectacled man with a shiny scalp.

"Look at him," Tarkovsky muttered so only Alexei could hear. "Head shaved slick as an Army recruit's. Maybe I'll address him as 'Comrade Private'."

"Pyotr Maximovitch," Alexei said urgently, "if you have no respect for what he is, at least remember what he used to be."

Tarkovsky was silent. That was one thing he didn't want to think about. The new Deputy Premier of the Politburo who was walking toward him was Sergei Nekrasov, and Sergei Nekrasov was, until his promotion, head of the KGB.

"Comrade Director Tarkovsky?" Nekrasov asked, holding forth a hand.

"The same," Tarkovsky said. The hand he shook was firm and dry. Everything about Nekrasov seemed dry. His skin, his shiny scalp, his voice, even the eyeballs behind the thick spectacles looked dry. Behind Nekrasov were several faceless men, so featureless that Tarkovsky had trouble counting them. KGB, he thought.

"You honor us with your visit," Tarkovsky said. In spite of his contemptuous words to Alexei, he felt distinctly nervous in the Deputy Premier's presence. Even the greatest scientist had to acknowledge the supremacy of the KGB, which the Deputy Premier probably still ran, despite his change of title. "Will you allow me to show you our new facility?" Nekrasov and Tarkovsky got into the rear of the staff car. One of the faceless men got in beside the driver. The faceless man carried a briefcase, presumably Nekrasov's. Alexei was left behind to return with the others.

Tarkovsky pointed out all the features of the modern spaceport, beginning in a bored, tour-guide fashion, but growing more animated as the tour progressed, unable to repress his enthusiasm for the project. As much as any single man can accomplish anything in the Soviet Union, the Tsiolkovsky Space Center was *his* creation. Nekrasov nodded politely and asked pertinent questions, but it was clear that space science was not of great interest to him, beyond its military applications. Tarkovsky wondered why the man had come.

At Nekrasov's direction, they drove out onto one of the piers and emerged from the car. Workmen nudged one another. Everyone recognized Tarkovsky, but who was the bald man? Somebody important, that was clear from the transportation and his fine, foreign-tailored suit. They tried to recall

his face. Was it one they saw on the balcony overlooking the May Day parades in Red Square? If so,
it was too far down the left end of the lineup of
notables to be remembered. They shrugged and
went back to work.

Nekrasov kicked at the steel decking and sniffed
the fresh breeze off the Aral. The big piers en-
closed wide basins. "It looks more like a naval
base than a space facility." He looked up. The sky
was clear, with some cumulus clouds massing on
the southern horizon. "I wonder what the Americans are making of all this? They must have plenty
of satellite pictures by now."

"If one just passed overhead," Tarkovsky said,
"some American will be studying your expression
this evening. Their high-resolution cameras are that
sensitive. We got orders just last week not to let
any sensitive documents be exposed to aerial surveillance. Personally, I don't believe their cameras
are that good, but one never knows."

"The order came from my office," Nekrasov said.

Tarkovsky's shaggy eyebrows went up a trifle.
Security orders for his project emanating from the
Deputy Premier's office? That sounded ominous.
This was no routine visit. He knew he was about
to hear some bad news.

"Let's take a walk," Nekrasov said. He set out
toward the end of the pier, nearly a third of a
kilometer out over the sea. Behind them, the brief-
cased KGB man trailed at a discreet distance. As he
walked, Nekrasov made polite conversation and
Tarkovsky was aware that every word was loaded.

"I've been keeping current with your end of Project Peter the Great, Comrade Tarkovsky. I'm very
keen on the space sciences, you see." Tarkovsky
knew this to be a falsehood but he let it pass. Like
most such men, Nekrasov was an ignoramus in
everything except power.

"Project Peter the Great is just one of many we shall be carrying out at this facility, Comrade Nekrasov, although I admit it's my pet. Since you have been studying it, you realize there are many experiments I wished to have included in it, but the budget—"

"I wish to speak to you about that." Nekrasov stared out at the piling clouds to the south as if trying to forecast the weather. He nodded to the KGB man and was handed the briefcase. The faceless man backed away out of hearing range. Nekrasov reached into the briefcase and withdrew a sheaf of papers. Tarkovsky recognized the title. It was one of his own scientific papers, but it now bore a security stamp above the title that had never been there before.

"Two years ago," Nekrasov continued, "this paper was brought to my attention. Do you recognize it?"

"My paper concerning the Tunguska event," Tarkovsky said. He wondered which of his colleagues had shown Nekrasov the paper. Probably no friend of his. His sense of foreboding increased.

"A most fascinating document, Comrade. Its implications struck me immediately. I have also read your complete, original proposal for Project Peter the Great. Far too grandiose, I was told, far too expensive."

Tarkovsky shrugged, hands in pockets. "It's how these projects work the world over. One proposes the optimum in hopes of receiving the minimum."

"Short-sighted fools," Nekrasov said. "They couldn't see what this means. Comrade Tarkovsky, from now on, my office is in full charge of Project Peter the Great. All results will be reported directly to me." Tarkovsky was stunned, but he was well-schooled in hiding such things. Nekrasov continued: "You will receive the fullest possible funding to carry out your project as first proposed."

"Comrade Nekrasov," Tarkovsky pointed out, "this will mean stripping half the projects in our entire space program."

"Just send your requests through my office," Nekrasov said. "If your colleagues have any complaints, they may address them to me." An oblique way of saying that there would be no complaints. "As of now, this project has Class One priority, right along with our missile defenses. It is also under maximum security." He took several more papers from the briefcase and handed them to Tarkovsky. "Here are the names of persons you have here who are no longer to work on the project. All of them are security risks."

Tarkovsky scanned the list. "But these are eminently qualified personnel, Comrade," he protested. "Some of them I have worked with for years. I am not sure I can carry out the project without them."

"Nonsense," Nekrasov said, coldly. "Your field is space science, Comrade Tarkovsky. Leave state security to me." A not-so-oblique reminder of his former position. "Dismiss these people. Other positions, less sensitive, will be found for them. Then send me a list of persons to replace them. Make it a long list, with at least three hundred percent redundancy factor. Many of those you propose will also have to be vetoed for security reasons."

Tarkovsky was stunned. Did this KGB paranoid think that qualified people were as easy to find as strongarm men for his goon squads? Even so, a Class One priority meant that he could transfer in personnel from almost any other space project. He had never had such power, such a budget, at his disposal. Very few Soviet scientists ever had. But it meant that Peter the Great was no longer his project. As of now, it belonged to Sergei Nekrasov. He lit one of his coarse, cheap cigarettes, stalling.

"Comrade, I have been involved with our space effort as long as there has been a Soviet space program. I am sure that none of my colleagues has ever received such a *carte blanche.* . . ."

"You want to know whether I have the authority to do this?" Nekrasov asked, bluntly. "I assure you that I have. Do you think such a thing could be carried out without the full support of the *highest* authority?" His glare was in no way mitigated by the thickness of his lenses. "Believe me, Comrade Tarkovsky, as closely as I shall be watching this project, they will be watching me."

Tarkovsky smoked the raw tobacco without tasting it. He had just been told that the Deputy Premier's future was in his hands. Failure might well prove fatal.

"It can be done, Comrade Nekrasov," he said. "Just as I proposed it. It will be done."

CHAPTER TWO

WASHINGTON, D.C.

Sam Taggart slapped his alarm clock into silence as he rolled from his bed. He ached all over. The months of therapy had put him back in operating condition, but it would be a long time before all the effects of his injuries wore off. He crossed the Spartan little efficiency apartment and went into the bathroom, switching on lights as he went. At six o'clock on a winter morning, Washington was still dark.

He splashed water into his bleary eyes, brushed his teeth and shaved. He was deeply tanned in winter because he had been recuperating in Florida. Against the tanned skin, the new scars on flank, chest and shoulder were pale pink. There were also older, whiter scars. Before leaving the bathroom he stepped on the scale and noted that he was still about ten pounds below his normal weight. He decided to step up his exercise program at the gym no matter what the damned doctors said and add a few more calories to his diet.

He dressed and went downstairs and across the

street to the early-opening diner where he usually had breakfast. He ordered ham and eggs and pancakes and hash brown potatoes, deciding to put his higher-calorie regimen into effect immediately. The waitress, who was familiar with his habits, left a pot of coffee on his table. She studied him from behind the counter as she waited for the cook to fix his order. He hadn't been in for a long time, and he had changed a little since she had last seen him. He was a little thinner, for one thing, and he hadn't had a whole lot of weight to spare in the first place. The skin was stretched more tautly across his prominent cheek bones. His already broken nose looked as if it had been broken again. Most of her early-morning customers were government workers heading toward their jobs. If he was a government man, it wasn't a desk job he was holding down.

Taggart read the newspaper while he waited for his order, downing half the coffeepot in the process. The news was about as bad as it had been every day of his life, no change there. The usual little wars were in progress. More little wars were expected soon in the usual hot spots. Typical day. His order arrived and he ate, listening to the inanities from the radio behind the counter. Afterwards, he got into his old Chevrolet and drove across town to a nondescript building in a nondescript neighborhood.

Inside, he stopped at a desk and picked up his ID badge. The man behind the desk grinned at him and shook his hand. "Good to see you again, Mr. Taggart. How are you feeling?"

"OK," Taggart said, slightly annoyed at the concern. "Is Morgan in?"

"He came in about fifteen minutes ago. Said for you to check in with him first thing."

"Thanks." Taggart pinned the ID badge to his

lapel and walked past the desk. The desk man watched him to see if he was moving unsteadily, but Taggart seemed to be in pretty good shape, if a little on the thin side. Not bad, all things considered. Getting four bullets cut out was no picnic.

Taggart took an elevator to the fifth floor and knocked on Morgan's door. "Come in." He went in and Morgan, a tall, beefy man in an expensive suit, stood and grinned and shook his hand. "Sit down, Sam. Good to have you back. How're you feeling?"

"Fine. The doc says I'm about ninety-five percent."

"Good. That's good to hear, Sam. Too bad about that last assignment. I want you to know I think you did the right thing."

"Of course I did the right thing. Who says I didn't?"

"Easy, Sam. Nobody does. Still, getting shot full of holes is considered by some to be an unwise move."

"Now, hold on a minute, nobody said—"

"It's a closed matter, Sam," Morgan said icily. "Now, I said I had something for you. We're going over to State to talk to a defector."

Taggart calmed himself with an effort. He knew his position with the agency was precarious. Best to play it cool. "A defector? That's not my kind of action. I'm a field man."

"Of course. But ninety-five percent's not good enough for field work. You've got to be one hundred percent."

"All right, I'll go along with that. What kind of defector, military or intelligence?"

"Neither. This one's an astronomer."

Sam wasn't sure whether to be incredulous or insulted. He decided on both. "You can't be serious. What good is a Russian astronomer?"

"Not Russian. Estonian."

"Jesus. A defecting astronomer from a satellite state. Is somebody trying to tell me something?"

Morgan was perfectly bland, which for him indicated intense satisfaction. "Only that someone thinks this is important enough to demand an operative of your caliber, Sam."

Taggart sat in stony silence during the drive to State. He had worked with defectors before, in the days before he got important field assignments. Mostly they had been high-up people from opposition intelligence agencies, people who needed protection and who had to be escorted by someone trained in eliciting and handling sensitive information. Once he'd nursemaided a Czech general for two months, picking up some good Warsaw Pact intelligence in the process. As much as a Czech general would be trusted with, at any rate. That was a long time ago. Being put back on that kind of duty was like a police captain finding himself back in uniform and pounding a beat.

At State, they had to go through the same rigmarole about ID tags before being allowed into the sanctum. They were guided along featureless corridors and past featureless rooms. Sam knew for a fact that these rooms were mostly inhabited by featureless people, which was a major reason that he had opted for hazardous field work as soon as he had suffcent seniority. Just being here was depressing.

In one of the rooms they met Steinberg, a man Taggart knew very slightly. Morgan walked over to a small window in one wall. "That her?" he asked.

A woman? Taggart took a look. The window was a one-way mirror. Sitting in the next room at a table was an attractive young blonde. He guessed her age at about twenty-five. She was nervously smoking, holding her cigarette in the underhanded style of Eastern Europe. She looked tired.

"Not bad duty, Sam," Morgan said. "I never got to work with a looker like that."

"Why's she important?" Taggart asked. "I'm told she's an astronomer. Something to do with missiles or something?"

Steinberg shook his head. "No, she's never been entrusted with anything really sensitive. You know they hardly ever let anybody from the satellites in on the really big stuff. No, she's been employed on scientific research since graduating from school. Some pretty important projects, though."

"Her?" Taggart said. "She's just a kid."

"Look again," Steinberg told him. "She's thirty, and her father was a pretty famous scientist, too."

"I have some things to do back at the office," Morgan told them. "I'll leave you two to it. Sam, don't let her get away from you." He left smiling. Taggart watched as the door shut behind him. Then he turned to Steinberg.

"So I'm going to nursemaid a defecting astronomer, huh? When do they put me on defecting athletes and musicians? This one looks like she could be one of those ballerinas they have such a hard time keeping."

Steinberg looked at him levelly. "As I understand it, Mr. Taggart, you were lucky to get even this."

"That's the word, is it? I'm glad to hear it from somebody at last." It wasn't as if he hadn't been expecting it.

"Word has it you're a prize eight-ball, Taggart. You've been losing friends fast, lately. They say you've gotten trigger-happy. Your agency's trying to play down that kind of action these days. It's bad publicity, bad for appropriations. I think you need to keep a low profile for a while."

"Yeah. No doubt. Well, if she doesn't know anything why don't you just turn her loose? The country's full of people like her. Half our instructors back in Army Intelligence school were satellite defectors. Hell, we even had real Russians."

"She's got an odd story," Steinberg said. "I don't know, there's probably nothing to it, but as long as there's a chance, we're supposed to look into it. I'll let her tell you about it herself. Come on, it's time for you to meet your charge."

They went into the little interrogation room and the woman looked up with weary, frightened eyes. "Miss Tammsalu," Steinberg said, "this is Sam Taggart. He'll be working with you."

Laine Tammsalu studied the man who had just come in. He was tall and rangy and good-loking in a tough sort of way. Men of his physical type were the kind that American movies always cast as cowboy heroes and Russian movies as fascists. He nodded at her curtly, clearly none too happy with his work. That did not look good. She had been hoping that the Americans would take her seriously. "Good day. Are you a scientist, Mr. Taggart?"

"No, I'm a grunt."

"I beg your pardon?" She was unfamiliar with the word and unsure that she had heard him correctly.

"I'm a standard field operative, Miss Tammsalu. No scientific background whatever."

"I see."

"Yeah, well, I was hoping for something else, too. What's the nature of your information?"

Tammsalu looked pleadingly at Steinberg. "Please, I have gone over this so many times. Must I do it again? At least, get me to somebody who will understand what I have to say."

"Sam, I think I can give you the gist of what Miss Tammsalu's told us," Steinberg said. "She is an astronomer, and has lived most of her life in her homeland, Estonia. Until just prior to her defection, she was assigned to a new Soviet space center on the north shore of the Aral Sea. Shortly after her security status was changed, she got an approval to attend an astronomical conference in Yugoslavia, where she managed to cross the border into Italy. She went to the American consul in Trieste and applied for sponsorship through the Estonian-American Society. She's been in debriefing for a week, now."

"Why was your security clearance withdrawn, Miss Tammsalu?" Sam asked.

"When I left Estonia," she said, undoubtedly for the hundredth time, "it was to work at the new Tsiolkovsky Space Center under Pyotr Tarkovsky." Taggart glanced at Steinberg.

"We have a file on him," Steinberg said. "Top Russian astrophysicist. One of the best in the world, but he's seldom been involved in military or defense-oriented work."

"I was to work on Tarkovsky's Project Peter the Great," Laine continued. "It was one of several important scientific projects to be initiated from Tsiolkovsky Center. One day, we received a visit from Sergei Nekrasov—a routine inspection, we all thought at the time."

For the first time, Taggart began to feel a stirring of interest. Nekrasov. He knew that name, for sure. No longer head of KGB, but the new head was rumored to be Nekrasov's man. Sergei Nekrasov was little known in the outside world, but real Kremlin-watchers considered him one of the four or five top up-and-comers among the present generation of Soviet leadership.

"The next day," she continued, "people began to be dropped from the project. Almost all personnel who were not Russian-born were dropped immediately. It was put under highest secrecy status and rumor had it that Tarkovsky was to report only to Nekrasov, that Nekrasov was taking personal charge."

"Do we have anything on this Project Peter the Great?" Sam asked Steinberg.

"Not a thing. It's not a military project and you know how they like to play their space stuff close to the vest."

"What does this project involve?" Sam asked Laine.

"Well, it is a comet research project involving a rendezvous of a spacecraft with a comet, and possibly a soft landing on the cometary nucleus, if sufficient resources were allocated."

Taggart sat and stared at her for several seconds. Then he got up. "Excuse me for a minute, Miss Tammsalu. Steinberg, let's step outside." He waited until the soundproof door was closed behind them before he turned to Steinberg. "Comets! What the hell is this? How in God's name has this got anything to do with state security? I know comets were big stuff in political circles in the old days; foretold the death of kings and the outcome of big battles and all that. Not lately, though. Is this somebody's idea of a joke?"

"I'll give it to you as straight as I can, Taggart. Nobody can make anything out of this, but every test we've got says the woman's telling the truth. If Nekrasov's in charge and a security lid's been clamped on the project there's got to be something of interest there."

"It's a goddamn red herring, is what it is," Taggart fumed. "It's a distraction. Let me guess: she was planning to defect even before her security clearance was withdrawn, right?"

"Right," Steinberg admitted reluctantly.

"So they found out about it and decided to make

use of her. You said yourself she had no trouble getting across the border. They loaded her up with this stuff so she could spill it to us and still be telling the truth as far as she knows it. It's not the first time they've done this kind of thing."

"That's been thought of," Steinberg said. "But this is a little clumsy, don't you think? Why not something more believable than comets?"

"It's working, isn't it?" Taggart said. "It's costing us time and attention we should be using on really important matters."

"It's your baby, Taggart. Until you're pulled off of it, you're to investigate. You've got the usual expense account. It's going to call for some travel. You'll probably be talking to a lot of scientists in the next few weeks."

"How the hell can I investigate when I don't even know what kind of questions to ask? She's right: If there *is* anything to this, she needs a scientist with her, not a grunt."

"It's your baby, Taggart," Steinberg reiterated coldly.

Wearily, Sam turned and reentered the interrogation room.

"You're free to go now, Miss Tammsalu," Steinberg said. "Mr. Taggart here will be your liaison with us. He'll see to all your travel arrangements. I know that these next few days will be difficult for you, Miss Tammsalu. It's never easy to relocate in a new country, but I think that Mr. Taggart will be of great assistance to you. If we can help in any way, please feel free to call on us."

"Yes, thank you," she said, knowing a pro forma offer when she heard one.

"Where are you staying?" Sam asked her.

"A hotel called the Wildner, on Connecticut Avenue."

"I know where it is. Come on, I'll drive you

over. Maybe we can have lunch somewhere on the way."

In the parking garage beneath the building, they got into Taggart's handsome red-and-white automobile. She was still having trouble adjusting to the sheer number of such vehicles she encountered every day. Where she had come from, possession of such a machine would have typed Taggart as somebody of importance. Here, as she was finding out, it merely meant that he was beyond his early teens and not blind.

"What kind of car is this?" she asked, not really interested, but wanting to end the man's sullen silence, which had made her uncomfortable. He patted the dashboard and she saw him smile for the first time, very slightly.

" '56 Chevy Bel Air. 'Chevy' is short for Chevrolet. This one and the '57 from the same company are the best products ever to come out of Detroit."

"So old?" she said. She had never heard of an old car being a status symbol. She had always thought that the newer the auto, the higher the standing of the user. He drove up out of the building and out into the traffic. His smile faded and he resumed the frown he had worn earlier, his momentary good humor at an end. Several times, in traffic, she saw people looking at them. That had always been a danger signal to her, but then she realized that they were admiring the Chevrolet.

"Your car has admirers," she said.

"Just wait," he said with another small smile. "Before we get to your hotel, somebody'll try to buy if off me. Custom car freaks love these old Chevys. They'll chop and channel them, jack up the rear end and fit them with oversized rear wheels, install superchargers, all kinds of crap like that. I keep this one just like it was when it came out of the showroom, though." She understood less than half of what he said, but it seemed to be a safe subject.

He pulled in at a small restaurant. It was early yet for lunch and the place was almost empty, but he went to a table at the rear of the dining room, near the kitchen entrance. He took a chair against the wall. She would have preferred a table near the front window, but she sensed that this was a habit with him. A waitress brought them menus and she scanned the lengthy list. So many dishes, and so few of them were fish. They ordered and he lapsed into silence once again. She found this annoying.

"Mr. Taggart, I am sorry that your assignment displeases you. I assure you that it was none of my doing."

He looked at her with what seemed to be genuine surprise. "I know that. It's certainly not you that's bothering me and I'm sorry if I've given offense."

The response startled her. She had expected an ill-tempered outburst. "What is it, then, if I may ask?"

He thought for a while, then: "I'm not really sure how to put this to you. Do you know what UFOs are?"

Caught off-balance by the obliquity of the question, she had to think for a moment. "Do you mean unidentified flying objects? Flying saucers?"

"Right. People are reporting them all the time. There are whole organizations devoted to studying them. They're always getting on the Air Force to study them, too. Some of them insist that the Air Force is hiding information about UFOs, so the Air Force had to establish a bureau to investigate UFO reports and convince people that they're not hiding anything."

"And so?" she asked, mystified.

"Well, I had a friend once, an Air Force officer. He had some problems which we won't go into just now, but they were causing him a lot of trouble with his career. One day, he found himself assigned to UFO investigations. You see, in the Air Force, assignment to that bureau is usually the kiss of death. Nobody in the Air Force takes it seriously, it's just a public relations gimmick they came up with to placate a bunch of crackpots. He told me that he knew it was time to resign his commission and return to civilian life."

She was not stupid. She saw immediately where this was leading. "Have you just been assigned to UFO investigations, Mr. Taggart?"

"I'm afraid so. When my boss told me this morning that I was going to work with a defector, I knew I had trouble. When I learned that the defector wasn't military or intelligence, I knew it was deep trouble. When I heard that bit about the comets, I knew I'd been kissed off."

"So, your government really is not interested in what I had to tell them? They think I am just another crackpot, like your UFO enthusiasts? Then why are they bothering? What will they do with our findings?"

"They'll make up a file. They're great ones for filing things. They'll look like they're keeping busy. And I'll be out of their way for a while."

"Is that a matter of some importance to them?" She did not want to rub salt in his wounds, but she had to know.

"It's beginning to look like it. You see, people like my straw boss, Morgan, or that man Steinberg back there, they're desk men. I'm a field operative. They call us spooks or cowboys but we just call ourselves grunts. That's a word that came out of the Viet Nam war. It meant an infantryman, a ground-pounder. Now it means the people who go out and put it on the line. The expendable ones."

Despite his colloquialisms, she could understand most of what he was saying. "There is little love then, between the desk men and the 'grunts'?"

In spite of himself, he had to grin at the pronunciation she put on the last word. He'd never heard it said that way. "Very little. And less every day. Years ago, they made heroes of us. It was taken for granted that we were in a war, even if it was an unofficial one, and rough stuff was expected. We got our assignments and we went out and accomplished them. Or we failed and that usually meant we didn't come back. In any case the hero stuff was a lot of crap but at least we were pretty free to do what had to be done.

"Now, they don't want field operatives to have any autonomy. And they don't like rough work. That's supposed to be a relic of the bad old days, before we all got civilized and polite. It seems that I'm a relic of the bad old days, too. My last couple of jobs got pretty rough."

Their orders arrived. So this was one of the American hatchetmen she had been hearing about all her life from official propaganda. He certainly looked tough enough, but he didn't seem to be a sadistic maniac. But then, she thought, what does a sadistic maniac look like? He had ordered the biggest steak she had ever seen. Americans, apparently, were beef fanatics. His potato looked like something that belonged in a sporting event. She had ordered only a salad, but even that shocked her. She had seen smaller gardens.

"Anyway," he went on, "the time came, as it had to, when I muffed one. I won't go into the details, which I'm not free to discuss anyway, but I got shot up pretty bad. Nothing much to be done about it, I took the only course open as I saw it, but it cost me. They had to put up with my cowboy antics as long as I turned in positive results, but they can be unforgiving when an operation goes sour. This is the first assignment I've been handed since that one. I was wondering what it would be."

"And now you know?"

"Now I know." He wasn't sure why he was telling her all this. It was none of her business.

She studied him differently this time. She should have seen the signs, she thought, but she was still unused to this alien physiognomy. His extreme gauntness was unnatural, but she came from a place where most people were either gaunt or overweight by American standards, and she was not used to deeply tanned men. Now that she knew what to look for, she could see that he was only recently recovered from severe illness or injury. Not fully recovered, at that. At least there was nothing unhealthy about his appetite. She would not have believed that a human organism could absorb so much protein without going into shock, but the steak was disappearing fast. She was more circumspect with her salad. The vegetables were excellent, but the dressing was unfamiliar. She supposed she would adjust. She had a lot of adjusting to do.

"Mr. Taggart—"she began.

"Make it Sam," he said, "since we'll be working together for a while." His tone conveyed little enthusiasm for the prospect.

This must be the famous American informality. "Sam, then. Despite what your people think, I believe that what has happened to Project Peter the Great is terribly dangerous."

"Do you think it's being used as some kind of coverup for a new military weapon? Something nuclear, or something along the lines of the satellite-killers we keep hearing about?"

She shook her head. "No. The boosters were already being brought in before I was dismissed. They are quite unsuitable for anything of a ballistic nature. These are for placing massive payloads into near Earth orbit. They are bigger than the ones used in your moon shots. Of course, the expedition proper would be launched from a permanent space station in orbit."

"Expedition? Are we talking about a *manned* shot?"

She made an expressively uncertain gesture with her hands. "I do not know. That was one of Tarkovsky's proposals but I do not think he seriously hoped to get funding for such a thing. Still, I don't see how an unmanned mission could have much significance beyond pure scientific research. Nekrasov would have no interest in simple data-gathering."

"What I'm wondering," Taggart said, "is why somebody like Nekrasov should have any interest in comets at all. I've heard that Hitler was pretty buggy about lights in the sky, but it's hard to picture a former KGB boss worrying about them."

A little stiffly, she said: "Mr. —Sam, you must not confuse astrology with astronomy, they are—"

"Hell, I know that," he interrupted. He reminded himself ruefully that her command of the language did not necessarily qualify her to recognize such subtleties as irony or even heavy sarcasm. "I was being facetious. My point is that I've never heard of the space sciences having any real military or security significance beyond the orbital phase."

"It was not so long ago," she reminded him, "that even sub-orbital rocketry was believed to have little military application. As for orbiting satellites and manned space flight and permanent space stations such as we have now, these were purest fantasy when I was a small child."

"Right," he admitted. "Buck Rogers stuff."

"Buck Rogers?" she said.

"American trivia. A comic-strip hero of the Forties, long a synonym for anything having to do with space programs. Even so, this comet business seems a little far-fetched. What's your guess?"

She was uncomfortable with the question. She was trained in rigid scientific disciplines and found premature extrapolation on insufficient data distasteful. "Are you asking me for—what is the expression I have heard since coming here—a stomach feeling?"

"Gut feeling. Yes, I guess that's what I'm asking for."

Gut feeling. How odd that Americans found viscera superior to brains for problem-solving.

"Very well. My gut feeling, for what it is worth, is that Sergei Nekrasov has seen in Project Peter the Great some implication that has escaped other people. It must be something that will give the Soviet Union some kind of advantage, either in space or on the Earth. The advantage will be of a military nature, otherwise a man like Nekrasov would not be interested. And he must have seen this implication in something submitted to him, perhaps in Tarkovsky's original proposal, perhaps in some earlier work by Tarkovsky or a close associate that was included with the proposal. He is not a scientist and it is unlikely that he will have formulated any original thoughts on his own. There is, of course, the possibility that someone else brought the idea to him. Whatever it is, it is something important enough to warrant the personal intervention of the Deputy Premier of the Politburo."

"You missed your calling. You were cut out for intelligence work."

She supposed that he was paying her a compliment. "In the sciences one is trained to reason along certain lines, with a certain discipline of thought, although one does not always succeed." Several teenage boys came into the restaurant and began feeding coins into a machine that stood by the door. Its television screen lit up with lurid, incomprehensible graphics and screeching sound effects filled the air. A thin, undersized boy in thick glasses began annihilating attacking space-ships with merciless ferocity. His friends cheered him on.

Sam glared at the boys. "Damn space cadets."

She smiled for the first time that day. "Your next generation of fighter pilots."

"So where do we go from here? I'll admit that this is out of my depth. If it was espionage or counter-terrorism or something like that, I'd know what to do next. But comets?"

"Comets. Exactly. It is time for us to talk to some people who know about comets. People who are familiar with Tarkovsky's work. We must consult with such experts as you have on the Soviet space program. That will be important. Space projects are enormously expensive and are run on very rigid budgets. A sudden expansion of one program will be reflected in many of the others. Resources will be reallocated, some projects will be set back or cancelled. We could extrapolate a great deal from that. For instance,—"

"Hold it," Sam said, palms out to forestall a flood of information. "One thing at a time. I think it's time to set up appointments with some people at NASA. We have a lot of time left today. Are you tired or would you like to go to work on this right away?"

"Just walk right in and talk with personnel at NASA? We could do that? But, yes, you have all the right clearances, don't you? They will talk with us if you show credentials."

He laughed aloud. She liked his laugh. "Credentials? My god, you don't need credentials to get those people to talk! The problem's in getting them to shut up once they've started on their pet subject. Believe me, if they're not involved in defense or intelligence work, you'll hear all you want to hear from them. More than you want to hear."

"Then let's go." Behind them as they left, loud cheers announced the destruction of another alien spaceship.

CHAPTER THREE

WASHINGTON, D.C.

Sam ducked into a telephone booth and made a few calls. He returned to announce that they were going to pay NASA headquarters a visit. "Is it that easy to get an appointment?" she asked.

"Appointments are things that bureaucrats cancel," he answered. "I avoid them whenever possible." With that cryptic remark, he put the Chevy in gear and pulled out into traffic. It did not take long to reach the corner of Independence and Maryland Avenues where, miraculously, Sam found a parking space almost immediately. He slid from under the steering wheel and extended a hand to Laine. A little uncertain about proper American automobile etiquette, she took the hand and slid across the seat and out in a single, flowing motion.

Across the street, an immense building immediately caught her attention. In contrast to the pseudoclassical architecture all around, it was severely modern, its surrounding terrace adorned with metal sculpture that looked like vegetation from another planet. A large number of people were milling about outside the building, many of them foreign tourists, as well as an animated group of school children. It did not have the kind of grim, authoritarian look she habitually associated with government buildings. "Is this NASA?" she asked.

"No, that's the Air and Space Museum. *That's* NASA." He pointed at a gray, nondescript building exactly like a hundred others she had already seen in the city.

"That is better," she said.

"What?"

"It restores my faith in the universality of government agencies," she said. This time it was his turn to be mystified. They entered the building by way of a gray foyer as anonymous as the exterior. The atmosphere inside was that of faceless civil service everywhere. Its function might as easily have been finance as space exploration.

The woman behind the reception desk looked up nonchalantly as Sam stepped up with an uncharacteristically ingratiating smile.

"Pardon me, Ma'am, but might I borrow a NASA phone directory for a minute? I need to look up a name." Wordlessly, she handed him the directory. He glanced through the organizational pages until he spotted the Associate Administrator for Space Science and noted the name and room number. He returned the directory. "Is this Federal Office Building 10?"

"That's right," the woman said, "FOB 10."

"Thank you," he said, his smile undaunted by her bored monotone. He took Laine lightly by an arm and guided her to an elevator. "We're going to call on the Associate Administrator for Space Science," he told her.

She was not familiar with official ranks in the U.S. government, but that sounded entirely too lofty a title to accept a casual, unannounced visit from a grunt. "Surely," she said, "*this* calls for an appointment."

"I guess so. But, it would probably take several weeks while his secretary tried to find five vacant minutes on his calendar. He may not be in now, anyway, not that it matters. Our business isn't with him just now. It's with his office."

"I don't understand, but lead on." She was beginning to enjoy this.

He favored her with another of his rare, tight smiles, quite different from the fake smile he had used on the receptionist. "Just stand back and watch a pro operate," he told her.

The office of the Associate Administrator for Space Science was only one floor up from street level, at the end of a hallway. As they walked into the pleasantly furnished anteroom, an alert, conservatively-dressed woman looked them over swiftly and asked pleasantly, "What may I do for you?"

"This is Dr. Tammsalu, and I'm Sam Taggart from the State Department. We're here on a matter of some importance. We'd like to see the Associate Administrator for Space Science, please."

The woman made a show of looking through her desk calendar. "Dr., ah, Tammsalu, was it? And Mr. Taggart? I'm sorry, I don't see any appointment here."

"Actually," Sam said, "Doctor Tammsalu has just arrived from overseas and the people over at State thought it important that she speak with the Administrator. Didn't anybody contact you?"

"From the State Department? I'm afraid not. In any case, the Associate Administrator is on the Hill today, all day, I'm afraid. His appointment schedule is full until next week. Would you care to make an appointment for next week? Or, could anyone else help you?"

"That's a pity," Sam said. "We truly are pressed for time. We'll talk to his deputy, or whoever else is in charge of the study of comets."

"Well, the Deputy Associate Administrator is currently overseas but let me see what I can do for you." She reached for her phone and began punching buttons. She spoke inaudibly to someone, then hung up and placed another call. This time she was smiling as she hung up. "A Doctor Ken Bridges, who is the Discipline Scientist for comets and several other research areas, is available and is expecting you now. His office is down the hall." She jotted down the room number on a memo slip and handed it to Sam.

In the hall, Laine said. "You never expected to talk to the Associate Administrator, did you?"

"Of course not. But if you want to see somebody in a big bureaucracy, start at the top. It's much quicker to get kicked down to the office you want than it is to climb up from the bottom. We've been here for ten minutes and we're going to see the man we want. It might've taken days to get past all the secretaries if we'd gone through channels."

She surprised him by laughing girlishly. "I've always suspected it worked that way, but I never had the courage to try it myself." The corridor seemed endless. "What is the Hill? That woman said the Associate Administrator was on the Hill."

"That's Capitol Hill. He must be up there lobbying for more funds for NASA. He may be the big shot here, but up there he's standing with his hat in his hand, smiling at some bunch of political hacks he despises, trying to pry nickels loose for the space program. Department heads are just beggars like everybody else on the Hill." She was surprised by the real bitterness in his voice, and she suspected that it had nothing to do with the woes of NASA.

The Discipline Scientist's office was a modest room with a fair view of Independence Avenue and the museum across the street. The man who greeted them was in his forties, with thinning hair, turning gray and square glasses. "I'm Ken Bridges. I take it you're Dr. Tammsalu?" He shook hands with Laine, then with Sam.

"Sam Taggart, from State," Sam said, bending the truth slightly for the sake of cooperation. People often clammed up at the mention of CIA. "Dr. Tammsalu is a refugee from Estonia, and she's come to us with a rather peculiar story. Since it involves your realm of expertise, we wondered if you'd be able to help us out." As always, he chose his words carefully while trying to seem spontaneous and casual. For some reason, most people reacted sympathetically to a "refugee" while a "defector" was often regarded with suspicion. One was a victim, the other a turncoat.

"Of course," Bridges said, "I'll be happy to extend any help I can. What's the nature of the problem?"

"I'll let Dr. Tammsalu explain," Sam said.

Resignedly, Laine launched into her story yet another time. She found it a bit easier though, since Bridges' occasional interruptions with pertinent questions and comments displayed understanding and interest. He did not dismiss her story as too far-fetched. As her recitation ended, he leaned back in his chair and laced his fingers across an incipient paunch. He looked distinctly puzzled.

"I'll confess," Bridges said at last, "that this has me stumped. We've known about the big Soviet push into exploration and exploitation of space for a long time, of course. We've been expecting them to announce a manned expedition to Mars, for instance. Mars makes sense. It could be colonized eventually, and it would be a massive propaganda coup. An exploratory mission to a passing comet makes sense, too. Even a manned expedition to a comet isn't out of the question, though it sounds awfully ambitious. But," he raised his hands in a gesture of helplessness, "why the cometary mission should be taken over and given top priority by the Deputy Premier I can't imagine. Current knowledge of comets is that they're just big, dirty snowballs. Most of them spend much of their time so far from us that Pluto's close by comparison. It would do no good to build a military base on one. An analysis of a comet's makeup would be of great scientific interest, naturally, but it could be done without a manned expedition, and it would be of no interest to the likes of Nekrasov, anyway. The expense would be enormous, too."

"Then they must be expecting to find something pretty valuable out there," Sam said.

"I can't imagine what," said Bridges. "Scientific value is one thing. Military or commercial value is another. Even the propaganda value isn't all that great. The typical layman doesn't even know what a comet is. Everybody knows about the Moon, or Mars." He thought a while. "Look, I'm not the best person to talk to on this subject. There's going to be a colloquium on comets sponsored by the International Astronomical Union week after next in Baltimore. It'll be at the Space Telescope Science Institute. I could try to organize a special evening session to have comet specialists listen to you. Maybe someone at the meeting could come up with an intelligent guess."

"Will there be a lot of Soviet bloc scientists there?" Sam asked. "At this stage, it would be a mistake to let them know that we're asking questions."

"It's an international colloquium. It'd look funny if we tried to exclude anybody. Let me talk to the chairman of the scientific organizing committee. He's an acquaintance of mine, from West Germany. I know we can trust him and he might be able to think of something. There may be nothing to worry about. This kind of event is like sports or cultural exchanges. When diplomatic relations are strained, the Soviets stay home in protest. Right now, relations are pretty strained."

"Tell me about it," Sam concurred.

Bridges turned to Laine. "I'm glad you've come to America, Dr. Tammsalu. Do you plan to go into teaching or research?"

"Research, if I can find a position," she said, smiling radiantly.

"What's your specialization in astrophysics? I may be able to help you. I'm afraid I'm not well acquainted with the names of astronomers in the Soviet Union."

"There is no reason for you to have heard of me. I was never terribly important. My personal interest has been high energy astrophysics, in particular gamma-ray astronomy. We have not done much experimental work in this field, although we did have a rather ambitious plan for gamma-ray and x-ray satellites as a scientific arm of Project Peter the Great. Now, I have no idea as to what will become of that project, much less about its scientific satellite programs."

"Let me look into it," Bridges said. "There may a good position open for you. Let me write some colleagues. Can't make any promises, of course. Funding for scientific work's gotten pretty tight again. A few years ago, you'd have had your pick of a dozen jobs."

"You are very kind. It is good to know that someone is willing to take in a wandering Estonian."

"Actually, you're not the first Estonian astronomer I've met. Back when I was a grad student, far too long ago, I attended a seminar given by Ernst Opik. It was a great privilege. After that, I specialized in symbiotic stars. Do you have a number where I can get in touch with you?" There was an exchange of telephone numbers, then Sam put on his best official smile and they shook hands with Bridges and took their leave.

"High-energy astrophysics," Sam said, as they trudged down the long hall, "x-ray and gamma-ray astronomy, symbiotic stars," head down and hands in pockets, he was a picture of perplexed dejection. "I haven't felt so lost since my first day in boot camp. At any rate, I think you've won a fan."

"It's good of him to want to help me," Laine said, "and if you *really* want to feel lost, try defecting to an alien culture. Your '56 Chevy is as strange to me as a gamma-ray telescope to you."

Sam released one of his infrequent laughs. "Thanks. I was starting to feel sorry for myself."

Outside, Laine pointed at the modernistic facade of the Air and Space Museum. "Could we go in there?"

"Sure. We're in no rush. I should've thought of it myself. Here you've been in D.C. for days and you haven't had a chance to be a tourist yet."

"How could I? I've spent all my waking hours since I got here in one of those interrogation rooms."

He took her arm and escorted her across the street. "Please, Ma'am," he said with mock gravity, "*We* have no 'interrogation rooms.' Those were *debriefing* rooms'."

"How can you take a briefing back from somebody?"

"True, but 'interrogation room' puts people in mind of blinding lights and rubber hoses. If you think 'debriefing' sounds evasive, I'll take you up

on the Hill and you can hear some *real* doubletalk."
At the entrance to the museum he remembered
something. "Wait here a minute." Laine watched
bemusedly as he ran back across the street and fed
coins into a meter next to his Chevy. He made it
just as a woman in a police uniform came into
sight mounted on an odd, three-wheeled motorcy-
cle. "Just made it," he said when he returned.
"D.C. cops are fierce about parking tickets. They
can't do anything about all the cars with diplomatic plates, so they take it out on the rest of the
citizens. Come on, let's go in."

The interior was immense. Apparently, the Americans were as fond of the grandiose as the Russians.
The scale was so numbing that she had no idea of
the true size of the place until she looked upward
to see the aircraft dangling from the ceiling on
cables. "Is that really a full-sized airplane?" she
asked, pointing at a twin-engine craft overhead.
She could see that it was an old design, but it had
marvelously graceful lines.

"It's a Douglas DC-3," Sam said. He stood looking up with hands on hips, smiling broadly. "Military designation C-47. It was the workhorse cargo
plane of World War Two. Most beautiful plane
ever built. You might call it the '56 Chevrolet of
airplanes. Used to see 'em flying a lot when I was
a kid. We lived near an airport. I wanted to be a
pilot more than anything."

So hatchetmen had childhoods, too. "Why didn't
you? Become a pilot, I mean?"

"I tried to get into flight school in the service,"
he told her. "They found something wrong with
my inner ear that only shows under very low pressure. They have medication for it now, though."
For the first time, she heard him laugh genuinely
and ungrudgingly.

They started at one end of the museum and

began working their way toward the other. The displays began with the earliest and crudest aerodynamic devices such as boomerangs. There was even a platter-shaped flying toy which a label identified as a "frisbee." There were spaceships and satellites at the other end.

From a balcony overlooking the main foyer, they rested. Busloads of school-children and tour groups were constantly arriving and leaving. A camera-draped pack of Japanese tourists was snapping pictures of everything. "Seeing this," Laine said, "it's hard to believe that your space program is in trouble." She thought for a moment. "I suppose I should say 'our' space program now, since I intend to live here and work in it if I can."

"Our space program is like our military establishment or our highways," Sam told her. "We're proud of it, but we don't like paying for it. The payoff from space exploration seems too remote and rarified for most Americans."

She studied an ethereal, pedal-powered aircraft hanging nearby. "But, there have been a great many advances in other fields because of the space competition: miniaturization, medical technology, a great many others. Every schoolchild learns that in my homeland."

"Maybe. But NASA suffers from bad PR." Sam said.

"What is that?"

"Public relations. There are agencies that do nothing but sell an image to people. I guess NASA never hired one. They've done a lousy job of selling themselves to the public. Besides, there isn't just one space program, there are a lot of them. I don't know much about NASA, but I've worked with others, and they're all about the same. The people working on manned expeditions worry if it looks like the unmanned probe crowds are getting too big a slice of the budget. The military starts interfering if they think the purely scientific programs are getting too much attention. Hell, for all I know, the infra-red astronomers are fighting tooth and nail with the ultraviolets for funding. In good times, when there's lots of money floating around for everyone, they're all one big family devoted to the betterment of mankind. Now, times are rough, the economy's down, and they have to fight for every dime."

"I suppose it's the same where I come from," she said. "But they never explain or ask our opinion."

"They never ask for mine either," Sam said. "I give it to them anyway. Maybe that's why I'm on UFO investigations."

Once again, Laine had the impression that he had gone off on some tangent of his own. It occurred to her that the man was not quite sane. Oddly, that made him a little more human and likeable. She was so tired of interchangeable government automatons.

"What an amazing place," Laine said as they emerged. "Boomerangs to moon rockets. That's a very large cultural jump." The streetlights were beginning to come on around the mall. "We must have lost track of time. I had no idea it was so late."

"Are you hungry?" Sam asked. "I'm starved."

She was ravenous and told him so. "Would you like to have dinner in Chinatown? It's only a few blocks from here."

"Chinatown? That sounds exotic. Yes, I would be delighted, if it doesn't interfere with your personal plans for the evening. I was resigned to eating alone at the hotel restaurant."

She got her first taste of Washington rush-hour traffic on the way to Chinatown. It took nearly half an hour to cover less than two miles. Unlike Sam, Laine did not fret over the delay. She was enthralled by the cosmopolitan quality of Washington life which was apparent even on the sidewalks. Blocks of slum housing stood cheek-by-jowl with rows of brightly-lit shops displaying expensive wares. Here, away from the tourists, the street life took on a kaleidoscopic quality that reminded her of some of the very strange films she had seen while she was in Italy. Young black men balanced huge, blaring radios on their shoulders. Teenagers strolled about in makeup and hairstyles from other planets. Dark arcades were momentarily lit by lurid flashes from the screens of video games. She pointed at a group of shaven-headed youths in orange robes and tennis shoes who stood on a street corner shaking tambourines and chanting and holding bowls out to passing pedestrians. "Who are those?"

"Hare Krishnas," Sam said. "Actually, they call themselves the Krishna Consciousness Movement or something like that. It's an American version of some Hindu sect. It was very popular for a few years. You don't see so much of them any more. If you think this place is weird, wait till you see California. It'll send you right into culture shock. Someone once said that America has a continental tilt and everything that's loose rolls down into Southern California."

Laine laughed. "Actually, I find this all terribly exciting and fascinating. So much color and variety! You have no idea how dull things are in the Soviet Union and the satellite states."

"Oh yes I have," Sam said, changing gears, "I've been there."

Chinatown turned out to be a small area of nondescript, rather dilapidated buildings. Laine was a little disappointed. She had expected buildings with pagoda facades and strange neon lighting and tong gangsters lurking in the alleyways.

"It's not like the San Francisco Chinatown," Sam said, as if in answer to her thought, "but there are some pretty good restaurants here if you know where to find them." He pulled into a customer's reserved parking space next to a restaurant whose exterior was nothing but a shabby storefront. Across the plate glass window was lettered, with incongruous grandiloquence, *Pearl of the Orient*. Inside, it was no more distinguished, but was scrupulously clean. All the other customers appeared to be Chinese, which Laine took as a good sign. As before, Sam chose a table in the rear, near the kitchen, and sat with his back against the windowless wall. A puffy-cheeked Chinese doll of a waitress brought them menus, but a middle-aged man came from the kitchen and spoke to her briefly in rapid Cantonese and she went to wait on another table.

"It's been a while, Sam," the man said with a smile that exposed several gold teeth.

"I've been out of town." He turned to Laine. "Would Tsin-Tao beer suit you to start with?" She nodded affirmatively. "Would you like for me to order? I know the menu pretty well here." Again she nodded. He turned to the Chinese man. "We'll start with the shark's fin soup and barbecued ribs, then the Peking duck and the Moses pork—"

"That's moshi pork," said the Chinese.

"You mean it's not kosher?" Sam said in mockhorror.

The man looked at Laine, deadpan. "Clowns they got working for the government these days. No wonder the country's in the shape it's in." He took their order back to the kitchen.

"Is he a friend of yours?" Laine asked.

"He's somebody I helped out in a jam once. His

name's Sammy Quo. A few years back he was having some tong trouble. I happened by when a couple of thugs were roughing him up and straightened things out. Since it wasn't official business, I didn't report it to anybody. That meant a lot to Sammy. Probably half the people working here are relatives of his who're here without proper immigration papers."

"Tongs?" Laine said. "Are they still active? I thought they were something from old films."

"Very active," Sam said. "They were pretty quiet from the twenties through the fifties. It was the big upsurge in the drug trade and illegal immigration in the sixties that revived them."

Their beer arrived and the Chinese doll poured it into tall glasses. Laine lifted hers in a silent toast and took a cautious sip. Surprisingly, it tasted much like the beer she was used to. She remarked on the fact.

"I'm not surprised," Sam said. "It was the Germans who started brewing in China before the First World War. They probably still make it the same way."

"You have a remarkably broad range of information," Laine said.

"You mean for a CIA thug?"

Laine flushed. "I meant no such thing!" She was embarrassed. He was right. She had not expected a government gunman to be so many-faceted. She wondered whether the KGB had such unusual men.

"Sure you did. That's ok, it comes with the job. Actually, I came by that last piece of information from my grandfather. He was with the Marines in Shanghai in the twenties. He was a mine of information about China in those days." Their dinner arrived and the quality of the food proved to be even better than Sam had hinted. The Peking duck, in particular, was roasted exquisitely crisp. They made small talk while eating, and Sam in his unobtrusive way managed to get a little background information from Laine without being obvious.

He learned that she had befriended a visiting American astronomer for a year or so while she had held a research appointment at the Sternberg Astronomical Institutute in Moscow. She had learned from him much of her American English. She displayed that rare ability to talk about her work without cluttering her speech with incomprehensible jargon. It was some time since Sam had found such a charming dinner companion. She had a wry sense of humor that came across despite her slight linguistic handicap.

Throughout the meal and the drive back to Laine's hotel, both were aware of a tension between them, a tension resulting from a mutual withdrawal from a mutual attraction. Sam rejected the temptation to involvement for professional reasons, Laine because she still did not trust her feelings. She wondered whether he would make a more determined advance. Experience told her that he would, but he didn't.

"Good night, Laine. I'll be by to pick you up at about nine in the morning." They parted with a mutual sense of diappointment.

CHAPTER FOUR

WASHINGTON, D.C. AND SUBURBS

The following morning, Sam got up just before the alarm rang at six. He turned on his radio for the early news broadcast as he forced himself through an intensive set of calisthenics of his own design. He was still far from his peak condition, and he promised himself that, as soon as his schedule straightened out, he would resume his judo workouts. For years, karate had been the glamour art, largely because of media exposure and Bruce Lee movies, but he still preferred judo. Dripping with sweat, he switched the radio off and went into the shower.

At 8:15 Sam phoned a number at Langley CIA headquarters. The phone was answered on the first ring. "Novak."

"Hello, Slats. Sam Taggart here."

"Hey, old buddy! What's new?" Novak's Alabama drawl sounded even more exaggerated than usual.

"Slats, I want you to do me a favor," Sam said, without preamble.

"What kind of favor?" Novak asked with sudden suspicion.

"I want a two-hour executive summary on Project Peter the Great."

"Where the hell did you come across that codename? You aren't supposed to be at this end of Company business." Novak's lazy drawl had disappeared.

"Never mind how. I'll be by with my partner at ten."

"You think I got nothing better to do than devote two hours of my busy day to you? Or even five minutes? Now that I think of it, last time I saw you, you were walking away with my girl."

"If I was walking away with her, she wasn't yours." Sam sighed. It was time for the ritual. "All right, I'll tell you why you owe me a favor: Istanbul, a dead female agent, your worthless ass on the line and—"

"Okay, okay," Novak said, hastily, "not on the telephone. I capitulate. I'll see you and your partner at ten."

Sam hung up. He and Novak had been partners on a number of occasions, years ago. Novak had owed Sam his life on more than one occasion. The time in Istanbul had not been one of them. Instead, it had been a tragi-comic affair that might have made them both laughingstocks if they hadn't covered up the evidence and beat a hasty retreat. Now that it looked as though they were safe from ever being connected with the incident, they sometimes reminisced about it over a few beers. Slats now held a desk job at CIA headquarters in Northern Virginia. He still liked to be reminded that he had been a cowboy once, too. His current specialty happened to be the analysis of Soviet potentials in space.

When Sam arrived at the Hotel Wildner he found

Laine already waiting in the lobby, looking stunningly beautiful with her long, blonde hair draped over her black overcoat.

"Where are we going today?" she asked as she climbed into the car.

"CIA headquarters."

"You're joking." She studied him. "You're not joking. Am I going to be interrogated again?"

"No. This time, we'll do the interrogating. That restricted badge they gave you will get you inside as long as you're with me. Consider yourself my partner for the duration."

Laine settled back in the seat. His partner. Did that make her a spook, a cowboy or a grunt?

Novak looked up as they entered his sparsely furnished office. His glance shot from Sam to Laine. His inspection of Laine was brief but thorough. "Haven't changed much, have you, Sam?" Laine was not quite sure how to take that.

"Not much," Sam said, "but the Company has."

Slats got down to business. "You asked for a two-hour summary of Project Peter the Great. It's the code name for the Soviet grand plan to explore, exploit and colonize the solar system. They plan to make much if not all of the real estate in the solar system Soviet fief. As Mother Russia expanded explosively under the leadership of Peter the Great, so shall she now expand into space, under less charismatic but more orthodox collective leadership."

Sam seated Laine in one of the chairs and parked himself on Novak's desk, shoving a pile of papers aside for the purpose. "Desk work hasn't blunted your taste for rhetoric, Slats."

Novak grinned. "Believe me, if it was just you, I'd be brief. But, how often do I get a chance to play to such an attractive audience?" He smiled toward Laine. She returned the smile nervously. "Very ill-bred of you to neglect introductions, Sam." Sam started to rectify his error, but Novak breezed right on. "I'm honored to make your acquaintance, Dr. Tammsalu. I hope you're enjoying your introduction to the U.S. Is your room at the Wildner satisfactory? Wouldn't you rather have a less scruffy escort?"

"I am, it is and I think I'm in good hands," Laine answered.

"Don't count on that last part," Novak advised her.

"I'll make you pay for this, Slats," Sam said, studying the nails of one hand.

"Back to business," Novak said. He leaned back in his swivel chair, lacing his fingers behind his head and causing his paunch to protrude somewhat. "You've got two hours of my exceptionally valuable time to receive an education on Soviet plans for space for the next fifteen or so years. Listen attentively and don't interrupt except with questions of the greatest pertinence." Sam gazed at the ceiling in disgust but Novak went on obliviously. "The initial phase involves permanent space stations, which are very much in evidence these days, and high-power solar satellites. The second stage involves lunar stations; we know they're at it in earnest. The forthcoming phase is expected to be manned deep space probes, manned missions to Mars, Martian bases, exploration of asteroids, even," he paused dramatically for effect, "terraforming of Venus."

"Fly that last one past me again," Sam said.

"Settle down. You'll get your chance for questions." Novak launched into his briefing. Apparently, it was one he was accustomed to giving for VIPs needing some background in Soviet developments in space. It seemed the Soviets had been investing a great proportion of their resources in Project Peter the Great. When a compromise accord had finally been reached in the East-West armament race, much of their ex-military industrial capacity was converted to the space program rather than toward production of more and better consumer goods. Much of this was in the name of efficiency, because of the common aspects of modern military technology and one space program. Instead of better ICBMs, they could develop better space trucks. Consumers could wait, as always. Patience was one of the Russian virtues.

More importantly, the Soviets saw little chance of winning the contest against the capitalist nations commercially or politically. In fact, they had been losing ground steadily for a number of years. They could from time to time establish some puppet government in some poverty-stricken part of the world, but keeping it within the Soviet sphere afterward was difficult and expensive. War, of course, was out of the question. It had been Russian military policy since Czarist days never to commit the nation to military solutions without at least a two-to-one superiority in armament. So far from achieving any such superiority over the West, their efforts to maintain mere parity had bled the economy white.

As soon as the armaments accord had been reached, the new program, long on the back burner, had been put into effect: If the East were to be victorious over the West, it would be through a vigorous exploration of space and utilization of its unlimited resources. Best of all, immense prestige would accrue to the Soviet Union and nobody could accuse them of military expansionism. The timing was perfect. The West seemed to be losing interest in the challenge of the space age. Political and industrial leaders advocated squandering the lim-

ited terrestrial resources for essentially nonpro-
ductive purposes. Those advocating the cause of
the high frontier were ridiculed as space cadets.

CIA information on Project Peter the Great was
not as complete as they would like, nor was it as
up-to-date as Novak would have preferred. However, one of the programs that the Soviets were
working on most feverishly was the development
of an ion-drive engine for constant-acceleration
flight in deep space. CIA information on it was
fragmentary, but apparently the Soviets were on
the verge of some breakthrough.

"Is this true?" Laine asked, interrupting for the
first time. "An ion-drive engine?"

Novak cocked an eyebrow at her, savoring his
little triumph. "Surprised we know about the project? It's supposed to be top secret, you know."

"Of course, I was not told of the project," Laine
went on, unperturbed. "My work was in astronomy, not spacecraft engineering. But a constant-
boost engine would open up all sorts of possibilities
in space. Imagine! I had thought that it would be
at least several decades before that sort of thing
would become practical engineering." She was
working hard at not being enthusiastic. She didn't
want to appear to be rooting for the wrong side.

Sam was intrigued by this sudden interest. "Why
is this constant-boost engine such a cause for re-
joicing?" he asked her.

"Well, the conventional engine is used primarily
for injecting a payload into a free-flying orbit. No
acceleration occurs after the injection except for
minor adjustments in the orbit. Using these engines, it takes months or years to get to another
planet. The rocket achieves its maximum velocity,
then it shuts off and coasts the rest of the way. It's
just a big skyrocket, enormously complicated, but
no different in principle from the kind used for

fireworks: just a big tube filled with explosive which is allowed to burn at a controlled rate. But, with a constant one-G boost engine, with a mid-course turnaround for deceleration, you can reach Mars within a week." She saw his slightly perplexed expression and added: "One-G stands for one Earth gravity, of course. It's the acceleration you experience downward at the Earth's crust due to its gravitational field. What it means in practical terms is that, with one-G constant acceleration, the entire solar system becomes as accessible as the coastlines of the world were to navigation in the Nineteenth Century."

It was a difficult proposition to swallow all at once. "If that's true, why aren't we going all-out for this ion-drive engine, too?"

"I can only make guesses," she told him. "For one thing, the ion drive is only one type of engine that is capable of constant boost, at least theoretically. There are other possibilities. Also, any form of constant boost engine has been considered by most space engineers to be merely a theoretical possibility, a dream for a future generation." She turned to Novak. "At least, so I thought until now. Besides, there are a number of practical problems to be solved, the primary one being the fuel or energy source and reaction mass." She waved her slender hands about in the immemorial gesture of the specialist searching for words comprehensible to the layman. "There are other problems, especially muzzle velocity."

Sam held out a hand in a silencing gesture. "Hold it. Muzzle velocity? Jesus, I thought only bullets had that. We'll talk about fuel and muzzle velocity later. I want to hear the rest of Slats' spiel. After all, we don't want to waste what he keeps reminding us is his valuable time."

"Hell," Novak admitted. "I sit around on my

rapidly-broadening butt all day with nobody to talk to. You know how much prestige this office has these days? Remember that Air Force guy we used to know? The one they put on UFO investigations?"

"Tell me about it," Sam said, wearily.

"Same thing here. If it's not orbital, if it's not military, they just aren't interested. You just watch, Sam. The bastards are going to steal a march on us, just like they did in the fifties, only this time it'll be a lot worse. And they're making no big secret of their overall plan, just certain crucial aspects."

"Before we get into the doomsaying," Sam said drily, "just how close are they to perfecting this constant-boost ion drive?"

"I wish we knew. What we do know is that they're devoting resources to the search comparable to their efforts to develop the A-bomb and the ICBM."

"Meaning that their security is probably comparably tight," Sam observed. "Anything else you can tell us about Peter the Great?"

Novak wrapped up his overview, noting that basic scientific research was an integral part of the project. He briefly described the nature of that research and added, "The head of the scientific program is Miss Tammsalu's former boss, Pyotr Tarkovsky, and the gamma-ray observatory had a high priority on his program. But from what your partner here has been telling us lately, it may not be a very live part of the program now."

"You've seen the transcripts of Laine's debriefings," Sam said. "What do you make of this business with Nekrasov?"

Novak leaned forward and rested on his elbows. "I'll confess it's the strangest thing I ever heard. I'd be willing to bet that what Nakrasov knows about the space sciences could be engraved on the head of a pin in letters a foot high. And as for the comet linkup,'' he shrugged helplessly, "I just can't feature the son of a bitch being interested at all. If ever there was a pure science project, it's that one. No military or intelligence potential at all. Sorry.''

"Look into it," Sam said. "I know you don't take your instructions from my boss, but I think we're all missing something important here. See what your computers can turn up. Anything on the project or on Tarkovsky in particular. It could be something Nekrasov picked up on that nobody else noticed, some paper he published or presented years ago. Whatever else Nekrasov is, he's not dumb.''

"You don't mind handing out hard ones, do you, Sam? Do you have any idea how much wordage a major scientist like Tarkovsky publishes in his professional lifetime? Not to mention that most of it's incomprehensible to anybody but his colleagues and a lot of it's under secret label to boot.''

Sam patted him on the shoulder. "I trust you, Slats. I know you can do it. Besides, it's got to be simple or Nekrasov wouldn't have seen the implications.''

"Get out of here," Novak said, wearily. "Dr. Tammsalu, I'm most pleased to have made your acquaintance. Come back some time without him. I'll be working on it.''

On their way back to the District, a late-model Lincoln pulled up next to them at a stoplight. The driver stuck his head out the window and shouted, "Wanna trade cars?''

"No, thanks," Sam said. The light changed and the cars went their separate ways.

"Was he serious?" Laine asked. "That looked like an expensive automobile he was driving.''

"Sure he was serious," Sam said, complacently. "But no way am I trading this beauty for some crummy Continental." He sounded as if his car had been insulted.

They stopped for a late lunch at the Marriott Inn. Although Sam fretted and complained about the service, Laine found it incredibly prompt. In a Moscow restaurant, a quick lunch meant anything under two hours. As usual, Sam tried discreetly to pump her for information. She decided to pump him instead.

"I know that you, or at least the officials you work for, must have some reservations concerning my allegiance," she said over coffee. "How is it that I was allowed in your discussion with Mr. Novak? I am sure it must have been highly confidential in nature."

"For one thing," Sam said, "since you've been turned over to me, it's my job to decide how far you're to be trusted. So far, you seem pretty plausible to me. Don't forget, I've worked with a lot of defectors. Some of them turned out to be phonies. You're measuring up pretty well, so far."

"Indeed?" she said, amused. "And just what makes you think I am not one of these phonies?"

"Well, I'd've been on my guard right away if you'd come on about how much you hate the Russians and how much you hate Communism and how you've always admired America and how you've always wanted to come here and help us destroy the evil Reds."

She laughed softly. "Do they really talk like that? The phony ones, I mean?"

"The dumb ones do. The smart ones are a little more subtle, but they can't seem to help thinking that something of that sort will allay our suspicions."

"Well, if you want to know, my feelings about the Soviets are a good deal more complex than that. For one thing, the antipathy between Russia and Estonia greatly predates Marxism. We've been enemies since the Middle Ages. I try not to let that cloud my judgement, but it is inescapable. Europe is far older than America, and we can't escape our history. Their takeover of Estonia in 1945 was just one episode in a long history of rivalry. The government they imposed is dreadful: Russians occupy most of the key positions. Lack of Party membership or patronage condemns you to second-class citizenship."

"No love lost between you and the Russians, then?" Sam said.

"I've worked and studied in Russia for a good part of my life. The Russians aren't so bad as a people. Not much different from Estonians or Americans. I got along well with most of my colleagues. Dr. Tarkovsky is a splendid man, very warm and humorous as well as brilliant and learned."

"And how do Americans stack up against Russians in your estimation?" Sam asked.

"I have been here only a short time," she said, evasively, "I have seen very little of America."

"Still," he persisted, "you must have some kind of feeling."

There he was with the "gut feelings" again. "All right, since you are so curious. From what I have seen so far, most Americans seem to be more superficial, less serious-minded than most Russians I have known. They seem more concerned with their immediate surroundings and problems, and less aware of the world at large."

"Go on," Sam encouraged.

She lit another cigarette, trying to find words to express her thoughts. "For instance," he said at last, "suppose you were to ask the average Russian why Estonia is part of the Soviet Union. He would tell you that all the Baltic nations joined of their own accord, because they wished to become a part of the family of Socialist Republics. He would say this because that is what he has been taught. But if you asked an American, I doubt if one in ten would even know where or what Estonia is."

"Probably not one in a hundred," Sam admitted. He looked at his wristwatch. "It's about two o'clock. There's one more expert on the Soviet space program I want to interview this afternoon."

"Who might that be?"

"You. Think you could give me an executive summary on what you know about the program?"

"I'm not sure," she said cautiously. "What is an executive summary?"

"It means a concise summary prepared for a busy executive who hasn't got the time nor the technical expertise to cope with a full report. The kind of report we just got from Novak."

"All right. On one condition."

"Name it."

"Please, no interrogation room. Even if you call it a debriefing room, I want no more of them."

"Any suggestions?" he asked.

"How about my hotel room? It's not luxurious, but it's adequate. Besides, all my papers and notes are there."

"You're on."

CHAPTER FIVE

BALTIMORE

In the week following their briefing from Novak, Sam and Laine, using introductions provided by Ken Bridges, visited a few cometary astronomers in the area to learn all they could on the state of research on comets. They spent an afternoon with a NASA official who described the principles of ion drive. Laine was still having difficulty with American colloquialisms, but she was at home with the technical discussions where Sam was utterly lost. They made a complementary pair. By the time the colloquium opened on Monday the following week, Sam and Laine felt prepared for it, if not individually, then at least as a team.

Sam's worries about the Soviet scientists' catching on to their investigation proved to be needless. None of the leading experts showed up. Tarkovksy had been scheduled to deliver an invited talk entitled: "Tunguska Phenomenon: A Quantitative Analysis." He sent a telegram to cancel his attendance, citing poor health as an excuse. A sudden cancellation of Soviet participation was nothing new to the scientific community and the meeting opened as scheduled, although some participants had been looking forward to Tarkovsky's invited talk at the colloquium banquet.

"In a way I'm relieved," Laine admitted. "It could be embarrassing, confronting a former colleague after defecting. What would I say to him?"

They attended several of the readings. Some of the speakers presented their work succinctly and interestingly, but others required perseverance to sit through. Laine had a greater tolerance owing to experience and training, but even she began to grow glassy-eyed by the end of the first day.

On the second day of the colloquium, after the traditional banquet, Professor Dr. Ehlers, of the University of Hamburg, chairman of the scientific organizing committee, called a special meeting of his committee. The only members missing were Tarkovsky, from the U.S.S.R., and Novotny from Czechoslovakia. The eight that were present came from the U.S., Canada, Western Europe and Japan: among them most of the best known names in cometary research.

Bridges sat between Sam and Laine, muttering thumbnail sketches of the members as they entered. Last to come in was a gnomish, bearded little man, not quite five feet tall. Sam had seen him around during the last two days, usually glaring about in a sort of silent fury, occasionally buttonholing some reluctant listener for a lengthy harangue on some esoteric subject. People seemed anxious to avoid him.

"And that," Bridges said with a chuckle, "is Dr. Ugo Ciano. Born in Brooklyn, teaches in Honolulu now. One of the most brilliant men working in the field today and a hundred percent certified loony. Astronomy and astrophysics are full of eccentrics, but Ciano has 'em all beat. He's always diving off the deep end into some fringe area. It'd be okay if he'd stick to his own field, where he's preeminent, but he's into all sort of fringe areas, you name it. He's living proof that a scientist can be levelheaded in his own specialty and an utter crank anywhere else."

Sam went to the table along one wall of the meeting room where a coffee urn was surrounded by cups and drew himself some fortification against the talking to come.

"I come allaway here from Hawaii and Tarkovsky don't show!" Sam looked around to find the source of the voice, then he looked down. It was Ciano. The tiny man stood not much higher than his elbow, filling a cup with coffee.

"That's tough," Sam said, noncommittally.

"I'll say it is," Ciano went on, oblivious to Sam's lack of interest. "I had a few words I wanted to say to him about that Tunguska business. I read his paper on the subject. I coulda got some valuable work done here, and now there's nothing to do but listen to these jerks mouth off."

Sam was intrigued. The voice was amazingly young. The man's dwarfish physiognomy and grizzled beard gave an impression of age, but he now saw that Professor Ciano was not out of his twenties. Ciano studied him as intently. "I never seen you before. You ain't an astronomer, are you?"

"No, I'm afraid not," Sam said.

"I didn't think so. You look like you got some brains. Well, looks like the old Kraut's gonna talk. See you later." Ciano went and took a seat. The two chairs flanking his remained conspicuously vacant.

Ehlers introduced the two special guests: Laine Tammsalu, formerly of the University of Tartu in Estonia and more recently of the Tsiolkovsky Center for Space Research, and Sam Taggart of the

Department of State. Sam, naturally, did not correct the slight misaccreditation. Ehlers yielded the podium to Laine and sat down in the front row.

Despite the slight handicap of expressing herself in English, Laine's presentation was incisive and fascinating and her audience listened with rapt attention. She was not at all handicapped by the fact that she was by far the most attractive astronomer in the room. Sam felt an oddly ticklish, totally unprofessional sense of pride. Then he noticed Ciano. The little man was not simply listening to Laine like the others. He was processing every word and turning them over in his mind, fitting them together in different combinations. Sam could all but hear the gears, wheels and tumblers whir and click in the man's head.

When Laine finished her talk, Ehlers rose to ask for questions or comments from the audience. Several questions followed but it was obvious that the other committee members were equally at a loss as to why deputy premier and former KGB chief Nekrasov had taken a personal interest in cometary probes and had given top priority to the manned missions to comets. No one could see any tangible scientific returns from landing a manned spacecraft on a chunk of dirty cosmic ice ball only a few kilometers across. The possible returns seemed wholly inadequate in consideration of the cost and risk involved.

Roger Marais, the Belgian astronomer with a serious interest in celestial mechanics, remarked, "The whole idea seems absurd. Even for a comet with a small eccentricity, an orbital inclination closely matching that of the Earth, and a favorable perihelion point, the fuel required for the safe return of the cosmonauts will be prohibitive. Unless, that is, Nekrasov plans to send his political opposition on a one-way trip, thus putting them on ice permanently, so to speak." The audience chuckled politely at his witticism.

When the comments were exhausted, Ehlers closed the meeting, asking the participants to get in touch with Dr. Tammsalu through the good offices of Ken Bridges at NASA, should they come up with new ideas concerning the subject matter, and to be discreet about the special meeting as it would not do to raise unwarranted publicity concerning the whole affair. Sam had little faith in this last point. The cat was out of the bag as of now, and he had little doubt that, within days, Nekrasov would know that questions were being asked in America about his pet project. No help for it, though. The only way to find out was by consulting with the experts.

"Sorry you weren't able to get more response," Bridges said as the meeting broke up.

"Well, maybe some of them will come up with something when they've had a chance to mull it over," Sam said.

Ehlers came over and shook hands. With deliberate Teutonic emphasis he said, "Cheer up, it could have been much worse. But, thank Gott, Ciano did not want to speak."

They left the room a little discouraged, but they had really expected no startling revelations from the colloquium. In the hallway outside the room, they found Ciano waiting for them.

"Dr. Tammsalu," Ciano said, managing a courtly bow despite his diminutive physique, "Mr. Government Man, allow me to introduce myself. I'm Ugo Ciano, and if you wanna know why this creep Nekrasov's taking over Tarkovsky's project, you've come to the right man."

"I know who you are," Sam said, "and we didn't come to you, you've come to us."

"Amounts to the same thing. Fact is, I'm the guy

with the answers. I didn't wanna say anything in there, because some of my esteemed colleagues would've given you a lot of bullshit, excuse me, Ma'am, about everything I said. So to save us all a lot of time I figured I'd talk to you after everybody else left. Buy me a drink and I'll tell you everything you need to know."

Sam considered it. Did he really want to waste time talking to this bizarre homunculus, considered as a crackpot by his own colleagues? On the other hand, maybe this was just what was needed: someone whose mind didn't work along accepted academic channels and was agile enough to make the intuitive leaps denied to the more ploddingly conventional. Besides, Sam was bored with scientists and bureaucrats and this little clown seemed to be entertaining, at least.

"There's a bar near here I know of. The jukebox is quiet enough for conversation without having to yell. Do you have transportation?"

"Are you kidding? On my budget? I'm staying in the cheapest flophouse in town and using the bus."

"Come on, then. My car's outside."

Laine smiled fetchingly at Ciano. "Now I remember! I read your paper on an alternative to the quantized Big Bang. I read it in translation, of course, including your name. Please forgive me for not recognizing you at once, but the Cyrillic transliteration of your name is very inadequate. It is a brilliant paper. Dr. Tarkovsky commented on it in a symposium he held for us while we were waiting for construction to be completed at the Tsiolkovsky Center."

Amazingly, Ciano blushed absolutely purple under the flattery. "Christ, you mean somebody actually *read* that? Everybody here gave it the dead fish treatment. Tarkovsky, though, he'd get my drift." He smiled up at Sam. "Superior minds understand one another."

"That's what I've always said," Sam assured him.

"You ain't really State Department are you?" Ciano said slyly as they rode down in the elevator. "What is it? NSA? CIA? Air Force Intelligence? Naw, not Air Force. You're no zoomie. You got that look, though. What was it kept you out of planes? Inner ear problems?"

Sam was flabbergasted speechless for one of the few times in his life. The man was crazy as a loon, but his intuition bordered on the supernatural. Of course, there was nothing supernatural about it. It was that rare ability to snatch up random pieces of information entirely out of context and rearrange them into a logical pattern. He had known only a few people with the ability, none of them so acute and none of them trained scientists. When they reached the car, Ciano careened off on yet another tangent.

"A '56 Chevy! I knew you was no ordinary G-man, Taggart. Only a person of real discernment would own such a vehicle. This is gonna be a real pleasure." He reached up to open a door and hauled himself inside like an ape.

Laine leaned close to Sam and whispered: "I like him. He reminds me of Dr. Tarkovsky."

"God help us," Sam muttered, "you mean there are *two* of them?"

During the drive to the bar, Ugo and Laine jabbered on about professional subjects, quickly switching to German as a more suitable mutual language for the discussion. Sam already knew that Laine had grown up, like many other Estonians, speaking German. It suited him because he could tune out the conversation and concentrate on the deadly traffic.

At one point during the drive an inept or possibly drunken driver pulled over without signalling, almost sideswiping Sam's classic Chevy. Laine was distracted from her conversation and saw Sam's hand dart beneath his coat as he bit out something pithy she did not understand. She knew he was reflexively reaching for a gun.

Ciano cackled and said, still in German: "God help the man who puts a dent in *this* car!"

The bar was, as Sam had promised, a quiet place. Sam ordered a double shot of Jack Daniels on the rocks and Laine a double vodka on the rocks. Ciano ordered Wild Turkey straight up. Sam was alarmed. The man couldn't weigh ninety pounds. His tolerance for alcohol had to be low. He hoped this wouldn't get sticky.

When their drinks arrived, they clinked their glasses.

"To Estonia," Sam said, diplomatically.

"To poor Pyotr Tarkovsky," Laine said, "wherever he is tonight."

"To Planck's Constant and the speed of light," Ciano said, apropos of nothing whatever.

They took their first sips and settled back in their chairs. "All right, Dr. Ciano," Sam said, "time to deliver. What revelation do you have for us?"

"The ion drive," Ciano began, abruptly. "It's still theoretical, but, theoretically, it can use anything for reaction mass. It's not like atomic reactors, where you gotta have something rare like uranium. Anything'll do, and the simpler the better. You can do it with water. Miss Tammsalu, didn't you say this new Tsiolkovsky Space Center was built on the Aral Sea, with docks out into the water like a navy base?"

"Yes—that's true. We wondered about that, but—"

"Hold it," Sam said. "I'm not an expert like you

two, but I know a little about planes and ships and such. It's not enough to have fuel to go out. You have to have fuel to come back again. Could they take that much water with them? It weighs a lot. I've hauled plenty of water buckets in my time."

Ciano shook his head wearily. "Jesus. You gotta lead them by the hand." Then, shockingly, he jumped up onto his chair, grabbed a handful of ice from Sam's glass and held it under Sam's nose. "Ice, you dumb jerk!" he yelled. Heads swiveled to see the source of this disturbance. "The frigging comets are made of ice! Weren't you listening? Ice is the solid state of water. They pick up their return fuel at their destination! Ice is the key to this whole business!" The little man dropped the ice back into Sam's drink and resumed his seat as if nothing untoward had happened. Sam and Laine sat and stared, utterly at a loss as to how to deal with this mad little dynamo.

"Okay," Sam said at last. "Now we know how they plan to carry the expedition off, but we still don't know why. How come Nekrasov's interested?" Sam saw Ciano's sly smile. "Hold it!" he ordered. "If you jump up on the table, I'll bat you across the room."

"No need," Ciano said. "It's the same answer. Ice." He sat back in his chair with a contented smile and drained his glass. Sam did the same and signaled for another round. When the fresh drinks arrived, he said, "Okay, enlighten us."

"They got food here?" Ciano said. "All of a sudden, I'm hungry." Sam glared at him, but decided that the little man really should get something in his stomach to soak up the alcohol he was absorbing. The waiter came and Ciano ordered barbecued ribs, french fries and onion bagels. Sam and Laine ordered a late supper as well.

"Jesus, I hate bagels," Ciano said.

"Then why the hell did you order them?" Sam demanded, almost at the end of his tether. Laine laid a restraining hand on his arm.

"All in good time," Ciano said. He launched into another technical discussion with Laine, in German. Sam stared into his drink, wishing for the good old days, when people just shot at you and you could shoot back. The food arrived and Ciano attacked his ribs wolfishly. By that time, it was time for another round of drinks. Ciano sat back, satisfied, sipping his third Wild Turkey, his bagel still untouched.

"Okay," Ciano finally said. "We got 'em to the comet, and we know how they're gonna get back. The question is why? You remember what Tarkovsky was supposed to speak about?"

Sam thought back. It was something that meant nothing to him, so he couldn't remember the title of the scheduled talk.

"It was something about the Tunguska event," Laine said. "It was—" her voice trailed off and she turned decidedly pale. Sam was alarmed. It was unlike Laine to lose her self-posession. "Ice!" she half-whispered at last.

"The light dawns," Ciano said. He looked sharply at Sam. "You know about the Tunguska event?" Sam shook his head. "Okay, lemme give you a rundown," Ciano said. "It was something happened in Siberia way back before the Revolution, a big blast that laid down hundreds of square kilometers of forest but didn't kill anybody because there was nobody there."

Sam's professional hackles stood up at the words, "big blast," and something about it shook a memory loose. "Hold it. I think I read or heard something about it, years ago. No remains, right? No crater or meteorites?"

"Exactly," Ciano confirmed. "Now, I got a lot of

friends who'll swear that what caused the blast was a UFO blowing up, or some kind of natural atomic explosion, or a whole lot of other explanations."

"Why an atomic explosion?" Sam asked.

Ciano grinned triumphantly. "Where the blast went off, the trees were still standing at the center. That's a torus effect, just like you get with an aerial atomic blast." He grabbed up his bagel and held it out. "That's a torus, a bagel, a donut, an inner tube. It means that the released energy is largely confined within this closed, tubular matrix and stuff standing at the epicenter stays standing. Get it? That's what happened at Tunguska, and that's what Tarkovsky was gonna talk about tonight."

Sam knew that this was what he had been searching for. He also knew that he was going to have to let this displaced Hobbit go about telling him his own way. "Go on," Sam said.

"A few years ago," Ciano said, "Tarkovsky published a paper. For some reason, it never made it into the major astronomical journals. I guess he yanked it shortly afterward to polish it some. I've done that myself. Anyway, I ran across it in a little Japanese publication I subscribe to. The Japanese are great comet-watchers, you know. Most new comets are spotted by amateurs, and Japan is the preeminent country for amateur astronomers." Sam didn't know that, but he let it ride for the moment in hopes that Ciano would get to the point.

"Now, Tarkovsky's point was this: he thinks that the Tunguska blast was caused by a collision with a chunk of cometary ice!" He paused for effect. "See, ice accounts for a lot of the anomalies in the Tunguska business: There were no meteoric particles found. Ice wouldn't leave any. There was a hell of a blast. Ice would make just such a blast."

"Just a minute," Sam said, "bear with me. Why would ice make a blast like that?"

"Look," Ciano said, "suppose you had a chunk of ice about the size of," he looked around, then spread his arms to their widest extent, "about the size of this bar. And suppose you detached this chunk of ice from its parent comet, as must have happened many times in the past, and suppose you chucked this hunk of ice right down Earth's gravity well. Well, right there you got mass and velocity, plus you got the effect of the ice, which is just water, flashing to steam when it heats up, and the result is," he rummaged in his pockets and came up with a pen and a pocket calculator. He began punching the calculator and scribbling down figures on the tablecloth. "You got an ice cube that's ten meters by ten meters and it'd mass a thousand tons. If it fell from outer space at zero initial velocity, it'd pack energy about the same as that of a twenty kiloton bomb when it hit. Only it probly wouldn't hit, because one that small would produce an aerial blast, like the Tunguska event. See what I mean? And see why this guy Nekrasov wants control of the project?" He looked back and forth at them, "Because, when that chunk of ice comes in—" he threw himself back in his chair, flung both arms out extravagantly, and bellowed: "KABOOM!" Once again, heads swiveled.

Now Ciano leaned forward across the table and said in a low, conspiratorial voice, "and the beauty of it is, it's one hundred percent clean. No radiation, no fallout, just one hell of a big bang." He sat back and took another big slug of Wild Turkey.

"It provides a great many answers," Laine said. "One of the great limitations on deep space travel has been the necessity of taking water along and recycling it. It's necessary for every biological function. The same with oxygen. With the ice in the comets, they will be able literally to mine all the water and oxygen they need."

"Kinda opens up all sorts of possibilities, don't it?" Ciano said. "Lunar colonies, Martian colonies, asteroid settlement, all kindsa stuff. All the water and oxygen you need, plus fuel for your engines. Jeez—"

"Speculate on that later," Sam said. His demeanor was as impassive as usual but he was feeling a cold sweat. "Let's stick to Project Peter the Great and Nekrasov's probable plans. How soon can he put it into effect? What are our chances of pre-empting his project by instituting one of our own? What are the best defenses against such an attack?"

This time, it was Ciano holding out a hand to stem the rush of questions. "Wait a minute. In the first place, you got no proof that what I'm talking about is what's going on over there. I'm pretty sure I'm right, but that's a long way from having proof. Plus, there's still a lot of things to iron out, like just how are they gonna make the ion drive work?" He jabbed a forefinger into the tabletop with every point.

"Don't you think," Laine said, "that the evidence now at hand is sufficient to assume that the ion drive is now at Tarkovsky's disposal? Surely such a commitment of resources would not have been authorized otherwise."

"Sure," Ciano agreed. "*We* can be pretty sure of that. Now, how about convincing somebody else? I think Mr. Taggart here can tell you how cooperative his superiors are when they're handed something really outlandish. Tell them we have evidence that the Soviets are planning to chuck big ice cubes at us or somebody else, and you'd get shown the door quick."

"And for once I'd agree with them," Sam said. "This whole theory has one great big hole in it."

"What might that be, pray tell?" Ciano asked.

"Just what advantage is this iceberg bomb to the Soviets? They already have plenty of nuclear warheads, even after the accords are fully effected. So have we. If they attacked us with ice bombs or anything else that big, the result would be the same: nuclear retaliation. So why bother?"

"That's a very astute observation," Ciano admitted, immediately qualifying it with: "Especially considering its source."

"Perhaps," Laine hazarded, "they intend to make it look like a natural disaster, like the Tunguska event."

"That'd make sense," Ciano said.

But Sam was shaking his head. "It'd be a hell of a risk for them to take. Consider: A big explosion going off without warning like that, or a whole bunch of them, wouldn't it look just like an atomic attack for the first few minutes? They'd be taking the chance that we'd launch a counterattack as soon as the first explosion went off, even before we knew what we were being hit with."

Ciano sat with his chin against his deformed sternum, thinking. Then: "Suppose they play it up for months ahead of time? You know, 'Big Comet Headed This Way: Sov Scientists Issue Warning!' That kind of thing. First it's in all the tabloids that they sell at the supermarket checkout counters, then it makes the respectable papers and the scientific publications. By D-Day, everybody's ready for it, only, of course, there's no way to predict where it's gonna hit. When it does, well, it just happens to be the Western Hemisphere, with maybe a few not-so random hits on Soviet soil for verisimilitude. How's that sound?"

"Better," Sam said. "But, it's still a hell of a risk. After all, if we decide that we're being weakened militarily for *any* reason, we just might launch a preemptive strike to keep the Soviets from picking up all the marbles. They'd sure as hell do it if the situation were reversed. Furthermore, they have to take into account that we might penetrate their operation."

"Yeah, that's so," Ciano admitted. "Still, you gotta take into account the fact that there are some real nutso cases in important positions all over the world."

"Astute observation," Sam said, smiling, "considering the source."

Ciano went on, ignoring him. "So, we got two major possibilities: (A)," he held up one finger, "Nekrasov's crazy and thinks he can get away with it, which is entirely possible, or (B)," he held up another, "he figures he's got an angle that's gonna let him get away with it, which is also quite possible. Of the two, I favor hypothesis (B), which presupposes that there's some factor here that we're missing which, if we had it, would make sense of this whole mess, and that, my friends, is the greatest likelihood of all."

"We must have more data," Laine said, somewhat more succinctly.

"No kidding," Ciano said. He looked to Sam. "Well, Mr. G-Man, that's your field. You're the intelligence man, we're just intelligent."

"Since when did you take over this operation, Ciano?" Sam demanded.

"Nature abhors a vacuum," Ciano said. "and always tries to fill it with something. Human nature abhors a competence vacuum. Here I am to fill it. You need me, Taggart. Dr. Tammsalu here knows something about the project, and she knows some of the people involved. You have access to a lot of important classified data that you'd never understand. I can put that data together and make sense out of it."

Much as he hated to admit it, Sam figured that the arrogant little dwarf was probably right. He'd already observed Ciano's ability to draw accurate conclusions from skimpy data.

"Won't they miss you back in Hawaii?" Sam asked.

"Naw, they're probably hoping my plane'll get hijacked to Antarctica or somewhere."

"What did we ever do to deserve the help of such a charming and popular scholar?" Sam mused.

"I don't know," Ciano said, seriously. "You musta been a real saint in some former life and all your good karma's come back to you in spades. I take it you got an expense account, right? You can establish me in some halfway decent digs handy to a facility with a good library, telex equipment and a really first-class computer setup. A good university would be better than a government facility. That way we can skip all the security crap."

"Anything else I can do for you?" Sam asked.

"I'll let you know. Leave me your phone number."

"Gentlemen," Laine said, just as Sam appeared ready to explode, "perhaps we should order a nightcap." Sam, somewhat defused by the interruption, ordered an Irish Coffee. Laine had another vodka and Ciano, predictably, another double Wild Turkey. The waiter looked at them strangely as he delivered the round.

"The Aral coast is a dull place," Laine said, as if somebody had asked. "A great tolerance for vodka is the natural result."

"Now," Ciano went on, "what we're looking for is changes in the priorities on this Peter the Great thing. If Nekrasov's going all-out on the comet project, other projects are gonna be cancelled or stripped of resources. Crucial materials are gonna be diverted from other projects. *That's* what's gonna provide us with our evidence."

"Speaking of security crap," Sam said, "you realize I could be committing a federal offense by smuggling any of this stuff out to you."

"I know you can do it," Ciano said. "Just put your low animal cunning to work. It's not like you're worried about keeping your job much longer, anyway."

Sam fumed. The little man was at it again. "Job, my ass. I could be looking at several years in a federal pen."

"Where's your sense of patriotic duty, Taggart?" Ciano chided. "You owe it to your country."

Sam slumped back in his chair, feeling very nearly defeated. "My God," he said, shaking his head. "It's going to be hard enough trying to sell my bosses on a Soviet comet attack. How the hell am I going to explain *you*?"

CHAPTER SIX

WASHINGTON, D.C.

The next morning Sam woke up with a mild hangover. He wondered what Laine and Ciano must be undergoing this morning. Double vodkas and Wild Turkey, for God's sake! He forced himself through his morning regimen of exercise, fortified with a handful of aspirin. He refused to let a self-inflicted infirmity be an excuse for slacking off. During the course of a very long, very hot shower, the fog began to dissipate.

At five after eight he phoned his boss' secretary and bullied her for an appointment later that morning. He immediately called up Laine and arranged to pick her up in time for the appointment. Then he pondered the wisdom of taking Ugo along as well. Was his boss really ready for something like Ciano? On the other hand, he needed an expert, an American expert, to back him up. He was going to be trying to put over a story so wild that his boss would never buy it on his word alone. Or so he told himself. But it was the mental image of Ciano confronting Caldwell that sold him in the

end. He just had to see what it would be like. He
called Ciano, then went out to lay in a substantial
breakfast against the coming exertions.

Theodore Caldwell's office was neat and under-
stated, with dark paneling and heavy furniture.
Most people would take it for a banker's office.
Caldwell sat behind a teakwood desk, complete
with a leather-cornered green blotter and a massive brass pen stand. Otherwise, the desktop was
utterly bare. At least, Sam reflected, Caldwell wasn't
the type who tried to make you think that you
were stealing his valuable time from terribly important business.

Caldwell himself was a tall, slightly jowly man.
Once upon a time he had been an athlete, but the
years and a sedentary job had taken their toll. His
hair, what was left of it, was gray and short. He
wore the anonymous, conservatively-cut suit that
constituted a uniform in Washington.

Sam made introductions. Laine Caldwell already
knew and, to his credit, he didn't turn a hair when
he saw Ciano. Sam suspected that somebody downstairs had tipped him about what to expect. Sam
wasted no time on pleasantries. As soon as Ciano's
professional credentials were established, he outlined their findings and suspicions, with emphasis
on the discussion of the night before, giving full
credit to Ciano's insights. To his relief, Ciano interrupted no more than a dozen times. Sam took
this to be evidence that Ciano was suffering from
last night's overindulgence. He was having a slow
morning. At least, the little man's interruptions
were for the purpose of setting him straight on
technical points, colorfully interspersed with Low
Brooklynese and an occasional sentence or even
entire paragraph in impeccable English.

Laine maintained a discreet silence throughout
all this. Caldwell said very little, merely sitting

back in his chair and giving the impression of full attention and interest. Sam knew this to be part of his bureaucrat's pose. For all he knew, Caldwell wasn't hearing a word. For about fifteen seconds after Sam's wrap-up, Caldwell remained silent.

"I must admit," Caldwell said at last, "that this is the craziest story that's come across my desk in a long time. Maybe in my whole career." He thought for a while. "Before we can take any kind of action on your report, we will have to have additional expert opinions. If there's anything to your theory, it'll have to go to the National Security Council, and they're not about to act on the unsubstantiated word of three . . . people."

"Whaddya need additional expert opinions for?" demanded Ciano in his inimitable manner. "You got *my* view, and believe me, that's the one that counts. You go asking my esteemed colleagues, and what are you gonna get? You're gonna get a hundred opinions from a hundred semi-morons with framed degrees on their walls and not an original thought to split among 'em."

Only slightly taken aback, Caldwell continued smoothly. "I understand what you are saying, Dr. Ciano, but I must first convince my superiors of the severity of the crisis before the matter may be brought before the decision makers." He paused for emphasis. "As Sam can tell you, the National Security Council means the President. Now, I may be convinced," Sam caught the weaseling "may" and wondered whether the others had, "but that won't matter as far as the NSC is concerned. Also, they'll be most displeased if we alarm the President without cause. We need a panel of expert advisers. We should probably consult with the National Academy of Sciences to form a panel."

This time it was Sam's turn for an outburst, causing Ciano to shut up before he could get a word out. "Damn it, we don't have time for that. They've stolen a march on us as it is. If we go appointing panels and instituting studies and turning them over to evaluating committees we'll be so far behind we'll never catch up! We know damn well how fast the Soviets can move when they commit themselves to a course of action like this. They did it nearly half a century ago with their A-bomb project." Sam got out of his chair and began to pace frenetically, forcing Caldwell to keep turning his head to follow his subordinate, "And don't give me that crap about the Rosenbergs selling them the secrets; they were ready to test their first device before they got word one from the Rosenbergs. They did it again with Sputnik in '57 and by God they're going to get away with it a third time with this Peter the Great business!" By now he was slapping the surface of Caldwell's polished desk.

"Tell him, Rev!" Ciano cheered.

"Now," Sam went on, somewhat calmer, "if the Soviets are going to outstrip us in space exploration, that's between their scientific establishment and ours, and it's not this bureau's concern. But this comet business is going to be used as an offensive weapon and that means national security and that means us! They're moving on it fast, and the reason they can do that is because they aren't appointing any goddamn committees! Nekrasov pulls the strings and Tarkovsky directs the project and that's it. Now, if we can't come up with something as streamlined as that, we're finished. We've lost before we've started." Actually, the Soviet structure was not as simple as all that and Sam knew it perfectly well but he chose to overlook it to make his point.

Caldwell sat through Sam's mini-tirade with the unperturbed air of a man whose job involves listening a great deal and saying very little. He was far from inept, otherwise he would never have been able to maneuver himself into his current position. If Taggart's report turned out to be as hysterical as it sounded, his reputation could be ruined for having taken it seriously. Conversely, if it should prove to be true, and if he had not acted promptly and decisively, he would be finished as well. He was, however, an expert at survival in this bureaucratic jungle. With a repressed shudder, he remembered the notorious Army Ordnance general who had staked his professional reputation on the belief that an atomic bomb was an impossibility. Ice bombs sounded absurd, but he wouldn't risk his reputation on the likelihood that he might be wrong. He'd pass that on to someone else.

"Sam, I'm setting up a task group on Project Peter the Great. You're going to head it. Even if it is a committee, it can't move too slowly with you at its head, now can it?"

"That depends on who's on it," Sam answered suspiciously. He sensed a trap.

"For one, Dr. Tammsalu, if she's willing." Laine nodded quickly. "Good. Then you are hereby assigned, at a salary commensurate with your training. Your appointment will, of course, be subject to further security clearance. This will also eliminate the need for you to find a suitable research position right away. Dr. Ciano, we would like to have you as a consultant to this task group."

"Well, OK," Ciano said with poor grace. Clearly, he thought he should head the group, but he would take a consulting position if that was all he could get.

"As you say, Sam," Caldwell went on, "this is a matter of utmost urgency. How soon can you get back to me with your panel report? You'll be given access to funds adequate to cover all related expenses, and I'm assigning five people to your task group, under your direction." Sam was ready for that. He had gotten most of what he wanted, after a fashion. Now he was going to have to do something for Caldwell. He took the list of names Caldwell had scribbled. As he had expected, all but one were from the UFO department. He was to keep them out of Caldwell's hair for the duration.

"Expect to hear from me in about a week. I should have our blue ribbon panel organized by then."

"Fine," he glanced at his watch. "Well, Drs. Tammsalu and Ciano, I won't detain you further. I hope we can contain this situation before it presents a national danger." As they got up to leave, he said: "Sam, may I speak to you in private? Our friends can wait in the anteroom. It'll only take a few minutes."

When the others had left Caldwell turned to Sam, his bland bureaucratic expression gone, replaced by the severe face of a superior about to give a subordinate a dressing-down. "Where the hell did you find this guy Ciano?"

"I didn't," Sam replied. "He found me."

"Christ, Sam, can you imagine taking him in front of the NSC or God help us, the Joint Chiefs?"

"He can't help the way he looks," Sam said. "Hell, even the way he acts isn't as crazy as some pretty highly-placed people you and I know."

"I know that," Caldwell said, impatiently. "When I was a kid at Princeton, I used to see Einstein sometimes, though I never took his classes. That old coot was a pretty bizarre sight, by early fifties standards. But at least his reputation was already made before he even came to this country. But this guy! Not only is he a screwball, he's just a kid. Will anybody take him seriously?"

"He's brilliant," Sam said. "Take it from me. He's not only an expert in his field, he's intuitive as all hell. I've never seen anybody who could pick up a few disparate facts and come to a correct conclusion like this guy. He's like those Intelligence wild men they used in World War Two to break the Japanese code, or crack the Ultra device."

"Yeah, I know," Caldwell said. "But why couldn't he be a nice, clean-cut Prussian like von Braun? Well, the hell with that. The other problem we have is you."

"Me?" Sam asked, innocently.

"Exactly. That little outburst you put on just now." Caldwell gazed at him with icy eyes. "I can put up with it, because I'm used to your little idiosyncrasies and you've done some good work in the past. You've earned a little latitude. Also, those other people in the room were nothing, this time. But," he paused and rapped out the rest in a deadly monotone, "if you pull that in front of any of *my* superiors, you'll be out on your can looking for work as a security guard." For once, Sam kept his mouth shut. "That's all, Sam. On the off-chance that you're actually onto something I look forward to hearing from you." Sam left. The ball was in his court now. He found his two companions in the anteroom and took them out of the building. Half an hour later, they held a war council over lunch in the restaurant of a nearby Holiday Inn. Sam was silent on the trip to the restaurant and so, for a change, was Ugo.

"What kinda yoyos did your boss saddle us with?" Ugo asked after they had ordered.

"Not as bad as I'd feared," Sam said. Laine noted that all his choleric temper of earlier in the day had disappeared. She wondered if it had all been an act to bully concessions out of his superior. "Of the five, four are on the outs with the organization. One for inefficiency, one for a drinking problem, but the other two because they're mavericks like me. Old-time hardliners being kept on the back burner."

"What are hardliners?" Laine asked.

"Actually, it's a matter of government policy," Sam explained. "Or rather style. In the fifties and most of the sixties, we played hardball with the Soviets; lots of confrontation and saber-rattling in public, rough games for people like me. The seventies and a lot of the eighties were a softline period; detente, arms talks, but little brushfire conflicts in the Third World. Then there was a period of really rough hardballing. That was when I got a lot of action. Now, we're back in a softline mode again. With the new arms accords apparently working and everybody backing down from armed confrontation, I thought it was going to stick. Now it looks like rough times again. The reason I'm still around at all, and these two men, Pearson and Camargo, are still on the Company payroll, is that we've been kept in reserve against a return to the bad old days."

"So we got a lush, a screwup and two cowboys," Ciano said. "Who's number five?"

Surprisingly, Sam grinned broadly. "That one was a big shock. Number five is Fred Schuster."

"Who's he?" Ciano asked.

"Fred's a she. Frederike Schuster. She's been a top operative for years, and she's in no trouble I ever heard of. That makes me wonder why she was assigned to us."

"Perhaps," Laine suggested, "since Mr. Caldwell gave you four misfits, he gave you this Frederike as compensation."

"Don't count on it," Sam cautioned. "If Caldwell assigned her to me, he's got some ulterior motive." He looked at Ciano with an odd cast of eye. "You'll like her, Ugo. She's your kind of person."

"I don't like the sound of that," Ciano said. Sam would say no more on the subject.

"What do we do now?" Laine asked as their orders arrived. "Won't it take several months to assemble this blue ribbon panel?"

"Why bother with a panel?" Ciano said. "Don't we got enough to take to the President as it is?"

"Look, Ugo," Sam said. "You don't just walk up to the President of the United States and say you want to talk about ice. Presidents are a shy breed and they're surrounded by people whose specialty is keeping people from seeing them." He sighed. Ciano's impatience and detachment from reality were going to be a problem. "Believe it or not, right now our most direct line to the White House is through my boss. It's going to take the Russians time to put this project together. They're going to have to strip other programs, train people, re-arrange budgets, all kinds of things. They'll be moving fast, but with any luck we'll have time to set up."

The waitress came back with drinks and salads and Sam continued outlining his plan of action. "If we're going to be taken seriously, we'll have to have evidence, lots of it. We'll need an impressive array of experts." Before Ciano could start his obvious outburst, Sam said: "I know what you're about to say, so keep it to yourself. We have to have them. Here's my plan for getting them: The top people are mostly so busy they're not going to be willing to just drop everything and hop on the first flight to Washington, right?" Ugo and Laine nodded agreement. "But Caldwell didn't say that the panel had to be locked up in one place to debate the matter. The answer is, we go to them. You two get to pick the names for the panel. They'll have to be nationally known, at least within the scientific community." With a pointed look at Ciano he added: "With *good* reputations among their peers." Ciano just sat and glared, while simultaneously wolfing down salad like a starving vegetarian. "We'll visit each one individually," Sam continued, "and try to persuade them of the gravity and urgency of the situation.

"Once we have them talked around, we'll ask them to come to Washington for a presentation to the Agency chief and maybe to the National Security Council. I figure we can swing it in about a month. We've got to do it in that time, because once this business gets in front of the NSC, things will start moving *really* slow."

"How can we be sure we will persuade them all?" Laine asked.

Ciano chuckled. "Relax. If I been reading this fella right, he's gonna load the dice in our favor."

"I beg your pardon, Dr. Ciano?" Laine said.

"Make it Ugo," Ciano insisted.

"What he means," Sam explained, "is that I'll only invite those experts whom we've persuaded. If we move quickly enough, we'll be able to set up the meeting for the Agency chief before the ones we don't persuade have time to yak to their friends in Washington. Remember, some of these people are likely to be pretty committed to the disarmament process. They're going to see us as alarmist freaks out to wreck the rapprochement and drag us all back into nuclear confrontation. So, when you make your list, make it a long one. We probably won't convince a third of them that this is for real.

"Of course, we'll try to forestall them as well as we can. We'll tell them before the interview that our little conference must be held in strictest confidence for at least five years. We'll scare them a bit by invoking the National Security Act or some such. That ought to keep them quiet for a while. I hope."

"I wouldn't count on that," Ciano told him. "You're dealing with the scientific community. Some of those people are real blabbermouths."

"You don't say," Sam said. A large steak had been placed before Ciano, and it was disappearing at an amazing rate. Sam wondered how such a diminutive man could support such an appetite. He decided that it must all go to sustain Ciano's hyperactive imagination, temperament and mouth. "Could you suggest some good names, Ugo? I think a panel of about six would be close to ideal: enough to be impressive, but not so many that everybody's bored before the last one's said his piece."

Ugo considered for a while, polishing off the steak and working on the french fries in the process. "Lessee, a panel of six means about eighteen to start with. There must be at least eighteen good scientists in astronomy and astrophysics who ain't altogether dumb. We oughta have a coupla comet specialists, maybe an astronomer or two, at least one good generalist. Of course, we already got one of them, but it looks like I don't qualify for the panel. Lemme make a few phone calls and I'll have the list for you tomorrow."

"What's a generalist?" Sam asked.

"A generalist is the guy who's bright enough to embrace the whole gamut of scientific knowledge and make sense out of what he knows. Sorta the Renaissance man of science."

"I thought the Renaissance man was an impossibility in the twentieth century," Laine said, skeptically.

"Not impossible," Ciano corrected, "just improbable. But such people exist. I'm living proof. I gotta admit, though, there ain't enough of us in the whole world to fill a decent-sized phone booth in Manhattan."

Ciano set to work on the cheesecake he had ordered. "Hey, Taggart, what do you say we get us a rocket jock for our panel?"

"An astronaut?" Sam said. His eyes lit as he grasped the possibilities. "Jesus, that's a great idea."

"An astronaut?" Laine said. "Why? Aren't they just glorified test pilots? They are highly esteemed in the Soviet Union, but mainly as popular heroes and role models for the young. Their scientific opinions would not carry a fraction of the weight of a real scientist's. Do you mean the kind who is really a scientist trained to work in space?"

"No, Ugo's right. He means a real rocket jock, the kind who actually pilot the ships. The guys with the right stuff."

"Right stuff?"

"She ain't been here long enough, Taggart." Ciano dropped his Dead End Kid persona a bit in order to explain the complex piece of Americana. "You see, Laine, America's a funny place. People complain alla time about how much the space program costs, but they worship the astronauts like crazy. The first bunch, the Mercury and Apollo guys, grabbed the national imagination like nothing else in our history. Now, to most Americans, they're like just what you said; popular heroes and role models for the kids. Every American kid wants to grow up to be an astronaut. Hell," he admitted, low voiced, almost embarrassed, "I did, myself. But there's more to it than that. To achievement-oriented Americans, the upper-middle-class elite, which let me inform you is the *real* elite in this country, these guys represent something special. They are absolutely as expert and tops in their field as any human being can be, and it's probably the most demanding field that's ever existed. These guys gotta have smarts, they gotta think fast and move fast, they got nerve that makes a marble statue look like a gibbering hysteric. They are unquestionably the smartest, toughest, most skilled and expert specialists this country's ever produced."

"And when Ugo talks about achievement-oriented Americans," Sam added, "he's talking about the kind of people who make up the National Security Council. The kind of people who are advisers to presidents. To hell with the old East Coast money families like the Rockefellers, the real power elite in this country are middle-class men and women with ambition and ability, and for some reason they've settled on those astronauts as their heroes.

"Exactly," Ciano said. "Most of those people we'll be trying to convince at Sam's agency and the NSC and the President's cabinet, they wouldn't know an astrophysicist from a paleontologist. But if we can put one of them old rocket jocks in front of them, and he fixes them with his patented steely-eyed gaze and tells 'em the Russkies are gonna chuck ice down our gravity well and blow Cincinnati all to hell, they'll believe him."

"The right stuff," Laine murmured.

"There's even a book and a movie about it," Ciano said. Laine was fascinated, not only by this peculiar look at the American mentality, but by what she had just learned about these two men. At last she had a handle on them, a single point the two wildly disparate men had in common: they were both frustrated spacemen.

"Now," Sam said, sipping his coffee, "we need a name for this project. Now, Laine, this codename, Project Peter the Great, it refers to the entire Soviet plan to expand into space and exploit its resources, right?" She nodded. "Did the comet project have a specific name?"

"Not that I ever heard. It was just one project

among many, although it was Tarkovsky's pet. And of course it had no military dimension at that time."

"Then we need a codename to pin on this. Now, if I was a typical Pentagon planner, I'd stick a name on it that would give nobody any idea of what was under study. I'd call it Operation Sunflower, or Plan Salami Sandwich or something. But we want something that sounds as ominous as what we're facing." He saw that he was faced with two mystified masks. "Don't laugh, dammit, I'm serious. If I was a Hollywood agent, I'd say we were putting together a package. We're dealing with people who think in terms of signs and symbols. We should have one for this project."

"Hell, that's easy, Taggart," Ciano insisted. "The peaceful uses of space come under the heading of Project Peter the Great, right?"

"Right," Sam concurred.

"Well, what we got here," Ciano ground a thumb into the tabletop, "is Project Ivan the Terrible."

CHAPTER SEVEN

TSIOLKOVSKY SPACE CENTER

ARAL SEA, U.S.S.R.

The snow storm that had raged for two days had stopped, but it was bitterly cold outside the Administration Building of the Tsiolkovsky Space Center. In weather like this, even the hardy native Siberians would not dare to venture outside without their heavy protective winter outfits. It was in just such outfits that Tarkovsky and his young protogé, Alexei Ilyich Kamarovsky, were attired as they mounted the steps, no longer smelling of pinesap, to the building. Kamarovsky was about to push open the door when Tarkovsky stopped him and turned, facing out over the docks and slapping at his sides with mittened hands. "Isn't it a fabulous sight, Alyosha?"

Alexei turned reluctantly to look. Yes, the docks were more complete now. The paving was being laid on the roads and more of the crude buildings had had their electricity connected. "Yes, it's beautiful, Pyotr Maximovich," he admitted. "But we can't admire it if our eyeballs freeze. Let's go inside."

"You know what happens if you go into a Siberian's house on a night like this, Alyosha?"

"No," Alexei said, patiently, "what happens?"

"Well, they'll have a big samovar full of hot tea, just like all other good Soviet citizens, but as much as you long for some of that tea, coming out of weather like this, they won't serve you any until you've been in the house for at least half an hour."

"And why is that, Pyotr Maximovich?" Alexei asked, now wishing the old man would stop stalling and go inside.

"Because, when you come inside out of a night like this, with temperatures so low, it is dangerous. When that hot tea hits your teeth, they can crack. What do you think of that, Alyosha?"

"I think the Siberians are superstitious. No matter what the temperature is outside, that in your mouth will remain at normal body temperature."

"You have no soul, Alexei Ilyich," Tarkovsky said, testily. It was very nearly the strongest insult that one Russian could give another, but Tarkovsky took the edge off with a self-deprecating admission, "and, yes, you are right. I don't want to go inside, and tell the people in there the things that must be said."

Alexei released a sigh and watched it drift away in steam on the stiff breeze. Darkness was falling, electric lights were blinking on all over the complex, the temperature was dropping rapidly, and it was only mid-afternoon. God, what a place this was! He dragged enough air into his lungs to tell Tarkovsky what had to be done. "Pyotr Maximovich, it will be unpleasant, and I would not be standing in your shoes, or whatever the Siberians call this footgear, tonight. But you have your instructions and it must be done for the sake of Mother Russia."

Tarkovsky looked at Alexei and wondered if he had guessed wrong, if he had let his affection for the father color his judgement of the son. The boy's father, Ilya Yurivich, would never have mouthed such a sentence with a straight face. Pyotr Miximovich Tarkovsky yielded to none in his love of Mother Russia, but he would never have sought to express his patriotism so pretentiously. "Yes, it must be done," Tarkovsky admitted at last, not taking his eyes off Alexei.

"Come on, old man," Alexei punched Tarkovsky hard in the ribs. "This isn't the way Papa said you were when the Fascists came to Leningrad! You were his hero then! Surely you can face down this pack of Moscow pimps."

"Right you are, Alyosha," Tarkovsky roared, hugging the younger man. "Your papa was just a boy then, not ten years old, and we were going out every day to scrounge food or try to kill a few Fascists. But I was big and tough. By God, I was seventeen years old and a match for anything Hitler could throw against us! All right, let's go inside and tell these people what's what." They pushed through the door and a blast of hot air enveloped them like a blanket. Tarkovsky felt no better about what he had to do, but he was greatly reassured about Alexei. The boy was all right, he just had a tendency to phrase even his most innocuous thoughts in official terms. And that, Tarkovsky knew, was not such a bad quality to have.

In the large anteroom, Tarkovsky and Alexei peeled off their heavy winter garments and hung them up to dry along with the other coats and hats. Tarkovsky noted the fine sealskin coats, even a few splendid sable coats and hats. These could only belong to senior Party members. With a snort of disgust, Tarkovsky hung up his good, if common, Russian sheepskin, first withdrawing a flask of vodka from the pocket and taking a long swig. He capped the flask. He could stall no longer.

Tarkovsky pushed into the heavily-packed Director's conference room. "Comrades," he announced, "I hope you've come prepared for bad news." With no more preamble, he launched into his briefing on the new order for project Peter the Great. His recitation was bleak, but the mood of many of the scientists was no less so. When he finished, he looked about for comments. He was pretty sure where the first and most vehement protest would come from, and he was not disappointed.

It was Buganov, the ambitious head of the High-energy Astrophysics Division, who broke the silence after the Director's briefing.

"So, that's the final word from Moscow, then; an indefinite postponement of our x-ray and gamma-ray satellite program while stepping up considerably the pace of your cometary program."

"So it seems," Tarkovsky said. "I know that this is a great disappointment to many of you. This decision was made at the highest levels by people whose major concern is that we must at all costs maintain our lead in the exploitation of the solar system. The United States, Japan and the European community must not be allowed to monopolize our solar system for capitalistic purposes."

"That much is understood," said Petrov, the diminutive vice chairman of the project. "With the new engines nearing the testing stage and the emphasis shifted to long-range missions, a greater effort to exploit cometary ice is quite understandable. But this new timetable," he tapped the folder on the table before him, "virtually scraps half our space program, the work of decades."

"I suggest," Tarkovsky said, "that you address further questions of policy to the comrades who on my right." He nodded toward the group who had flown in from Moscow the day before. Most prominent among them was a bulky man in the uniform of a full general. Tarkovsky did not need to introduce him. Everybody here was familiar with General Doroshenko, who had been involved with the military end of the Soviet space program since he was a major.

"Comrades," Doroshenko began, "I have been assigned to take over as military director of Project Peter the Great. I will be replacing Colonel Kalashnikov in that role. This project, especially the cometary phase, is now perceived to be of utmost importance to national security, and military participation is to be emphasized accordingly." The general spoke with a heavy Ukrainian accent. "You may expect to see a great deal of me and my subordinates. Comrade Tarkovsky and I shall be, in effect, co-directors of this project." He scanned the table and saw only bland faces. Any discontent would from now on remain unvoiced.

Later, in his office, Tarkovsky poured glasses full of vodka for himself and Alexei. Glumly, Tarkovsky drained his and poured himself another.

"At least," Alexei said, "now you'll have no trouble out of Buganov and the rest."

"That's true. But now I am co-director with a uniformed flunky and we're both working for Nekrasov. And just what is *that* madman up to?"

"I think he sees that exploitation of the resources of the solar system is the wave of the future," Alexei answered. "The more he can expand his influence in the space program, the stronger his position will be in the future. With the new engines and the plans for expanded lunar activity and eventual exploitation and settlement of the asteroids, the need for cometary ice is crucial. Even Nekrasov knows that."

Tarkovsky shook his head. "No, I have talked with the man. He doesn't know the relative positions of the planets. I tried to explain to him the principles behind the new engines. He didn't understand and he doesn't care. No, his aim is something much narrower. What's worse, he got the idea from me."

Alexei sat on the corner of the desk and poured himself another vodka. "Explain, please."

"It was the Tunguska paper. You remember it?"

"Of course," Alexei answered.

"Somebody brought that paper to Nekrasov's attention, and I think I know who. The possible military applications of the project were explained to him. His only interest in cometary ice is in making ice bombs, to reproduce the Tunguska blast in places more interesting than Siberia."

Alexei stared at him blankly. "It makes no sense. What would be the advantage? Such weapons would set off a world war as surely as a nuclear missile attack."

"That is just what I do not understand. Such a blow could indeed be devastating, and it would produce no fallout, but how can he expect to get away with it? He assures me that his plans have the approval of his superiors, but is that true? And granted that he does have their approval, what story has he given them?" The old scientist shook his shaggy, graying head. "I don't like it. I've devoted my entire professional life to making this nation preeminent in space. Project Peter the Great was intended to assure that preeminence. Now I deeply fear that it has become a vehicle for the ambitions of one man, and a terrible threat to peace."

"Could it be a power play?" Alexei refilled his glass yet again.

Tarkovsky chuckled without humor. "A power play? You are too cautious. It could well be the weapon he needs to pull a coup."

The word brought Alexei up short. "Coup? That's a word from the old days, from before Stalin. I thought we were long past that kind of thing."

"It's still a perfectly usable word. The time is right for it. The economy is not healthy, our forays into the Third World have come to very little and our quest for military superiority has cost us most of our material prosperity without even, except for a few brief years, achieving parity. The West can always outspend us. The only area in which we are still ahead is space. I had always hoped that we would finally beat them out there, peacefully, because our system is better. The West, particularly the Americans, suffer from short-sightedness. Like all capitalists, they want a quick profit on any expenditure. As soon as times are difficult, the space budget is the first they cut and this is how we have maintained our edge in space.

"Now Nekrasov is going to throw that advantage away. He does not understand the overwhelming importance of the peaceful exploitation of our solar system. All he sees is the chance to make himself a new Stalin. Somehow he must expect to gain dictatorial power out of this. What do you think?"

"I think," Alexei said, unsteadily, "that we have both had too much to drink. We should not be talking like this." He looked around the office nervously.

Tarkovsky poured himself another, slopping a few drops of vodka onto the papers on his desk. "Are you worried about listening devices? They are there, all right, but it's hard to eavesdrop on a man who knows his electronics. Just now, our monitor is listening to a conversation we had in my quarters last week. I think the subject was the budget. Those little Japanese recorders are handy things. I always pick up one or two on my trips abroad."

"What are you going to do?" Alexei asked.

"There is only one thing I can do. Somehow, without Nekrasov's knowledge, I must speak to the Premier."

"And if Chekhov is aware of this plan and approves?"

"Don't even think it," Tarkovsky said low. "That would mean Armageddon."

MOSCOW

Nekrasov did not bother looking at the papers before him. He knew they were in order. The overhead lights reflected from his spectacles and his shiny scalp as he surveyed the men sitting around the long table, meeting in secret session to review the revised Phase I for Project Peter the Great. This was the Politburo of the USSR and Nekrasov's future rested in great part on the outcome of this meeting.

The building that surrounded them, the Kremlin Palace, showed centuries of use in the multitude of decorative styles, but this room was severely modern, and except for the inevitable portraits of Marx, Lenin and Engels it might have been a government or business meeting room in Bonn, Tokyo, Paris or Washington.

Even for the Politburo, this was an extraordinarily secret session. At the insistence of the Deputy Premier, even the personal assistant to the Premier had been forbidden to enter. Preliminary remarks were over, and it was time for Nekrasov to come to the meat of his proposal. At the far end of the table sat Premier Chekhov, his face a bland, noncommittal mask. Nekrasov detested Chekhov.

The Premier was a softliner, a man who, in Nekrasov's opinion, had conceded too much to the capitalists and had missed many golden opportunities to gain ascendency over the West. Chekhov was, however, an adroit, skillful politician and diplomat. One does not become Premier of the Soviet Union by being inept.

"In brief," Nekrasov said, "the first manned expedition to a comet will be to bring back two cometary icebergs approximately ten to fifteen meters across."

"Just what benefit could we get from these icebergs in space?" asked Denisov, whose portfolio included international trade. "Can they be sold? Anything that would reduce our trade deficit would be welcome. We're importing grain in tremendous quantities again this year." The Minister of Agriculture, sitting on Nekrasov's left, could only glare silently at this implied attack.

"Comrade Denisov," the Deputy Premier said, "this project means a race for our very national survival. It is unquestionably the most important race for superiority since the early days of atomic weapons. This is the last frontier, make no mistake about it. If we lose this competition, we may as well concede defeat and become slaves to the capitalists." He had their attention now.

"So what do you propose to do with them?" said Marshal Petrovich. His voice was deep enough to rattle the water glasses on the table.

Nekrasov was glad that it was Petrovich who had asked the question. "We'll let them fall on two designated spots in Arctic Siberia."

"What will that accomplish?" Petrovich demanded. "There's no shortage of ice in Siberia."

"But they will not quite reach the ground," Nekrasov said. "We plan to inject them into the atmosphere at a precisely computed speed and angle. They will explode just before reaching the ground." He paused for effect and surveyed the puzzled, incredulous faces around him. "The explosion will precisely duplicate the Tunguska blast of nineteen hundred and eight."

Premier Chekhov immediately grasped the military significance of what Nekrasov had said but he did not speak yet. Instead, it was Petrovich who spoke again. "Who did the technical analysis on the impact of these cometary icebergs?" Apparently, the general was not pleased that his extensive technical staff had never suggested such a possibility to him.

"It was Professor Tarkovsky, lately of Moscow University currently the director of the new Tsiolkovsky Space Center. As you know well, he is widely considered the world's foremost authority in this area." He picked up a thick typescript. "Here is the text of his complete work. Naturally, I have classified this paper class A secret and stopped its publication in the Soviet Astronomical Journal. I caught it before an official approval was given for publication and no preprint had been sent out. At least, none to overseas addresses."

Nekrasov saw that his audience, except for the Premier and Marshal Petrovich, still looked a bit mystified. It disturbed him that the Premier showed so little amazement. He reminded himself that the man was a politician and diplomat, well schooled in hiding surprise and indecision.

"The effect of the blast," Nekrasov went on, "should be comparable to a 20 to 50 kiloton bomb. With one major exception: No fallout. Thus, a by-product of this exercise is the testing of a new type of clean bomb, much cleaner than a neutron bomb. Besides, since nobody in the West knows about it, there is no known defense against the iceberg bomb."

"Two blasts of that size," interjected Premier Chekhov, "will be picked up by every detection system in the world. I take it you have plans for a cover story?"

"The beauty of this weapon," Nekrasov said, "is that it is absolutely indistinguishable from a natural meteorite fall. Siberia has always been nature's favorite target for such missiles. Two more will not raise a ripple in the West. We shall report a pair of unusually large meteor strikes. In the absence of massive radiation there will be no suspicion. Western scientists will ask permission to travel to the fall sites in search of meteoric material. Permission will be routinely denied for reasons of state security." He glanced about the table and saw that he had made a few people nervous by blatantly referring to the iceberg bomb as a weapon. "Of course, you understand that this is basically a peaceful space experiment that happens to have a potential military application."

Marshal Petrovich persisted: "Why do you test only cometary icebergs as bombs? I would imagine that chunks of asteroids would serve as well. I understand that there are a lot more asteroids available than comets."

Nekrasov answered: "I am told that there are probably many more comets in the cloud surrounding the solar system than there are asteroids, but it is true that there are many more asteroids in the inner system, as you say, available. However, our new ion-drive engine cannot use asteroidal rock for propulsion. Thus, we couldn't shift an asteroid's orbit to coincide with a target on Earth unless we took a large amount of extra fuel, which would require a very much larger spaceship. As it stands now, we are counting on the use of cometary ice as reaction mass to bring back both ship and iceberg. Also, despite recent advances in laser technology, we still lack a means of efficiently slicing up an asteroid. We do, however, have an easily transportable laser gun that can cut ice quite well.

"In addition, ice is easy to tailor to size. If the mass of an impacting rock were too large, the results could not be controlled." Nekrasov stopped short of admitting that the size of the infalling object, whether ice or rock, must be tailored to suit military objectives. He was sure, though, that General Petrovich understood. So, unfortunately, did Premier Chekhov.

Most members of the Politburo remained impassive, a wise course to take considering the immense complexity and delicacy of the issues involved. It was Foreign Minister Kostenko who next attacked the subject. "Some years ago," he began, "a book was circulated among us. It was a romance by an American author with a German name and it involved a lunar colony in rebellion making use of lunar rock as missiles, using some kind of moon-based apparatus to launch the rock instead of conventional rockets. Attached to the book we received a report by a panel of our own scientists, Tarkovsky among them as I recall, stating that this plan was quite feasible. At present, all powers with space capability have established surveillance systems against just such an attack in the future. Wouldn't your iceberg bombs be detected by such systems, Comrade Nekrasov?" The small, bespectacled Foreign Minister studied the Deputy Premier with little favor.

Nekrasov did not need to answer. "No," Marshal Petrovich said, "they would not. Lunar activity is monitored by spy satellites orbiting the moon itself. Any kind of missile would be far easier to detect leaving the moon than nearing the Earth. Recently, the European Space Agency's moon base successfully tested a mass-driver using solar energy. Such a thing could be used as a weapon in the near future, but we had pictures of the test within minutes. We could easily destroy any such facility at the first hint of hostile activity and so could the Americans. But these surveillance systems watch only the lunar surface. All others watch for missiles launched from the Earth or from orbiting satellites or space stations. These ice bombs, if they need no high-powered rockets to be injected, would be virtually undetectable before impact."

Behind his bland mask, Premier Chekhov was deeply disturbed. It sounded practical and logical, but it did not sound like Nekrasov. The Deputy Premier had high ambitions; Chekhov knew that. He knew as well that Nekrasov had been carefully and expertly coached prior to this presentation. By Tarkovsky? Somehow, Chekhov was certain that it was not. Now, however, was not the time to take decisive action. Chekhov needed more time, and Nekrasov needed a little more rope.

"I know this man Tarkovsky," Chekhov said. "He is a capable man, and I would like to have his technical assessment before we take a vote on this matter. In the meanwhile, Comrade Nekrasov, you have the necessary authorization to proceed with the accelerated pace you have requested. You are not, however, to drop these icebergs until we have conferred further on this matter." He looked around the table. There was no dissension.

Later the same afternoon, Nekrasov sat in his office overlooking Red Square, reviewing the events of the meeting. It had gone better than he had expected. It bothered him that Chekhov had raised no more objection than he had. It suggested that the Premier would be engaging in some game of his own. Nekrasov got up and crossed to a wooden cabinet where he kept his favorite brandy from the Caucasus. A voice on his desk intercom announced the arrival of KGB chief Boris Ryabkin.

"Good evening, Boris," Nekrasov said as the man walked in. "Care to join me for a brandy?"

Ryabkin accepted the delicate cognac glass and the two men sat on opposite sides of a tea table. The KGB chief sank heavily into the overstuffed leather sofa as he sniffed the bouquet of the fine brandy. He took a sip, sighed in appreciation, and launched into his unofficial briefing.

"The Estonian woman is now under the protection of the CIA. I have learned from a reliable source that she showed up at an international conference on comets held in the United States. As you may recall, that was the meeting Tarkovsky was planning to attend. In a special meeting arranged by Professor Ehlers of Hamburg Observatory, she asked the assembled world authorities on comets what they thought about the Soviet plans for a manned mission to a comet. Apparently, she drew a complete blank. Incidentally, she was escorted by a man who was later identified as a CIA operative."

Nekrasov studied his former deputy over his glass as he swirled the volatile liquid in its bottom. "The woman could cause us some problems. On the other hand, if we were to liquidate her now, it might tip the Americans that there is something to her allegations. It would not take long for them to figure out our probable course."

"The Estonian knows very little," Ryabkin said. "She left the Tsiolkovsky Center before the new timetable came into effect. She doesn't know the revised plans for Project Peter the Great and she can't reveal what she doesn't know."

"Let's not assume that. She may have kept in touch with others still on the project after she left but before her defection. Keep her under the closest possible surveillance."

Ryabkin nodded. "That is what I'm doing now."

Nekrasov punched a combination on his desktop intercom and spoke into it: "Dr. Baratynsky, come to my office, please." He turned to Ryabkin. "I think it is time for some expert advice."

Ryabkin shrugged. He did not like Nekrasov's scientific *eminence grise*, but the man was necessary to the operation.

"Who is the man escorting the Tammsalu woman? Is it anybody we have encountered before?"

"That is a very odd thing. Do you remember the one called Samuel Taggart?"

"Taggart? Indeed I do. He was one of their most effective field operatives several years ago. He shortened the careers of some of my best agents when we were playing rough games with the Americans. Didn't I read a report that he had been killed in Central America several months ago?"

Ryabkin shook his head. "Shot and severely wounded, but not killed. This is the first we've seen of him since the incident. He's a tough one, though. He took at least three hits before those Indians got him into a truck and away."

Nekrasov was puzzled. "Taggart is a gunslinger of the old school. Why would they put him on the Tammsalu case instead of one of their scientific people?"

"I think it's a good sign," Ryabkin said. "Our reports have it that the man has been on the outs with his agency for some time. His official CIA rating is comparable to our KGB captain. One would think that his record would have earned him much higher rank long ago. The operation with the counterrevolutionaries in Central America was the first important assignment he had been given in a long time, and he botched it. There was little he could have done, according to the report I received, but his superiors seem to have used it as an excuse to take him out of circulation."

"So they've put the old warhorse out to pasture?" Nekrasov said. "It could mean that they don't take the Estonian's story seriously. Again, it could be a subterfuge. Best to take no chances. Keep them both under close **obse**rvation and be prepared to take them both out should it prove necessary."

Ryabkin's glass stopped midway to his lips. "Take direct action against a CIA operative? It's been many years since we've done that." Traditionally, CIA and KGB killed off each other's expendable foreign agents, but avoided killing actual American or Russian operatives.

"An accident might have to be arranged," Nekrasov advised. "Something of a compromising nature involving the two of them. It would be helpful if the CIA found it embarrassing enough to do some of the covering up themselves. Put the Bulgarians on it. It's all they're good for in any case."

There was a knock on the door and Dr. Yevgeny Baratynsky entered. He was very tall but overweight and soft-looking, with round features and pudgy hands. His clothes were expensive and stylish and he was noted for his luxurious tastes in clothes, housing, food and women.

"Sit down, Yevgeny," Nekrasov said. "Have a brandy."

Baratynsky took a glass and dipped his bulbous nose almost into the brandy as he inhaled loudly. Ryabkin refused to show his distaste. If he could stand the Bulgarians, he could stand Baratynsky. In any case, Nekrasov's takeover of Project Peter the Great had been Baratynsky's plan to begin with, and they depended on him. Ryabkin and Nekrasov would be lost in the world of space science and policy without the gross but brilliant Dr. Baratynsky, who had once been Tarkovsky's student. In a system whose respect for seniority was second to none in the world, Baratynsky had nudged aside many senior scientists in competition for important positions in the Soviet space program with insolent, contemptuous ease.

Nekrasov outlined such parts of his recent conversation with Ryabkin as he considered important for Baratynsky to know. "Did Tammsalu get no reaction at all from the comet specialists?" Baratynsky asked Ryabkin.

"When she and the CIA man left, they were accompanied by an odd-looking little man identified as Ugo Ciano. I am told he has a teaching position in Hawaii but nothing else."

"Ciano," Nekrasov said. "Is he from Italy?"

Baratynsky laughed loudly. "No, I have met Ciano. He's a native-born American, although he might dispute the fact. He comes from the New York borough of Brooklyn, whose natives believe themselves to be a sovereign nation."

"Could he be a danger to our work?" Ryabkin asked.

"He could be, but he won't be," Baratynsky said, cryptically.

"Please explain," Nekrasov asked patiently. He put up with more from the scientist than he would accept from anyone not a political superior, and there were few in that category these days.

"Ciano is unquestionably one of the West's most brilliant generalists," Baratynsky explained. "If that were the only consideration, I would consider him to be the most dangerous man we could possibly have working against us."

"But?" Nekrasov prodded, now leaning forward in his chair and fighting an urge to squeeze some answers out of the fat throat.

"But, he's such an eccentric that no responsible scientist in America would take him seriously. He has never accepted their scientific dogma and is a notable champion of ideas which most Western scientists, especially the Americans, consider to be crackpot. We have done extensive research and made valuable findings in parapsychology, ESP and the like, but most Western scientists refuse to accord them the status of true sciences."

Nekrasov nodded as if in agreement. Personally, he considered these things to be merest drivel and the "findings" highly suspect, but he was willing to humor his pet scientific plotter. Nekrasov knew little in the hard sciences, but like any intelligence man he was interested in any new developments in the field of information gathering and spying. In his younger days, he had made an extensive study of the Soviet parapsychology program, in the hopes of developing a new, apparatus-free means of eavesdropping. He had been disappointed, and had found that the vaunted "discoveries" in these fields were grossly exaggerated to impress the Western press with the superiority of Soviet science. Still, Baratynsky was basically correct: Soviet policy on scientific research *was* more open to radical ideas. There was still the possibility of achieving a scientific coup in a field that Western orthodoxy declared spurious.

"Men like that," Ryabkin said, "are often disparaged by their peers. But sometimes they can gain a popular following. Look at Velikovsky and Von Daniken. It has happened here as well. Look at what that fraud Lysenko did to us, especially our agricultural programs and our genetics. Is it possible that Ciano could win such attention?"

Baratynsky looked at the KGB chief in exaggerated surprise. "A most astute observation to come from you, comrade." Ryabkin almost came out of his sofa at the insolent, patronizing tone, but Nekrasov made a barely perceptible gesture to calm him. Ryabkin settled back and forced a friendly smile. Time to deal with this impossible fool later.

"What of it, Comrade Baratynsky?" Nekrasov asked. "Could Ciano circumvent his colleagues in the scientific community by going for popular appeal instead?"

Baratynsky leaned back and laced his fingers over his large belly, tilting his head back to study the baroque decoration of the ceiling. "A most intriguing possibility. The Americans have a great fondness for their sensationalist press. Quite aside from the question of Ciano, we could make some use of that ourselves."

"How?" Nekrasov asked, this time without impatience. It was for this kind of thinking that Baratynsky was so valuable.

The scientist took a sip and sloshed it around in his mouth, sucking in air at the same time to build up a heady fume and air mixture, like some kind of human carburetor. "I have made a number of trips to America, and studied a bit of their popular culture. Their tabloid press is similar to that of Britain, France and West Germany. It is luridly illustrated, with large, eye-catching type. There is a very narrow range of subjects, repeated endlessly." He ticked off the subjects on his fingers, "First and greatest, there are the doings of celebrities, film and television personalities preferred, although political figures sometimes appear, if their private lives are messy enough. Second, anything having to do with losing weight. The Americans are fanatics on the subject. They always want to read about a new weight-loss technique, especially if it is instant and does not involve limiting food intake or increasing exercise.

"Tied for third place are miracle cures for cancer and other diseases and the ever-popular paranormal phenomena: ESP, unidentified flying objects, 'proof' of life after death, ghosts, etcetera. Combinations of several of these motifs are popular. A typical headline will involve a dead celebrity speaking from beyond the grave."

Ryabkin shook his head. "How did these people ever become a threat to us?"

"What use might we make of this press?" Nekrasov asked.

"Closely related to the paranormal and miracle-cure subjects," Baratynsky explained, "are discoveries, as they quaintly put it, 'from behind the Iron Curtain'."

"Damn Churchill," Ryabkin muttered.

"You would be amazed at the things they have attributed to Soviet scientists. I suppose we brought it on ourselves, by looking into subjects Western science refuses to touch. Now, if we leak to these representatives of the 'yellow press,' as it is called for some reason, the information that Soviet scientists are predicting a great increase in meteoric activity, Americans will not only be prepared for such events, they will be disappointed if they do not transpire."

"Unusual," Nekrasov said, "but an excellent idea. Ryabkin, put some of your people on it. Comrade Baratynsky will put together an information package to be leaked to the Western press through the usual channels, with emphasis this time on the lurid tabloids." He considered for a moment. "At the same time, you might as well add Dr. Ciano as one of the subjects of our cleanup mission. The three will probably be traveling together, so there would be little suspicion should all perish in the same accident. After all, one Estonian defector, a CIA man who was already on his way out, and a crackpot scientist would not be missed."

"I'll put the Bulgarians to work on it immediately," Ryabkin said.

"But take no action until I give the go-ahead," Nekrasov cautioned.

"Of course, Comrade Nekrasov," Ryabkin concurred.

CHAPTER EIGHT

WASHINGTON, D.C.

It was late afternoon when Sam pulled up in front of Laine's hotel. He glanced at his watch, finding that he was several minutes early. He wondered whether he should go up to her apartment or wait down here. He hadn't seen her or Ciano for several weeks. He'd been persuading people to appear before the Security Council and strongarming the University of Hawaii into giving Ciano indefinite sabbatical leave. To this last end, he got a friend in CIA to put in a word with a major funding agency which in turn called up the Provost's office, causing permission for the sabbatical to appear as if by magic.

Most difficult of all had been lining up an astronaut. They were busy men, even if they no longer were working in the space program. He'd called on an airline executive, a college president, an oceanographer, two senators and a state governor before finding an ex-rocket jock who was interested, believed the problem to be serious, and was

118

willing to get up in front of the Council and the President and say so.

He was opening the car door when Laine appeared in the hotel entrance. He almost whistled but decided that it would be too crass. She was stylishly dressed and impeccably coiffed. Her makeup had either been applied by a professional, or she was taking lessons somewhere. Most of all, her walk was springy and confident, perfectly poised. Gone forever was the fatigued, confused refugee he had met a few weeks before. She smiled broadly and waved as she saw his red-and-white Chevy.

Thoroughly liberated by now, she opened the passenger door without waiting for him to do it. "Sam! It's so good to see you." She slid onto the seat smoothly. Already, her accent was fading. She studied him. "You're looking well, Sam."

He grinned at her. "I could say the same for you." His weight was almost back to normal, and he had worked himself to within a fraction of his top condition. "I see you're adjusting to your new life pretty well." He pulled out into traffic and glanced into the mirror. The white Volvo was still there.

"I'm over the worst of the culture shock," Laine said. "The lady across the hall from me runs a beautician's school and she got me to let her students work on me. Now she's after me to go to modeling school. Do you think I should give it a try?"

"Probably make a hell of a lot more than you would as an astronomer."

She laughed. "I'm not serious. I mean, she really did say I could make it as a model, but I would never do it. It sounds terribly dull."

"Most people think cuddling up to a cold telescope is dull," Sam commented.

"I suppose it's all in the temperament. How was your trip?"

"Overall, it was successful. I'll tell you all about it when we get to Ugo's." He glanced at the mirror again. "Anybody new moved into your building in recent weeks?"

"I don't know," she said, puzzled. "It's a residential hotel, I suppose there may have been several. Why?"

"Just a suspicion. I'm going to have to look into it." He changed the subject and they discussed inconsequential matters until they reached the building where Ciano was ensconced.

They found him sitting amid a litter of papers and empty Wild Turkey bottles. Most of the furniture was littered with more papers and books but an immaculate, late-model computer sat in splendid isolation on a table. He looked up from the surrounding mess. "Welcome home, Taggart. And you, too, Laine."

Sam crossed to a window and looked out onto the street below. "Did you know we're being kept under surveillance?" Sam asked.

Ciano scrambled to his feet and ran over to the window. "No kidding? We got a tail, just like in the movies? Which one is it?"

"I don't see them now, but there was a white Volvo following me from the airport. Question is, are they just dogging me or are they watching the two of you as well? It could be just me, for something that's not connected with our project."

"Don't count on it," Ciano said. He gestured toward a pile of tabloids on the floor. "Take a look at those. They're starting already."

Sam picked up a few of the papers. They were mostly titles he was familiar with, from hundreds of supermarkets, but he could not remember ever having looked into one. "You want to lose weight,

Ugo?" he asked. "Or are you just one of those who keeps hoping Elvis is still alive on a UFO?"

"Look closer, dingaling. The stuff about comets and meteors and Russian scientists."

Laine picked up some of the lurid tabloids. "Look at this." She held out a paper which bore on its cover a fuzzy, badly-reproduced photo of a flattened forest. Above it, giant, screaming red letters spelled out: SIBERIAN MYSTERY BLAST DUE AGAIN! Below that, in smaller type: *Sov Scientists Say Earth In For More Hits Soon! Is End Near*? They thumbed through the stack of tabloids. Every one of them featured a similar story on its front cover, some involving Tunguska, others showing file photos of the big meteor crater in Arizona or pictures of meteorites from museums. The articles were at best semiliterate, full of innuendos and wild distortions.

"They all appeared in the same week," Ciano explained. "You really gotta start keeping your eyes open, Taggart. What this means is, they leaked it all at once, and they went straight to the tabs, every one of them."

"I don't understand," Laine said. "Why these publications?"

"It's subtle," Sam said. "If you'll remember, Ugo suggested something like this that first evening, but I never expected anything this thorough. Who do you think is behind it? Tarkovsky?

Ciano shook his head. "Naw, he's strictly a science man. I got a suspicion, though. There's a guy I've met at a few international conferences; a big, tall, fat guy named Baratynsky."

"Never heard of him," Sam said.

"I've seen him," Laine said. "He's some kind of high-up administrator in the space program. He visited Tsiolkovsky Center a few times. He was always trying to corner me in a vacant room on his visits. I took to calling in sick when I knew he was coming down. Tarkovsky detests him."

"That's our boy," Ciano agreed. "He's ten percent scientist, ninety percent politician, and a hundred percent son of a bitch. Knows his space science, though, and he keeps up on military and civilian applications. I think he'd've defected years ago for the sake of higher pay, but nobody'd have him."

"So," Sam said, "if this man Baratynsky is playing Dr. Strangelove to Nekrasov—"

"Then we're in first-class trouble," Ciano finished for him.

Sam glanced through one of the tabloids as he crossed to the window. He never ceased to be amazed at what people would believe if they saw it in print. Still no Volvo, but he knew it was out there, or another surveillance vehicle might have taken over. He saw a tall but foreshortened figure striding toward the entrance. "Here comes Fred," he announced.

"So at last we meet the mysterious Fred." Laine said."

"I hope she's more interesting than those other guys your boss put on the team," Ugo interjected.

"What were you expecting?" Sam demanded. "James Bond, for Chrissake? These people are toilers in the vineyard of national security. In this business we prize anonymity. Fred's a little different, though." He was holding something in, and Ugo eyed him suspiciously.

There was a knock on the door and a female voice asked: "Sam, are you in there?"

Ugo crossed to the door, opened it and then looked straight up. The woman in the doorway was over six feet tall, with curly blonde hair and a face from a Mayan temple sculpture. She looked down and stuck out a hand. "You must be Ciano."

Ugo took her hand and said with awe: "Lady, where did you get them genes?"

Fred looked down at her pants. "These? At Saks."

"No, I mean the ones in your cells. The double-helix stuff. Hell, don't just stand there, come in. Have some Wild Turkey. I know I got a clean glass around here somewhere." He wandered off toward the kitchen in a half-daze.

"Fred," Sam said, "this is Dr. Laine Tammsalu."

Fred smiled and took Laine's hand. She had the largest, whitest teeth Laine had ever seen on a woman. In her strange, dark face they looked perfect. "I'm very pleased, Dr. Tammsalu. Sam briefed me on the project in Hawaii a couple of weeks ago. He was very enthusiastic about you and I can see why."

Laine blushed fetchingly. "He's been very mysterious about you. I think he was saving you for a surprise."

"He does that sometimes." She walked to the window and looked out. "Sam, about two blocks from here there's a white Volvo—"

"I saw it. It followed me from the airport to Laine's and then here. Anybody we know?"

She turned back. "When I walked past it, the guy on the passenger side tried to turn away fast, but I made him first. Remember the Bulgarian I deep-sixed in Rome two years ago?"

"Right. What was his name? Debelianov?"

"That's the one," Fred confirmed. "Well, this one was his partner, Liliev. I couldn't make the driver."

"Bulgarians?" Ciano said, returning from the kitchen. He handed Fred a glass full of straight Wild Turkey. "Here. This one didn't take much cleaning. Did you say Bulgarians? Ain't they the hatchetmen for the KGB?"

Laine smiled. Hatchetmen. Sam was a hatchet-man.

"That's right," Sam confirmed. He went to the telephone and punched a number, then spoke into the phone. "Paula? Sam here. See if you can find anything on a Bulgarian KGB man named Liliev." He spelled the name. "Don't dig for his whole file, just see if he's been reported here in the States lately."

While Sam waited Ciano protested. "Hey, Sam, if those people are watching us, this phone might be bugged!"

Sam looked at him. "Sure. So what?"

"Well, hell," Ciano said, "I don't know, I just thought that—"

"Relax," Fred told him. "The Bulgarians know they've been spotted. It makes no difference what they hear on that phone. Hell, I almost leaned in the window and said hello to old Liliev. It seems like old times with him around."

"You said you 'deep-sixed' his partner," Laine said. "Does that mean what it sounds like?"

Fred took a substantial sip of the high-proof whiskey. "Exactly. I caught him drawing a bead on a person very important to us whom I'm not free to name except he's a close adviser to a man often seen in a white hat on a balcony overlooking Saint Peter's Square on Sundays. I shot the son of a bitch right off the Sant Angelo bridge."

"Hey," Ugo said enthusiastically, "just like the movies!"

So, Laine thought. Fred was a hatchetman, too. Hatchetwoman? Hatchetperson. "Do you think we are in danger?" she asked.

"Maybe," replied Fred. "All we know so far is they're tailing Sam. Could be for something else entirely, though I doubt it. There's an outside possibility it's me they're after and they got word

Sam was supposed to meet me today. Most likely it has something to do with you two, though." She nudged a pile of tabloids with her toe. "I've been seeing those stories lately, since Sam briefed me." She looked at Ugo. "Germany and Mexico," she told him.

"Huh?" Ugo said. "Oh, the genes. How'd you get that mixture?"

"My father was German. He managed a bank in Yucatan. My mother was Indian from Cozumel."

"Now *that's* a genetic mixture," Ciano enthused.

Sam hung up. "Liliev arrived in D.C. last week, under a diplomatic passport."

"You two gonna do something about him?" Ugo asked. "Go take him out or something?" he suggested hopefully.

"Take him out?" Sam said. "Have you been watching TV or what?"

"Well, hell," Ciano fumed. "He's the enemy, ain't he? One of the bad guys?"

"He's just a guy doing his job," Fred told him, shrugging. "Just like Sam and me."

"That's right," Sam said. "If he makes a move for one of us, I'll ice him, or Fred will. Until then, he's got diplomatic immunity. You stick to the scientific stuff. Leave the rough work to Fred and me."

"I'm still waiting to hear about your blue-ribbon panel recruiting drive," Laine said.

"I'm starving," Sam said. "You want to continue this at a good restaurant somewhere?"

"And have those creepy Bulgarians following us everyplace?" Ciano complained. "I'd rather send out for something. There's a good pizza joint a couple blocks from here."

"I have to watch my sylphlike figure," Fred said. "I vote Chinese."

"Pizza sounds good to me," Sam said. "With pepperoni and anchovies and jalapenos and—"

"Sausage and onions and pepper and all the rest," Ciano said.

"I'd prefer Chinese," Laine maintained stoutly.

They compromised. Forty-five minutes later arrived a lavish Chinese dinner in paper cartons and two thirty-inch pizzas with everything. "There's beer in the fridge," Ciano announced, balancing two flat, cardboard boxes of pizza on one hand while Sam trailed behind him with the Chinese food.

Fred got up and went into the kitchen. "Dos Equis! Bless your little heart, Ugo!"

Eventually, they all sat in a circle on the floor, Ciano as close to Fred as he could manage within the bounds of decorum, discussing their problem.

"Not a bad bunch of scientists," Ciano said, studying the list Sam had ended up with. "Damn near everyone is a friend of mine, and that's no coincidence. Did you bag us an astronaut?"

"That was the coup of the whole operation," Sam said, complacently. "Do you remember Colonel Bart Chambers?"

"Do I?" Ciano said. "The guy has a profile like Mount Rushmore. He was one of the early ones; I think he was on the moon. They got his portrait blown up billboard size right across town at the Air and Space Museum! You couldn't get a better man!"

"I had to work my way through a bunch of them before I got to him," Sam admitted. "Most are too busy, or they have political careers and don't want to rock the boat, but Colonel Chambers spends his time these days as a volunteer administrator in the Veteran's Administration. He was a hotshot fighter jock in Korea when he was about twenty, remember? I walked into his office and started my spiel but he already knew about it from colleagues who'd turned me down. Unlike them he's pretty sure that there's something to this. He'd read that Heinlein book you showed me and he knows damn well that rock and ice are viable weapons when they come from space. He'll be ready to talk to the NSC."

"Ugo," Fred asked, "do you have any contacts with the UFO cultists? I mean the organized ones."

"Sure," Ciano said. "I get stuff from them all the time. I've even attended a few of their meetings. They assume because my esteemed colleagues consider me kind of a maverick, I must be a sucker for every pseudo-science that comes along. Some of 'em aren't as nutty as you'd think, though. What did you have in mind?"

"Those people probably keep in contact with these tabloids. We might find out who's been supplying these supposed Soviet findings. It might give us a little more evidence that they're up to something."

"I'll make some phone calls," Ciano said. "In fact, let's let *them* call up the tabs and ask where those stories came from. Save us a little legwork."

"Now you're learning to think like an Intelligence man," Sam commended.

"Why? Letting other people do the work? What do you think professors have been using grad students for since the Middle Ages?"

"I hate to bring this up—" Laine began hesitantly.

"What is it?" Sam asked.

"What if, despite all our work and all the evidence we have been able to assemble, they still don't believe us? Do we just give up?"

"They gotta pay attention to this!" Ugo insisted. "The evidence we have here is overwhelming!"

"Not to a bureaucrat defending his job," Sam

said. "You of all people should know that. Remember Billy Mitchell?"

"Who is that?" Laine asked.

"He was the man who more than any other built American air power from the ground up. He ran afoul of some entrenched military interests when he insisted that battleships could be sunk by aerial bombing. He was accused of being a hyperimaginative egomaniac," Sam wiggled his eyebrows at Ugo, "and he demanded a trial. Not far from here, off the Virginia coast, the Navy let him have a try at it. First, they saddled him with a bunch of unreasonable handicaps like having to fly too high and limiting the number of bombs he could use and the amount of time he had to drop them. This was before the Norden bombsight, remember. To top it all off, they gave him the *Ostfriesland* as a target. She was a German battleship, taken as reparations after World War One and believed by most Navy men to be unsinkable. The demonstration was witnessed by the whole Atlantic fleet, along with most of the Navy Department and a slew of foreign observers. Mitchell's bombers sank the *Ostfriesland* in less than twenty-two minutes."

"Then he was vindicated?" Laine asked, wondering what the point was.

"Uh-uh," Ugo said, taking up the story. "They *still* refused to believe that it could be done, even after it'd been demonstrated right in front of their collective nose. Those people believed in the invincibility of battleships, and they weren't going to let an irrefutable demonstration of their error stand in their way. Later they court-martialed Mitchell for making some off-the-cuff remarks about his superiors on an unrelated matter, something about a dirigible crash. They wanted to shut him up bad. Nearly every one of his predictions about the future of air power was borne out, but the U.S. was the last country to take him seriously. In 1945, he was cleared of all charges and fully vindicated by Congress. They gave him the Medal of Honor and promoted him to major general. He'd been dead for nine years but it was nice of them, anyway."

"Sounds like you're an expert on prophets without honor," Fred said with a big-toothed grin.

"Hey, what can I say?" Ugo shrugged elaborately. "I feel a certain kinship with the guy. But Sam's right: We gotta put together an airtight case, 'cause there's people on the Hill who, if they think it'll improve their careers, will tell you the sun don't shine even if you stake 'em out in the Mojave desert at high noon with their eyelids cut off, which for some of them is just what they deserve."

Laine lit a cigarette. "In an extreme case, should they prove to be as willfully blind as your admirals with Mitchell, what can we do? Suppose we went public? Might we not call a press conference and put our case before the public?"

"We'd have to be awfully quick about it," Sam said, "and it wouldn't be terribly advisable. Fred and I belong to an agency that's notoriously intolerant of operatives who blab to the press. In fact, they'd lock us up before we finished talking to the reporters. I might add that you're in this country through the good graces of that agency. They'd get you deported back to Italy, if not all the way back to Yugoslavia. As for Ugo, he can say anything he wants to anybody he wants."

"One little problem there," Ugo commented.

"Right," Sam said, "anybody who wanted to refute him could line up about a hundred prominent space scientists to testify that Ugo's a notorious crank."

"Some people have no perception of true genius," said Fred as she smiled down at Ugo.

"Are you married?" Ugo asked.

"Not lately," she said.

Sam pointed to the little computer. "The agency sunk a lot of money into that thing. Have you been able to get any use out of it?"

Ugo dragged his attention away from Fred. "You bet. Your buddy Novak came through with a lot of good statistics on the latest Soviet timetables, and he hooked me up with a computer they got monitoring Soviet imports of space-related materials. It's pretty complicated, but what it boils down to is this: Most programs have been curtailed or cancelled. The UV and IR satellites that were gonna be launched this year weren't. They were gonna start collecting material for a big, permanent lunar base this year and have it in near-Earth orbit, ready to go by next year. That program's been set back for four years.

"And, you know the big space station they built a couple of years ago? The one they devoted so much publicity to, that was gonna kick off their peaceful space program? Well, it's up there, fully staffed, and it's doing nothing! A whole staff of cosmonauts are sitting on their thumbs, if you can do that in zero gravity. Only some astronomers have been brought down. That's billions of kopecks down the tubes and what does that tell you?"

"They're going to be put to work on something else, soon," Fred answered.

"Right. Because one thing we know about the Soviets: They get their money's worth out of their space budget."

"It's good, but it's not conclusive," Sam said. "The cutbacks could always be explained by their economic difficulties, like maybe they needed the rubles to buy soybeans or something. Keeping the space station staff on hold is better, but most of our bureaucrats are so used to wasteful, half-assed practices that they won't think it's odd."

"Well, what the hell would it take to convince them?" Ugo cried in exasperation.

"If we could get Nekrasov to come and testify it'd help," Sam said, straightfaced. "But I wouldn't count on it."

"They might say he was lying, anyway," Fred added.

Laine looked from one to the other. "You two sound terribly pessimistic."

"Work for the government long enough," Sam asserted, "and it becomes a self-defense reflex. We're just preparing you for the worst possibility. All we can really do is put together the best case we can and hope for a fair hearing."

Ugo turned his attention to Fred once again. "Fred, what do you do besides shoot people? They sure as hell don't use you for clandestine surveillance."

"Mostly I specialize in guerrilla operations in Central and South America. I'm pretty good with computers, too, and that's about all I'm allowed to tell you."

"That's a real nice cross-section of talents," Ugo assured her. "We got a lot of computer work to do, and with them Bulgarians creeping around, I'm gonna need a bodyguard. I think you better stick pretty close to me from here on in."

"She takes her instructions from me, Ugo," Sam said, sternly. He faced Fred. "Fred, stick close to Ugo."

"Whatever you say, *jefe*."

It was after midnight when Sam drove Laine back to her hotel. The city had largely shut down for the night, and such inhabitants as were still out in the streets were of the exotic, phosphorescent variety that seldom shows itself in the light of day. "I like Fred," Laine said. "I think I am going to enjoy working with her."

"You don't like her anything like the way Ugo likes her," Sam said.

She laughed unrestrainedly. "I think he's in love. What a couple they would make! Do you think he really has a chance?"

"You can never tell. Fred's tastes in men can be peculiar. It's rumored that her first husband was an albino tackle for the Pittsburgh Steelers. She divorced him when he decided to turn gay and have a sex-change operation." He eased onto an on-ramp and pulled into the southbound lane.

"You're making that up!" she accused.

"I said it was just a rumor. I'd like to believe it, though." He glanced into the mirror. "No Volvo. They might be using another car, or they might be waiting ahead to pick us up farther on."

"I don't like this," Laine said.

"Don't worry. They may have just gone home for the night. I don't think they'll try anything overt against us. Not here in the States, and not when we're softballing it. I want to keep an eye on them, though. It doesn't pay to take chances."

He pulled into the parking garage of the Wildner and parked as near as he could to the elevator. He scanned the garage as he opened her door and helped her out. "No enemy in sight," he reported.

"It's good to have my own bodyguard. Are you always so protective of your charges?"

"It's a part of the job, Ma'am," Sam said, with great gravity.

Going up in the elevator, she felt again the sense of tension between the two of them she had felt on that first day. She wondered what it would lead to. At least, this time she felt far better able to cope with her new life and therefore with her emotions.

At the door to her apartment she searched for her key. "Would you like to come in? I don't have any of Ugo's favorite Wild Turkey, but I may have some Chablis."

This time, he was quick to accept. "Certainly. Besides, I have to check under your bed for Bulgarians." They went inside and, to her surprise, he actually went into her bedroom and looked under the bed. She watched bemusedly as she found the wine and glasses. He went over the whole apartment, checking lamps and paintings, examining potted plants, getting down on his knees to look at the edges of the carpet. Finally, he seemed to be satisfied.

Laine gave him a glass. "I thought you were joking. Do you really think there might be listening devices here?"

"I had to be sure."

She shrugged. "But, I'm not likely to say anything of use to anybody here. Usually, I am alone." Why was he behaving so oddly?

"I know. But I don't want anybody listening to what I'm going to do next."

"And what might that be?" She was very still as he set his glass down, then took hers and set it beside his. He took her face between his hands and kissed her, lingeringly and expertly. She released a long-pent-up sigh of relief and her arms went around him. She closed her eyes and leaned back in his arms and her hands explored his broad back. She had never touched a body so hard.

Reluctantly, she broke away for a moment. "If you found no Bulgarians under the bed, I think that would be a good place to go now."

As they undressed each other she said, "I expected you to do this that first night."

He carefully lifted the turtleneck collar of her blouse over her head to minimize the damage to her coiffure. "I wanted to. You wouldn't believe how much."

"Then why didn't you? I don't think I would have said no." She was having difficulties with his belt buckle and he had to help her with it.

"I didn't want you to think I took advantage of helpless refugees." He removed her final item of clothing and applied himself to her with great intensity.

"Sam!" she said, getting breathless. "You mean you've been a gentleman all this time?" They collapsed onto the bed, thoroughly entwined. After a few moments, she gasped: "Sam, stop being such a gentleman! I'm not that fragile."

Two hours later, she sat up in the bed, the rumpled sheets at her waist, smoking just like the mistress in a French movie. In the dim light of the bedside lamp she examined Sam's body. It would have been an absolutely perfect male body, she thought, if it weren't for the scars.

"I'm glad I checked the place for bugs," he said in an exhausted voice. "They'd have had plenty to listen to. I wish I understood Estonian."

"You'd have been pleased, but not shocked, I'm afraid. Estonian is not as rich as English in those basic, lewd words. I am learning them, but it will be some time before I can use them spontaneously." She ran her fingers along a ridge of scar tissue that slanted from his left hipbone across his abdomen to the base of his rib cage on the opposite side. "Sam, you really must find some other line of work."

"Now who's being protective? That was a machete. He almost had me that time. It was in a filthy jungle and it got infected, that's why the scar's so thick."

"These little round ones are bullet wounds, aren't they?"

"That's right. I've got to do what I'm good at,
Laine."

"You can't be all that good if people keep shooting and cutting you," she said, practically.

"Maybe you're right. Anyway, we make a nice
contrast this way."

She looked down. He was right. His body was
hard, tanned and scarred. Hers was soft, white
and smooth. "Still, I think you need to think about
the future."

"That's what I'm doing," he insisted.

"And what have you decided?"

"I think that it's time again." She stubbed out
her cigarette and, with a contented sigh, rolled
into his arms again.

CHAPTER NINE

The light reflected in rainbow colors from the wet road and through the Chevy's windshield as the wipers flicked back and forth across Sam's field of vision. There was a soft sound of snoring from the back where Fred leaned against the seat, her head tilted back and her mouth slightly open. Ciano lay on the seat with his head pillowed in Fred's lap, a contented smile in the middle of his beard.

"I think your Colonel Chambers will be valuable to us," Laine said, somewhat unsteadily. "If he speaks before the Security Council as well as he entertains, in any case. Is that a Texas tradition?"

"Seems to be. If we'd been at his place outside Houston he'd have thrown a whole steer on the fire for us." He slowed for a sharp curve in the narrow road. "Down in those parts they take it as an insult if you go home sober or unstuffed. Every male considers himself to be the world's best barbecue chef, too. I've seen shooting break out over the proper way to cook chili."

"It sounds as if you picked up some of their habits of exaggeration," she said. She leaned towards him and his arm went around her shoulder. She sighed contentedly and found herself drifting toward sleep.

"Like the barbecue sauce," Sam explained. "it adds flavor to what might otherwise be—" She snapped awake as he jerked his arm from behind her shoulders and took the wheel in both hands. "Are you strapped in?" he snapped.

"Yes." She slipped her arm under the chest strap. The car was filled with light from a vehicle coming up fast from behind.

"Fred!" Sam barked.

"Whaa?" Ugo got no farther as he was catapulted to the floor. Fred had twisted around to the rear. Her hand dipped into her capacious purse and she pulled out a large, businesslike automatic. Her thumb rested on the safety as she studied the situation. "Strap in, Ugo," she ordered.

"Who are they?" Ugo demanded as he fumbled with the seat belt.

"Where's that famous intuition, Ugo?" Sam said.

"Shall I open fire?" Fred asked.

"They haven't broken the law yet," Sam said.

The hell they haven't!" Ugo squawked. "They're speeding! Shoot 'em!"

The car behind was coming up from their left rear, pulling out as if to pass, but instead catching their bumper and accelerating. Sam had to accelerate and compensate to keep his rear end from throwing them into a spin. They could see the other vehicle now. It was a four-wheel-drive offroad truck, much larger and heavier than Sam's ancient Chevy. Its bumper was heavily reinforced.

"Christ! They're driving a tank!" Ugo gabbled.

Fred had her window rolled down. "Gimme a clear shot, Sam." Sam jerked the Chevy to the right and braked. The truck came almost even with Fred's window and she triggered three quick shots. Ciano squawked as a hot shell casing went down the back of his collar. The driver of the truck was too experienced to allow the bullet impacts to force him away. He slammed the truck against the side of the Chevy and sparks flew as the lighter vehicle slewed sideways and its righthand hub caps went up onto an embankment. Sam fought it back onto the road and hit the gas, and the responsive old engine yanked the Chevy well ahead of the ORV. Laine closed her eyes and tried to remember the prayers her grandmother had taught her.

"We dead yet?" Ciano asked, face pale and sweating.

"Not yet," Fred reported. "Don't you just love it, Ugo? Just like the movies." She leaned her whole upper body out the window and fired a string of shots. Sparks jumped from the hood of the truck and it swerved slightly, but maintained its course. Fred pulled back in and dropped the empty magazine from her pistol and slammed in a fresh one. "Whoever their driver is, he's good."

"Why aren't they shooting back?" Laine asked, fighting down panic.

"They want this to look like an accident," Sam said. He spoke calmly despite his frantic driving. "Otherwise they could've just taken us out with a sniper. Now listen, everybody: Up ahead of us, there's a series of sharp curves. There's a high bank on the right and a sheer drop on the left. That thing they're driving has a high center of gravity and it can't take the corners as fast as I can. I'm gonna get ahead of them on those curves." His speech was punctuated with four more shots from Fred. "On the last curve, I'm going to stop the car. Everybody jump out and scramble up that bank as fast as you can."

"Will we have time?" Laine asked.

"Plenty of time," Sam assured her. "Four, maybe five seconds." Behind them, Ugo groaned.

The curves loomed ahead. Each time the follower got too close, Fred drove it back with a few calculated shots. Then they were in the curves, their stomachs lurching as Sam whipped the Chevy around each in succession, the ORV falling back, finally dropping out of sight. Fred reloaded her pistol again, then dropped it into her heavy shoulder bag. "Hands on seatbelts, folks," she said.

The tail of the Chevy whipped wildly as Sam decelerated, then the car was stopped, slanted across the road with the tail toward the bank and the nose toward the guardrail. "Everybody out!" Sam barked. There was a simultaneous snapping of seatbelt buckles and the doors on the right slapped open. Laine and Ugo piled out, Sam and Fred a split second later, then all four were scrambling up the embankment.

They were twenty feet up the embankment when the truck came tearing around the last curve. The driver saw the car slanting across the road but it was much too late. He tried to take his chances with the embankment, but never quite made it. His bumper hooked the tail of the Chevy and the truck spun around, smashing the smaller vehicle broadside, throwing both into a ponderous spin, smashing them into the guardrail, the two vehicles hopelessly twisted together. The guardrail crumpled and the mass of metal tilted precariously for a moment, then toppled majestically over the edge. There was a series of diminishing crashes, then silence.

"Jeez!" Ciano half-whispered. "It coulda been us!"

Laine began to shake convulsively and Sam put an arm around her as she broke into sobs. Ugo started to stand up, but Fred took his arm and pulled him back down. "Uh-uh," she cautioned, "it's not over yet. They don't travel alone."

They sat in silence for several minutes. A car passed, then another. Except for some scattered pebbles of glass and the gap in the guardrail, there was nothing to signify what had happened. Then another car came by, travelling slowly. As it passed the gap in the guardrail it slowed. They saw its backup lights flare as it reversed and came back to the gap. When it stopped, a man emerged from the passenger side with a long flashlight in his hand but he did not turn it on. Slowly, he crossed the road and shone the beam of the flashlight down the slope.

Fred drew her pistol from her purse and snapped the safety off. She looked at Sam and he nodded. Unwinding her long legs, she stood and brushed mud from the seat of her pants, then she wiped her hand dry on one of the less wet spots on her blouse. Ugo stuck his fingers in his ears. Fred thrust two fingers between her teeth and whistled shrilly. "Hey, Liliev!" The man spun and leaned into a sprint that would have taken him back to the car but before he could set his foot down Fred's shot knocked him back over the cliff.

The car slammed into gear but Sam was standing now, and he held an automatic larger and heavier than Fred's. It roared three times and there were three closely-grouped stars in the windshield of the car on the driver's side. Then there was no sound or motion from the car. Cautiously, Fred descended the slope, pistol at the ready. She peered into the car, put her safety back on and dropped the automatic back into her purse.

"*Now* all's clear," Sam announced. He helped Laine to her feet and steadied her as they went down to the car. At the car she drew away. "I am all right," she said. Sam left her alone for the nonce. She had just seen a whole pack of hatchet-men at their work, and she didn't like it at all.

Ciano walked around the car, averting his eyes from the figure slumped on the front seat. On the left rear door he saw three ragged holes, the metal twisted outward where Sam's bullets had exited the vehicle. The slugs had slanted through the windshield, the driver, the seat and had still retained enough force to punch their way out through the door. "What kind of cannon you packing, Taggart?" Ciano asked, "A forty-five?"

"Ten millimeter," Sam said, jamming the pistol back into its holster beneath his arm. "It has much more penetration. That's a cut-down forty-five Fred carries." He opened the driver's door and Ugo looked away as he began to go through the corpse's pockets. Fred came up and looked at the dead man, grabbing his hair and tilting his face up for a better look. "Anybody you know?" Sam asked her.

She let the head drop forward. "Never saw him. I have a suspicion the Bulgarian embassy's going to be needing some new staff people, though."

"Hey, folks," Ugo said, "I don't like to complain, but it's past my bedtime and I'm standing out here on a deserted road getting rained on. How we gonna get home?" He thought for a moment, then: "Hey, we got a car here, don't we?"

"No!" Laine protested, vehemently. "I'm not riding in that car!"

"Don't worry," Sam told her. "We're not taking it. We can't leave it here, though." He shoved the corpse to the passenger's side and sat behind the wheel. Leaving the door open he restarted the engine and the others backed away. He drove the car very slowly to the gap in the guardrail and simply stepped out of it just before the car went to join the others.

As the sounds of the crash faded away, Ciano walked to the edge and looked down. "In the movies, they always blow up when they hit the bottom. Howcome—" then he saw the look on Sam's face. "Hell, Sam, I know how you must feel. If I had a hat, I'd take it off. They don't make 'em like that old Chevy no more."

"They'll pay," Sam said grimly.

"Hell, that bunch paid already," Ugo said. "Now, how we gonna get home?"

"We'll hitch a ride," Sam said.

"Sam, I hate to tell you this, but it's past midnight and we look like drowned rats and you ain't as good-looking as the rest of us. Who'd pick us up?"

"Not you and me, Ugo: Laine and Fred."

At sight of the two blondes standing by the road with their thumbs out, the driver of the car hit his brakes so hard the car skidded. The tires spun furiously as the car backed to the two women and the driver flung the passenger door open, unable to believe his luck. "Hop in, ladies! Where you headed?"

Sam leaned into the driver's window. "We need a ride, buddy. Mind if we join you?"

The man slapped the steering wheel disgustedly. "Shit! Every goddamn time! I see a broad hitchiking, I stop, and some bastard jumps out of the bushes!" He started to throw the car into gear and Sam thrust a badge into his face, letting his coat fall open to reveal the butt of his pistol. "U.S. government, friend. This is national security and I can toss you out and take your car if I want to."

Ugo chinned himself up to the window. "Yeah, jerk, we gotta go see the President, so don't give us no lip!"

The driver looked down at Ciano. "Who the hell're you? One of them atomic mutants I keep hearing about?"

"Sam, you gonna let him get away with that?"

"Ah, hell," the driver said, "get on in. You two bastards ride in back, though."

Fred slid in next to the driver and gave him a sloppy kiss on the cheek. "I knew you'd see your patriotic duty. Just get us to a telephone and I'll light candles to you every time I go to church." Laine remained subdued for the ride into town, slightly amazed at the driver's nonchalance in picking up such a crew in the middle of the night in the middle of nowhere.

Their reluctant chauffeur dropped them at a roadside diner on the outskirts of town. While the others fortified themselves with hot coffee while waiting for their nerves to calm down, Sam went to the public telephone in the back. He punched the twenty-digit combination that would give him Caldwell's super-secure home phone.

"Yeah?" said the sleep-befuddled voice. "Talk to me, and make it good."

"It's hardball time again, sir," Sam said. Quickly, he outlined the night's events.

"Oh, Christ!" Caldwell said when Sam had finished. "You offed three people who were probably on diplomatic passports?"

"Three for sure," Sam said. "There may've been more than one in the ORV. As for their passports, I wasn't asking for any ID. Just get the D.C. cops to declare it an accident. You know the Bulgarian embassy will go along with it."

"Well, your credibility just went up another notch, Sam. It's been years since they made a try against one of our operatives."

"And you know where that order had to come from. Sir," Sam said, pushing his new advantage as hard as he could.

"No kidding. Now we have ammunition to use in front of the NSC."

Sam smiled. Now it's *we*, eh? he thought. It was good to feel the political winds shifting.

"Look, Sam," Caldwell went on, "give me the exact location of the incident. I'll get a team to go over the wrecks first, then we'll inform the D.C. police. Get your people home and I'll have security people there to protect them. Then get some rest yourself and see me in my office in the morning. And Sam—"

"Sir?"

"Sorry to hear about the Chevy."

Back at the table, Sam explained how things stood. Laine seemed to have regained her composure. She had repaired to the ladies's room and was as presentable as the night's events permitted. Sam noted that she was still a shade pale, though.

"I don't get this," Ugo protested. "Whaddaya mean, you guys hardly ever go after each other? I thought CIA and KGB and all them was shooting it up all the time."

Fred was shaking her head. "Uh-uh. The rough stuff is mostly confined to the agents we both use."

"You mean you two ain't agents? I thought you were all agents."

"Common misconception," Sam said. "Terms like 'secret agent' did that, and it doesn't help that we're called an agency. Actually, Fred and I are operatives. Agents are people, usually foreign nationals, we employ to do work for us."

"And those people are expendable?" Laine said.

"We're all expendable," Sam said, "but some of us get expended a little more readily than others."

"But Fred tells me you got shot up in rare style not long ago," Ugo persisted.

"That was different," Sam told him. "I was working in one of the little brushfire wars. You go messing around where people are firing automatic weapons, you risk getting shot. No, this is something completely different. What happened tonight was direct action against two Company operatives, and within the U.S., to boot. Orders like that had to be cleared through the head of KGB, if they didn't originate there."

"That's this guy Ryabkin?" Ciano asked.

"Make it Nekrasov," Fred said. "Ryabkin wears the hat these days, but Nekrasov is still in charge."

"Then they know," Laine said. "They don't just suspect, they know for certain that we are on their plan and they want to eliminate us."

"That's how it is," Sam agreed. "Ever since the Fifties, we've laid off each other's operatives except in the most extreme cases. We're an extreme case."

"This time they tried to make it look like an accident," Laine pointed out. "Now they have shown their hand, will they try to stop us openly?"

"Good question," Sam said. "I doubt it, simply because they would only further establish our credibility without slowing down the enquiry. Too many people know about it now. My educated guess is that they'll lay off us now. Their future moves will be diplomatic."

"Yeah," Ugo chuckled, "it's gonna take some real diplomacy to explain away what they tried tonight."

"There won't be any explaining about tonight," Sam said. "What happened out there was a regrettable accident, and that's what it'll say in the papers."

"What!" Ugo choked. "Them sumbitches tried to kill us!"

"Keep your voice down," Sam said. The waitress, the only other inhabitant in the diner, was looking their way curiously.

"So what if they tried to kill us?" Fred said,

patting Ugo's ruffled hair. "We're all playing for keeps, remember? The Bulgarian embassy will be told that their people are dead in a car wreck. They can accept that, or they'll say that a bunch of their people, lousy with diplomatic immunity, were murdered by the nasty Americans. Remember, they weren't shooting. All the empty shell casings will be found in Sam's car. Chances are, though, they'll say it was a regrettable accident and let it go at that."

"Don't seem right, somehow," Ugo grumbled.

"Welcome to the world of higher diplomacy," Sam told him.

On the street outside Laine's hotel, Sam noted the Company car on watch. By now at least one of the hotel's domestic staff on each shift would be one of theirs and assigned to Laine's floor. At the door to her apartment, Laine turned to him. "I'd rather you did not come in tonight, Sam."

"You saw something tonight you didn't like, didn't you?" Sam said.

"Yes. Please, Sam, I don't want you to think I condemn you in any way. It's just that I have never seen personal violence before. It's unsettling. And the way you and Fred acted tonight; so cold and detached, so—" she groped for the right words.

"So professional?"

"I suppose that is what I want to say. I realize that those people were murderers, and that had they succeeded the consequences for the whole world would have been unspeakable. It is just that knowing it objectively and seeing the killing are two entirely different things."

Sam managed a faint smile. "And now you're feeling a gut reaction, is that it?"

"I am. And there is something else. I have the distinct impression that had you and Fred been ordered to ambush those people as they did us, you would have done it with no more compunction than did they."

"If we had those orders," Sam said angrily, "you're damn right we would! Listen, lady, this is a war. Just because nobody's signed any papers or made any speeches, don't think it's not. We've been killing each other since *nineteen seventeen*, for Christ's sake, with a few breaks when we had common enemies. And those bastards are not going to do to my country what they did to yours." Sam visibly calmed himself. "You'd better get used to it, because you might be seeing more of it soon. We have to assume you're still Target One."

"I suppose I'll have to. Good night, Sam." She went into her apartment and closed the door. Sam left, needing to find an all-night bar and tie one on, but knowing better.

CHAPTER TEN

WHITE HOUSE

It occurred to Sam that the crucial turning points of history had been as dull as this. There must have been endless haranguing and hassling over the wording of the Declaration of Independence. The French Revolution had probably been preceded by long, dull discussions of whether to storm the Bastille on the 14th or the 15th. A huge conglomeration of politicians, generals and maybe even astrologers had probably been empanelled to decide whether or not Hitler should invade Russia.

Now, in this room, men were facing the greatest crisis of the most powerful nation in history. What was decided here would determine man's future in the solar system. Sam was having trouble staying awake.

The blue ribbon panel had spoken, their recitations received with blank expressions, but Sam knew that meant nothing. Bart Chambers spoke most persuasively, and although his scientific credentials were the least impressive, his words carried more weight than the rest of the panel put together. There was just no beating the right stuff, Sam reflected. It also occurred to him that Chambers might have an iron of his own in this fire. If a new space program were to be formed specifically to meet this threat, Chambers might well get a high position, even the directorship. He certainly had the experience and seniority.

At least Ciano livened things up in his inimitable fashion. The President's scientific adviser turned green whenever the gnomish little man erupted to his feet to make a point. On the whole, though, Ciano behaved less outrageously than usual. Whatever his mannerisms, Ciano's data on the diversion of Soviet space resources were well-organized and convincing.

A short recess was called and the members of Taggart's panel were dismissed from the executive session to follow. For security reasons, only Sam and Ugo would attend this stage. In the anteroom, the two drew coffee and prepared themselves for the final session. Ugo spoke to Sam in a prison-yard whisper: "What do ya think, Sam? They buying it?"

"There's no way of knowing until we hear the summation. From the look of it, though, we're ahead. None of the military people were fidgeting or playing with pencils or staring at the ceiling. That means they're interested and taking us seriously. The civilian contingent, I don't know. I think some of them look bored for a living."

They were summoned back to the conference room and resumed their seats. Vice President Hernandez opened the executive session, "To begin, let's review what we know before we speculate on possibilities. We now have substantial evidence that the Soviets are planning a series of manned missions to comets. Their primary interest seems to be the virtually unlimited availability

of ice in comets. Of those things we can be almost
certain. There is a high level of probability that
the impetus for this project comes from the Soviet
development of a nuclear propulsion system including an ion-drive thruster for maximum efficiency. In addition, they appear to have solved the
problem of shielding their cosmonauts from radiation hazard without resorting to a prohibitively
massive radiation buffer. So much for the certainties and the greatest likelihoods." The Vice President tossed the papers he had been scanning to the
table and looked at the faces around him.

"Now for the speculations: Just what the hell do
they really intend to do with all that ice? Specifically, are they really planning to hit us with iceberg
bombs, as these people suggest? Frankly, I don't
see what they'd have to gain by it. They must
know that we'd retaliate with our nuclear arsenal.
By now they must know that we have suspicions
about their intentions. The attempt on the lives of
Dr. Tammsalu and Mr. Taggart and the others a
few days ago supports their argument, but it is in
no way conclusive."

Ciano almost came out of his seat, but Sam laid
a restraining hand on his arm.

"After all," Hernandez continued, "Mr. Taggart
has had an active career, as has Ms. Schuster, and
either of them or both might have been the intended target for reasons totally unconnected with
this Project Ivan the Terrible. Having established
our certainties, liklihoods, and mere possibilities,
let's hear the thoughts of the Council members on
this matter."

First to speak was General Moore, Chairman of
the Joint Chiefs. He was tall and whip-thin, one of
the few Korean War aces still in uniform. "Grant-
ing that these iceberg bombs are feasible, and my
scientific staff assures me that they are, what the

Russkies have here is a strategic rather than a tactical weapon. It looks like they think they can get away with a sneak attack and convince the world that it's a natural disaster. That sure as hell isn't going to work because we already know about it. My people also tell me that these missiles, being ice, can be destroyed by nuclear bursts. That can be done in space with no harmful radiation reaching Earth. The problem is, we don't have the satellite defense system that would be necessary for early warning. Orbiting lasers could cut the things up into little ice cubes, but I'm told that the technology for that is still at least ten years down the line.

"But, hell, we don't really need to do all that. Why not just tell the Russians that we'll launch our birds the minute anything big and loud goes bang on U.S. soil? Their plan, if it exists at all, hinges on our not knowing what the hell's going on. Since we know, why not tell them so? First they'll act all hurt and offended that we'd ever accuse them of such a thing, then they'll abort the project: end of problem. Just use the Red Phone."

Actually, these days the Washington-Moscow hot line was a desktop computer that provided simultaneous translation and screen readout in the receiving language and the thing was perfectly white, but the old name still stuck.

This time it was the President who spoke. "Gentlemen, I don't have to tell you that this business couldn't have come along at a less opportune moment. Since taking office, I've striven to lessen tensions between the United States and the Soviet Union. God knows we both face enough problems without having to face a war, nuclear or otherwise. We've succeeded in this, without weakening our position, largely by building a personal rapport with Premier Chekhov. I believe he sincerely wants peace. If I were to accuse him of plotting war against us on no more evidence than we have, three years of painstaking labor in the interests of peace would be lost. The very fragile trust we've built would be shattered for good."

"There is always the clandestine route, sir," said Caldwell. "We could leak our suspicions to a known KGB operative. It'd get to Chekhov, and it needn't touch your office. If this Ivan the Terrible project doesn't exist, they'll assume that it's just another nutty suspicion from the extreme Russophobe faction here."

"I think that would be best, Brad. See to it. And now, gentlemen, I think it's time we addressed the longstanding problem of our orbiting defense system. I don't mind telling you I was shocked to learn that an enemy could throw ice at us, *ice* for God's sake! And there's nothing we could do about it except wait for it to hit. You've all seen the pictures of the Tunguska blast. If Tarkovsky's right and that really was caused by a chunk of ice from a comet, then from now on we'll have to assess all such interplanetary debris as potential weaponry."

"Then, Mr. President," the National Security Advisor said, "we have to massively increase our space defenses. Such orbiting hardware as we have now is too little and out of date."

"That's because we've been struggling along on a starvation budget for a decade," the head of Space Defense Agency, General Hart, said heatedly.

"Gentlemen, no finger-pointing, please," said the President. "Granted we need to increase our presence in space, but I have no wish to touch off another arms race."

"Hell, that's easy, Mr. President," Ciano said.

The President looked at him. "Easy, Dr. Ciano? If it is, then it'll be the first easy solution to a problem that's confronted me since I've been in office. Please go on."

"Well," hedged Ugo, "maybe not exactly easy, but simple. We just do what they been doing the last ten years. What made Project Ivan the Terrible possible was Project Peter the Great. Announce that we're not gonna let the Russians get ahead of us in the *peaceful* development of space. Get us what we shoulda had a long time ago: really big permanent space stations, a lunar base, maybe a Mars base and manned asteroid probes. Friendly competition, see? Just what they claim they want. And the technology will be there if we gotta go to wartime status.

"Plus, unlike missiles in silos, this project can pay its own way in scientific and industrial benefits. And we gotta do it now, Mr. President, because I got a hunch the Russians have that ion-drive engine. I think your science advisers will agree with me that, if they got it, then it's like they got jet fighters and we got Sopwith Camels."

"Hmm," the V.P. said. "I am not at all sure that the American public can be sold on yet another massive space venture."

"Like hell!" Ciano said, jumping to his feet. Uh-oh, Sam thought. "Did J.F.K. get any lip from the public when he said we'd put a man on the moon by the end of the decade? No, he didn't. Why? Because he was an inspiring leader and because it's what they wanted to hear, that's why! Americans don't like the idea of being second-class in anything, and for the last ten years, all the major advances in space have been scored by the Europeans, the Japanese and the Russians. I submit that the American President who goes public and says that America's gonna be tops in space again," he grinned craftily, "I don't think he's gonna lose any votes thereby."

The men around the table sat awestruck by Ciano's incredible gall. Sam groaned inwardly. Don't ruin it for us now, you little jerk!

"Be that as it may," the President said after an audible pause, "something must be done to close this gap in space expertise between us and the Soviets. I shall be calling a series of meetings with key members of Congress to lay the groundwork for expanding the American role in space. In the meantime," he looked at the head of NASA, "I think we should go out and have a look at those comets we've heard about, and any Soviet spacecraft that might be hanging around them. Can it be done?"

The NASA chief, David Blaustein, had done his homework. "There is nothing to stop us, Sir. Using our intelligence apparatus and good sense, it shouldn't be difficult to pick out which comets the Soviets are most likely to go for. We could follow their craft to the comet and observe them. It wouldn't take long to figure out whether their object was in line with Peter the Great or Ivan the Terrible. Of course," he remembered that he was speaking to laymen, "one spacecraft doesn't follow another like two cars on the highway. The flight plan would have to be carefully computed, using a high capacity computer, expecially for a constant-boost spaceship, but, yes, it could be done. Now, if it turns out that the Soviets are really going to use those comets as weapons, our spacecraft should be equipped with devices—" Sam smiled thinly at the way the man was bending over backward not to say "armed." "That can obviate the threat out there, long before it can endanger us."

"It sounds simple," the President said. "I smell a catch. What is it, Dave?"

"The catch, Mr. President, is that it will take a

minimum of five years, but probably closer to ten, to develop a tested spaceship for the purpose."

A pall of deadly silence fell on the table. Even Ugo was subdued but it was, predictably, he who broke the silence. "I think, Mr. President, that the main stumbling block we got here is this word, 'tested'."

"Right," concurred General Moore, "how fast can we do it if we have some people in those ships who're willing to take a chance on not coming back?"

"Hold it!" Blaustein protested, "Throughout its history, NASA has given its highest priority to the personal safety of the personnel in space. Barring accidents on the ground, we've had an unbroken record of—"

"Hell with that," Moore said. "This is a national security issue. Hell, test pilots are killed all the time, and it never gets farther than the local papers; there's no national coverage. Mr. President, I was a fighter jock myself, once, just like Colonel Chambers. I guarantee you that if we get the ships cobbled together, there'll be no lack of volunteers to man them, even if the chances of coming back aren't the best."

Until now the President had mainly listened, and spoken interrogatively. Suddenly that changed. "Gentlemen," the President said. "I am not at this time invoking my presidential war powers, but you will proceed as if I damn well had. I'll be calling emergency meetings soon to settle this with Congress, but I'm sure most of them will agree with me, and the rest will go along when I make clear the alternatives. I see three important points. First, we must develop deep-space nuclear missile systems; discreetly, of course. Second, we must have a stepped-up manned program for deep space, with the emphasis on developing and testing a high performance nuclear propulsion system capable of using cometary ice as reaction mass. Third, we have to focus our intelligence apparatus on the Soviet manned space program." He gave the others a few moments to digest that. "Now, our first project is to track Russian's probe to their comet. Let's call it Project Bounty Hunter. This project is going to need a director." The President turned a frosty gaze toward Ugo. "Dr. Ciano, could you suggest such a person?"

Sam watched Ugo turn purple. I could've told you, he thought. He's going to nail you for that crack about votes. Here's your rope, you crazy gnome, now hang yourself. Ugo got to his feet once more and managed to strangle out some words that obviously cost him a lot. "Mr. President, I can't think of a better man for the job than Colonel Chambers."

The President and everyone else seemed genuinely surprised and touched. It was as if John Dillinger had walked past an open bank vault without going in. The President looked at the NASA chief. "Dave?"

"Top man for the job, sir, and long overdue. I think," he had to force out the last words, "that Dr. Ciano, in light of his unique familiarity with all elements of the problem, should have the number two position in the project."

"Then he has it," the President said. He looked at his watch. "Are there any further comments before we adjourn?"

Sam spoke up for the first time in this session. "Mr. President, gentlemen, I want to point out something Dr. Ciano and I discussed recently that hasn't been brought up here. All the people here who are charged with such responsibility are going to leave this room ready to push buttons when something big goes bang on the American continent. I have to point out that there is a tiny but finite possibility that a *real* meteor or comet strike could occur at any time and it'd be a real shame to wipe out life on Earth because a brainless chunk of rock or ice hit us at the wrong time. From what Ugo tells me, comets often break up in the inner solar system, so there could be *repeated* hits, just like a real attack."

"Come on, now," General Moore said, "the chances are so small that—"

"Small or not, General, they're there," Ugo said. "Gentlemen, since we're on the subject of ice let us not forget the *Titanic*. That ship was as unsinkable as the technology of the time could make it. To sink, she just about had to collide with an iceberg, and she had to collide just right to open up her bottom. The chances were a million to one that the two would hit just right and they did. First time out."

The President steepled his fingers and thought, not for the first time, that he should have taken his mother's advice and become a priest.

"Missed your chance, Ugo," Sam said as they walked away from the White House. "Why didn't you tell the President you should head the project? He probably would've given it to you, out of sheer spite."

Ciano grinned slyly. "Think you're smart, don't you? Well, old Ugo's smarter. I don't wanna be head of the department, even if I am the man best qualified for the job."

"How come?" Sam asked.

"Because the head of a U.S. government department don't get to go up in no rocket," Ugo said. Try as he might, Sam could get no more out of him.

CHAPTER ELEVEN

SOVIET SPACE STATION VOLGA

The red light came on above the communicator and it whistled shrilly for attention. "*Nevsky* to *Volga*! *Nevsky* to *Volga*! Korsakov here. My intership scooter is not operational. Glitch in the propulsion system. I need someone to come and fetch me."

"Hold on a minute, Korsakov," the communicator on duty said. He punched a switch to alert the crew quarters, interrupting a game of free-fall handball. "Attention! Korsakov needs help. He's stuck on the *Nevsky*. Scooter's down."

"Again?" said Bulganin, the chief pilot. "Tell him we're on our way."

The communicator addressed the *Nevsky*'s pilot. "We'll send out rescue within five minutes. Can you hold out?"

"No problem. I have enough oxygen for two more hours at least."

"We'll haul you back here well before two hours are up. *Volga* out."

"Thanks, *Volga*. *Nevsky* out."

Fifty minutes later, the hermetic inner lock of

the space station opened and two bulky, space-suited figures floated through, already undoing their helmets. Korsakov was a small, middle-aged man with a deeply-seamed face. Just now his graying hair was confined under the close-fitting coif that the cosmonauts had nicknamed the "bathing cap." He climbed out of the spacesuit and arranged it carefully in its locker, then he kicked the locker door shut with a practiced foot, turning the motion into a push-off toward the door to the main work area. He pulled himself along, utilizing struts and handholds, acknowledging the greetings of his fellow cosmonauts. Like him, they were clad in gray jumpsuits and white coifs.

Space Station *Volga* was a Spartan work-place, as bare and functional as a ship under construction. Simulated gravity was to be induced by spinning the entire station, but that could not be done until the station was fully operational. Then it would be relatively comfortable, with furniture and recreation areas—but not for four more years.

Korsakov pulled himself into a small office marked "Station Director." "Korsakov reporting, Comrade Director." The Director himself was floating in the center of the office, upside-down to Korsakov's orientation, but one quickly lost all sense of proper juxtaposition in free-fall. Korsakov hooked his boots into a pair of slots in the surface that one day would be the floor. From a big leg-pocket in his jumpsuit he took a small plastic flask and tossed it to the director. It crossed the room in a perfectly straight line, without the gravity-induced trajectory of earthly missiles.

The director caught the flask expertly. "Thanks, Aleksandr." He flipped the cap from the tube and took a sip, then tossed the flask back.

"Report," the Director ordered.

"Comrade Director, *Pionyer I* is now fully equipped and ready for testing."

"Excellent! Tomorrow, we check out the entire system except for the thruster. The nuclear-powered ion-drive system will be field-tested after everything else is checked out and proven satisfactory. Wouldn't want to send the test crew out on an inadvertent cosmic Odyssey without a fully operational life-support system, now, would we?"

"No, Comrade Director," Korsakov concurred, taking a nip of the vodka and tossing the flask back to the Director. "If that thruster malfunctions, even just a little, it would be a long time before we could get a rescue party to them."

The Director took another drink and made a face at the flask. "It never tastes the same when it's been put in plastic. If I had my way, Korsakov, I would test the thruster in a much safer environment. According to our original timetable, this phase of the testing was to begin two years from now. We could still make it to Mars and back by the official date, if we cared to. Not only have they changed the destination to a comet, which is a most flimsy target, if you ask me, but they have stepped up the schedule dangerously. The risk factor is much too high now. What do they think this is, a war?"

Korsakov declined to answer the rhetorical question.

"I wonder who our administrators have been listening to of late. I can't imagine that Tarkovsky is doing this. His projects are ambitious, but he's the most careful planner in the whole space program. Well, it's not the first time the amateurs have taken over. Have you heard that there's a faction that wants a political education officer assigned to every space station? Political education! As if we were a pack of teenaged Army privates. Ah, well, we can only do our best to stay ahead of the capitalists." This last was added pro forma to avoid sounding like a dissident.

Korsakov carefully paid no attention to the Director's grumblings. He wasn't interested in politics. What Korsakov liked was engines. The new engine was the greatest propulsion system ever devised. "If all goes ahead on schedule and barring any problems in the life-support systems, we should be able to blast off for the comet rendezvous in two weeks." Korsakov was as enthusiastic as the Director was doubtful. "With the tankful of water coming up on the next space truck, the reaction mass tank will be full and have enough left over for fine maneuvering to match the comet's velocity perfectly at the time of encoutner."

The Director just grunted and took another sip of the vodka. He did not like sending men out on what might be a one-way mission, but he was merely director of Space Station *Volga* and just now he was glad that he did not hold a higher post. "You may get there alive, but if you don't succeed in securing enough ice to feed your thruster, you won't be coming back. Besides, if there is too great a concentration of dust grains and rocks in the ice, I am not that confident that the water separation system will work."

"You sound like my maiden aunt Nina," Korsakov said. "She's a chronic worrier, too. Look, should it turn out that way, I won't be the first cosmonaut not to come back. If we'd wanted to be safe, we could have nice easy teaching jobs back on the ground. This time the risk is worth it, for sure. We've been in orbit and on the moon for years, but always within the Earth's gravity. This is man's first expedition into deep space, and I'm the pilot."

The Director tossed back the vodka flask. "You're crazy, Korsakov, but I wish I was going along."

CHAPTER TWELVE

WASHINGTON, D.C.

General Stephen Hart was Administrator of the United States Space Defense Agency, known in the popular press as the Star Wars program. The chatter of conversation in the briefing room died down as he came in, dressed in his civvies. It was a habit he had acquired from his early press conferences. It seemed to make people nervous to see men in military uniform running space projects. He took his place at the head of the long table, setting his briefcase neatly next to his chair. At his nod, the Marine MP stepped outside the room and shut the door. Others seated at the table were Hart's top administrators and his two new acquisitions: Sam Taggart and Ugo Ciano.

"Ladies, gentlemen," Hart began, "you have had two weeks to assess our options to counter the threat posed by Project Ivan the Terrible from the viewpoint of your own specialty." He glanced at the piles of reports neatly piled in front of each participant. He continued, his voice neat, clipped, accustomed to commanding undivided attention.

"We'll start with an overview. Regi, go ahead with your report."

Reginald LaCroix, Associate Administrator for Future Planning, stood up and made his way to the end of the table opposite the general. He was dressed in a fashionably-cut brown suit, artfully tailored to minimize his middle-aged midriff bulge. He ignored the modern vuegraph projector on the table. The General's aversion to darkened meeting rooms was well known, and the idiosyncrasies of generals were usually honored. In any case, all the tables and figures were in front of all the participants.

"As you'll see on the cover page summary, it will take a minimum of one year to adapt the prototype of the nuclear fission powerhouse to the engineering model of the ion drive. It's a miracle we even have those models, with the budget that department's been operating on.

"Our first manned interplanetary probe ship was planned with an engine using liquid hydrogen for maximum efficiency and not atomic hydrogen obtained from water for reaction mass. The use of ice water from comets, broken down to hydrogen and oxygen, is an intriguing possibility. Unfortunately, we have not been working on that."

Deputy Administrator Gerald Hayward spoke up at this point. "Why did nobody in our agency or NASA suggest this idea? It seems simple and obvious. The Russians have been working on it for a number of years."

"It was the usual failure of two departments to make connections. No astronomer thought to point out to our engineers that comets are basically gigantic cosmic iceballs. Likewise, nobody on the engineering end thought to mention that ice would be nice to have for manned interplanetary flight. I suspect, though, that if we studied all the minutes of all the planning meetings we've had and went through all the reports and suggestions and helpful letters that have been sent to us, in all probability we would find exactly this course suggested to us. Perhaps many times.

"We all know, though, that once an agency is committed to a particular course of action, it becomes next to impossible to change that course. All such alternatives are waved away while we proceed with the original plan. Now, let's look at what's on hand."

Fussing with his glasses, LaCroix consulted his notes.

"There is a long range program to consider the use of pulverized asteroidal rocks for reaction mass but that won't be a practical engineering proposition, probably for a few more decades. A bright young man in the engineering development division thinks that we might be able to develop the capability to use water in our nuclear propulsion system in about three years, if given enough resources."

Administrator Hart spoke up. "Could you speculate for us on the time it might take for us to send a round-trip mission to a comet dogging the heels of the Soviets in order to monitor and, should it prove necessary, interdict their mission?"

LaCroix poured a glass of water before answering his boss. "The possibility of sending our manned mission to a comet within one year is so slight as to be negligible. The chances of being ready in two years are remote but not ridiculously so. In my opinion, if given top national priority, it could become a practical proposition in three years."

"If the Soviets," Hart went on, "manage to complete their Ivan the Terrible mission in, say, two years, what options do you see for us?"

"This is something Dr. Ciano and Mr. Taggart

and I were discussing recently," LaCroix told him. "I think Dr. Ciano should give us his thoughts on this matter, which I am sure you will all find very well taken."

Ciano cleared his throat and put on his best ivy-league voice. Sam had been insisting that Low Brooklynese was a no-no in the world of high achievers. "Tarkovsky is a Russian, and like most Russians he's careful and cautious. They're willing to take big risks but they're seldom reckless. I don't think they'll try a massive ice-bomb attack without testing it first. I'm sure that their first mission will be to go out and bring back some cometary material and place it in Earth orbit where they can study it, maybe make last-minute trimmings so they can be absolutely certain how much mass they're dealing with.

"If current theory is correct and comets are of mixed ice and rock, there'll be some of each brought back. When they're ready, they'll inject it at the trajectory they want and study the results. Most probably they'll drop them on Siberia. There's a remote possibility they'll try an ocean drop, with a Soviet fleet or scientific station nearby. Sometime in the next couple of years we're going to hear about one or more blasts in remote areas, with little or no loss of life. I'm ninety percent sure that the figures will be consistent with a mixed drop of ice and rock. When that happens, we'll know that they're ready to get serious."

"Would they tip their hand like that?" objected Hart.

Sam held up a stack of tabloid clippings. "They've been softening us up for it for months, now. Everywhere you go you see these things. There's even a few books out now on meteor and comet hits. Astronomers and nutcase alarmists are all over the talkshows. A new book has come out on the

Tunguska blast and I heard there's even a movie in production about it. Apocalyptic fundamentalists are claiming that all the signs are in order for the end, or at least for a big disaster to punish us all for our worldliness. Hell, in the atmosphere that's developing, people are going to be disappointed if something big *doesn't* drop from the sky.

"Incidentally, concerning these stories that started showing up in the tabs: we've determined that the initial stories of supposed Soviet scientific predictions were leaked to the sensational press by the information office of the USSR's London embassy. It seems that American and British tabs exchange stories a lot." There was a subdued mutter at this revelation.

"That still leaves us with the question of our options in case the Soviets get their offensive under way before we send a mission to track them," Hart said, bringing the discussion back on course. "What then?"

LaCroix resumed his recitation. "Our first option is to shoot the Soviet mission down while it is still near the Earth. Clearly, we have the capability to do that right now. The price of that course could be to touch off a war, perhaps a nuclear one. This option would therefore be acceptable only if we are *already* in a state of war with the Soviets."

"Let's not discount that possibility entirely," Hart said, coolly.

"Um, yes, well, our second option would be to send a multi-megaton warhead to every comet with an orbit attractive for Ivan the Terrible. There aren't that many suitable comets, so the scope of this task is logistically manageable. The technology for it is already here. There are, however, major objections. On the diplomatic front, it would certainly create an uproar in the international community, enabling the Soviets to do a great deal of damage without dropping a single iceberg on us. Besides, as Dr. Ciano has pointed out, we would be destroying irreplaceable assets for our future exploration of the solar system.''

"Precisely," Ciano said. "To do that would be the equivalent of—" he waved his hands, searching for an analogy, "dealing with the Indian wars by permanently poisoning every water source west of the Mississippi. Those comets may be absolutely essential to sustaining viable colonies in space.''

"That brings us to option number three," LaCroix resumed. "Establishing an in-depth, layered, defense system against the iceberg bombs, in essence a whole battery of defenses, forcing them to run a veritable gauntlet before getting a clear shot at us. Once again, our course would be littered with obstacles. For one, it would be frightfully expensive. For another, conventional explosives might only result in altering the trajectories of the icebergs without vaporizing them. We would almost certainly have to use nuclear warheads, with all the problems that entails.

"The greatest problem, though, is how to find the damned things. The icebergs will be towed back to Earth by continuous-boost spaceships and it'll be almost impossible to anticipate their trajectories. The main problem here is that the icebergs are much too small for detection by any surveillance system in operation or on the drawing boards. We might look for the firing of the auxilliary rockets on the icebergs but they'll be activated only briefly and even that will probably take place just before their entry into the atmosphere. It would be futile to aim heat-seeking missiles at the exhaust from the auxiliary rockets.''

"Lasers?'' hazarded somebody.

"Way down the line," LaCroix answered. "They've been greatly overrated for long-range defense. Even under crash priority we couldn't develop an orbiting laser system that's up to this job in under ten years. And ten years we just don't have."

"So there are our options," Hart announced. "All of them have serious ifs and buts, which we'll now discuss in depth. Our one saving advantage, if it exists, is Dr. Ciano's assertion that the Russians will want to test their new technology first. That makes sense to me, and I think it's about the only thing that's going to save our butts." For the first time, he leaned back in his chair. "Now there was a time not so long ago when the first option anybody would've considered is the one nobody has mentioned here: a nuclear strike with ICBMs. The one way to preempt such an attack as we think they're contemplating is to hit them first and without warning. Well, there was a time we could've done that, but not now; they've been getting ready for that for forty years now. Good thing, too, since it seems that even if they never got off a shot our weapons alone could touch off an ice age that'd finish us as surely as losing a nuclear exchange. That's the past, anyway. Let's talk about the present and the all-too-near future."

The conference went on for the rest of the day. In late afternoon, Hart called a short coffee break. It was perfectly plain that nobody was going to be home for supper this evening. Everywhere, the chill-eyed presence of the MPs was a sobering pall. "Jeez," Ciano muttered to Sam, "I feel like a goddam convict."

"Do secret work for the government," Sam told him, "and you'll always feel like a convict. Start acting like one, too."

"Yeah?" whispered Ugo out of the side of his mouth. "How do ya mean?"

"Well, for instance," Sam murmured confidentially, "you start whispering when you could be talking right out loud."

"No shi—" Ugo began to mutter, then his eyes went wide. "The hell you say!" he shouted. He turned and stamped away in a diminutive huff. Sam smiled for the first time that day.

They returned from the coffee break to find that Hart had been busy even during the brief rest period. "Gentlemen, ladies, I've just been informed that we have a new status. This is now the first executive meeting of the Department of Space Defense, of which I am now Secretary, pending a routine ratification and confirmation by Congress. Head of Project Bounty Hunter," he winced slightly at the title, "will be Colonel Bart Chambers, who is at this moment selecting his team for the pursuit and interdiction mission.

"Make no mistake about it: what we have here is a crash priority program in which time is of the essence, far more so than in the moonshot program or even the Manhattan Project. We'll be taking chances we would ordinarily consider unacceptable. Lives may well be lost. This is a matter of national survival, and sacrifices will be made accordingly. On the plus side, you won't have to contend with the usual media coverage and interference."

"You realize, of course," Ciano put in, "that this means our contributions to the future of man in space may go uncredited. If we do our work right, we'll have laid the groundwork for humanity as an interplanetary species and prevented a world war, and nobody will *ever* know about it, or what really happened."

"I'm sure we can all live with that," Hart said. "Ladies and gentlemen, let's get to work."

In the parking lot, Sam headed for his new car, a late-model Japanese import that he preferred to recent Detroit products, but which was a poor substitute for his old Chevy. Ciano caught him before he could reach his new, unfamiliar machine.

"Look what I got," Ciano said, pointing at a massive limousine with a uniformed driver leaning against its fender.

"You're coming up in the world, Ugo. Congratulations."

"Sam," Ugo continued, "I made an appointment for us to meet with the Assistant Secretary for Crew Training at ten tomorrow morning. Guy by the name of Hubert Rollins."

For a moment Sam didn't say anything, just stood there looking troubled. Then, "Look, Ugo, I'm not a scientist, I'm not an astronaut and I'm not an administrator. You don't need me any more. I've pretty well wrapped up all my reports. My presence at this meeting today was mainly to provide continuity between the initial investigation and the inception of the space defense project. I've put in for a transfer. With rough times in the offing, my superiors have started being polite again. There's talk of some important missions for me."

"Not a chance. Cancel your request. You and me and Laine and Fred are sticking together until Ivan's finished. I wouldn't feel the vibes was right if we was split up. Right now I can just about write my own ticket, and I can do it for the rest of us, too. Between my new position and your connections in Intelligence, I think we can get what we all want.

"Look, you and Laine get together with me and Fred tonight at my new, bug-proof, bulletproof digs and I'll outline my proposition. After that, if you still wanna go be a cowboy you can, but I don't think you'll wanna pass up my plan."

Intrigued, Sam agreed.

That night, Caldwell got another late call. "Sam?

Don't you ever call at a decent hour? Who's tried to bump you this time? What do you mean, you want to be assigned as permanent Company officer on the Bounty Hunter project? Sam, I've been holding that Paris position open for you for six weeks while you wrapped up this space business! Do you realize how many senior men want that job? All right, all right, I'll do it for you, but you've used up all your credit with me, Sam, don't come to me for any more favors. And don't ever call this late again." Caldwell slammed the receiver down. Cowboys. He'd never understand them. At least this would keep Taggart out of his office for a couple of years. He couldn't very well turn him down, though. Sam Taggart was the President's fair-haired boy right now. But why the hell would he want a dead-end position on a project dominated by whiz kids and rocket jocks?

Whatever purpose the building had last served was high-security. It looked like a modern office building but was laid out like a prison, with checkpoints and spy cameras and guards everywhere. Instruments were being installed, desks being arranged and signs put up. Coffee machines were already perking as Sam and Ugo pressed their thumbs to the screen of the late-model ID machine. The suspicious guard seemed satisfied and he waved them in. He looked less suspicious and far more interested when Laine and Fred pressed their thumbs to the screen. Fred was flamboyantly dressed in the loudly-colored pants, bolero jacket, ruffled blouse and bow tie that were all the rage in the pop-music crowd lately. Laine was stunning in a simple charcoal suit over a white turtle-neck sweater.

At the metal detector, Sam and Fred handed over their guns and stepped through.

They proceeded up one of the endless hallways which echoed with the sound of hammering and power tools. Sam was out of his Agency gray for a change, looking casual in a handsomely-cut blue blazer and open-collared shirt. Even Ugo was presentable this morning, due more to his efforts to keep Fred happy than to his new status.

When they reached Rollins' office, the workmen were just finishing the lettering on the windowless door. They were greeted by a secretary, who asked them to wait while the Assistant Secretary finished a phone conference. She brought a tray of coffee and tea and looked at Laine for a moment. "Excuse me," she said, "but weren't you on the cover of *Vogue* last month?"

"No, but thank you anyway," Laine smiled. She looked at Sam. "See?"

Ugo took a sip of the tea. "Ahh, institutional Lipton's, straight from the bag. Some things never change."

Assistant Secretary Rollins was a small, black man with the barest trace of a Virgin Islands accent. He had been a Space Shuttle crew chief but had been grounded after twenty missions because of a heart ailment. "Dr. Ciano, Mr. Taggart," he shook hands with both, "and Dr. Tammsalu and Ms. Schuster," he shook hands much more lingeringly, "I'm very glad to be meeting you all. How may I be of help?"

While Ugo gently stroked a model of the old shuttle on Rollins' desk, Sam, as previously agreed, opened proceedings. "Mr. Rollins, as you know, our current assignment requires us to maintain a close, first-hand contact with all aspects of our undertakings against Project Ivan the Terrible." Rollins nodded. In fact, he wasn't sure just what Taggart's assignment might be. "So far," Sam went on, "all officials of the Department of Space Defense have been extremely cooperative in this respect. But, there's one major obstacle and you are just the person who can remove it for us."

"How can I help?" asked Rollins, who knew a pitch when he heard one. Laine smiled radiantly at him and he smiled back.

"The problem is we're barred from going into space. We must have first-hand knowledge of our preparations in space, but we can't go until we are first space-qualified. We'd like you to put us through your training program."

Rollins stroked his chin and looked at his model of the shuttle. Frustrated zoomies, longing to get into space. Well, he could sympathize. He'd do anything to get back into space himself. He looked at Sam. "I see. All four of you?"

"Absolutely," Ugo broke in. "I hope I don't sound immodest if I point out that my scientific expertise could make the difference between success and failure for this whole mission, and Dr. Tammsalu is my Astronomical Assistant." He had thought up the title the night before and had it made official earlier that morning. God, but it was fun being powerful!

Rollins turned his gaze to Sam and Fred. "And you two will be observers?"

"Officially," Sam said, "but don't think we'll be dead weight. I'm licensed to pilot just about anything that flies, including helicopters and high-performance jet fighters. Fred is a licensed pilot as well. We're all up on our physicals. Is there anything to keep us from going up?"

"Well, we've recently instituted a one-month training program for the scientists who need to go into space to perform important but somewhat limited functions. Their duties don't include, for example, piloting intership scooters or any sort of extravehicular activities. If you pass the program's specialized physical, I can put you through that course. Would that be satisfactory?"

Having received this concession so quickly, Sam used the golden opportunity to push his luck. "Yes, that would be satisfactory," then he qualified, "for a start. But I think we'll need to become fully qualified for all space activities, including piloting the shuttle."

"Hold on a minute!" Rollins protested. "It no longer takes as much experience or as many flying hours as they used to demand, but shuttle piloting is still a top professional's job. Now the other functions like EVA activities and scooter piloting I can probably get you into. But shuttle pilot, I don't know. Look, I'll get you into the full-scale training program, but I can't promise anything further until you've all undergone massive testing."

"That'll do," Sam said, scarcely able to believe that he'd done it so easily.

"Now," Collins said, opening up his desk calendar, "when would you like to take that physical? You'll have to fly out to Vandenberg."

Sam looked at his watch. "Do we have time for lunch first?"

"You came ready, didn't you?" Rollins said, shaking his head.

"Like General Hart said," Ugo told him, " 'Time is of the essence'."

Later, driving back to Washington, they made plans for a victory party. Rollins scheduled a physical exam at Vandenberg two days hence.

"I can't believe it!" Laine said, still laughing. "It was so easy! Yesterday we were scientists and observers. Now we are astronauts!"

"If we pass all the tests," Fred cautioned.

"No problem," Ugo assured them. "It ain't like the old days when you had to prove you were Superman with ten thousand flying hours before you could get into the program. Lots of people qualify now. It's the opportunity that's hard to come by. We had the opportunity dropped in our laps and there was no way I was gonna let it pass. How about it, Fred, think you're gonna like being an astronaut?"

She examined her blue-lacquered nails. "Sure. It's time I got out of this sneak-and-shoot business anyway, while I'm still alive. How about you, Sam?"

He draped an arm around Laine. "I guess I have to grow up sometime. You can't be a cowboy forever. Hell, I tried once and they turned me down. Not many people get a second chance."

"Well, this is what I was born for!" Laine said. "There was no way an Estonian woman could ever get into cosmonaut training but here I am going to do it! Ugo, did you really clear all this with Colonel Chambers?"

Ciano shrugged. "Bart's a busy man. There's no need to burden him with all the petty little details."

CHAPTER THIRTEEN

MOSCOW SUBURBS

The dacha was little more than a cottage but it was surrounded by a tall iron fence and there was an armed guard at the gate. The brand-new black Lada pulled up to the gate just as the sun was setting. Early summer was the best time in Moscow, the guard thought. Long days, trees in full leaf and the songs of nesting birds everywhere. It was no substitute for his home village in the Ukraine, but winter duty here could be truly miserable, when it was a race to see whether the cold or the boredom would kill you first. He leaned down to the car window and a fat face turned to glare at him.

"Baratynsky to see the Deputy Premier," announced the fat face. Just that. Not "Yevgeny Baratynsky," not even "Comrade Baratynsky." Just "Baratynsky," as if he were some big-shot Western orchestra conductor or artist, which reminded the guard that he was to meet his girlfriend for an evening at the ballet as soon as he got off duty, in just a few minutes. He waved the Lada in, wondering if he would ever be able to afford his own car. Barring an unforseen promotion from private to colonel, it wasn't very likely. He turned to more cheerful thoughts as the Lada passed through the gate and he shut it. His girl shared an apartment with only six other students, and they would all be going to a party after the ballet, leaving the apartment conveniently vacant. He wished his relief would hurry up.

Nekrasov opened the door at Baratynsky's ring. "Come in, Comrade Yevgeny," he said. He turned and went back into the parlor with Baratynsky in tow. "I've given my household staff leave for the evening so we can speak frankly."

Even here, Baratynsky thought, even this man. Everyone must be careful. Baratynsky wore a heavy cableknit Arran sweater, souvenir of some visit to Britain, against the still chilly evenings, and his shoes were expensive, custom-made Italian creations. No Muscovite would mistake Baratynsky for an unimportant man. He sank his immense bulk into a sofa facing Nekrasov's chair. The Deputy Premier handed him a glass of Caucasian brandy. "I've read the abstracted report on the testing of *Pionyer I*, but I want your personal report. Was the field-testing as successful as that report would have me believe?"

"An unqualified success, I assure you," Baratynsky boomed heartily. "Our investment in the nuclear-powered ion-drive engine is finally paying off! The years of research have not been wasted. It is just as I predicted."

"Then, we'll be able to go ahead with the cometary mission as scheduled?" asked Nekrasov.

"Most definitely. The target is a periodic comet and it is on its expected course. For an optimum rendezvous with it, *Pionyer I* should boost off from Earth's vicinity in about one week."

"Excellent. I shall pass orders to Comrade Tarkovsky to proceed on schedule. A few months ago, you gave me odds for success at 50-50 Now that the field-testing has been done, are you prepared to give me better odds?"

Baratynsky took a generous gulp of the brandy and Nekrasov poured more from the decanter. "I personally oversaw the construction of the continuous-boost engine," Baratynsky said, wiping the furry back of a hand across his bushy eyebrows. "It is marvelous. I was never in any doubt of its success. The uncertainties were and still are primarily from our lack of precise knowledge of the physical conditions of particular comets. As you've seen in our projections, conditions may vary quite a bit from one comet to another. Our success will depend on whether or not this comet is indeed of the ice type as Tarkovsky has predicted." It did not escape Nekrasov that Baratynsky always took full credit for successes and certainties, while he was always generous in sharing uncertainties, variables and failures.

"It will also," Baratynsky continued, "depend on whether the cosmonaut can operate the lasersaw properly to cut off an iceberg of appropriate size for *Pionyer-I* to use as reaction mass and at least two more icebergs for our experimental drops."

"And the rock missiles?"

"That could prove even more difficult. Here I agree with Tarkovsky: it is ice we want to work with. Of course, for experimental purposes, we'd like to have some rock as well, but if it comes down to a choice, the cosmonauts have their orders to bring back ice."

"And if we don't succeed the first time, we should have better luck the second time around?"

"Decidedly. Even if *Pionyer I* fails to return, the

information sent back will prove invaluable. We will know a hundred times more about comets than we know now, and would have almost a 100 percent chance for success on *Pionyer II*." Baratynsky chuckled, causing his multiple chins to quiver. "Tarkovsky would prefer this first probe to be unmanned, just sending back scientific data, maybe the first two or three. But Cosmonauts are like any other soldiers. They are expendable. If they die, the glory of their cause will live forever." He took a long drink from the brandy glass. "Besides, nobody is watching. Can you imagine having a thousand ignorant journalists hanging around your neck, asking impertinent questions, the way they do in the West? Madness!" He looked at Nekrasov. "Speaking of secrecy, are you really keeping all of this secret from Premier Chekhov?"

Nekrasov stared at him coldly. "You need not concern yourself with that, Comrade Baratynsky."

"I suppose not. And those Americans?"

"They are being dealt with. There is no evidence that they have done us any harm so far, and I soon expect word that they will be beyond harming anybody."

"Well, at any rate, even should *Pionyer I* fail nobody will know and we'll have gained valuable experience. *Pionyer II* will have additional propulsion systems for separate cometary icebergs, and it will certainly be completed in time for the next optimum opportunity. That's expected in about two years."

Nekrasov studied his science adviser narrowly over the rim of his brandy glass. The man was overly ambitious in a system that did not consider ambition a virtue, not that Nekrasov cared about that. Well, Baratynsky had better be right this time; Nekrasov's neck was stretched out, right on the block. He was gambling on his KGB connec-

tions and on the vagaries of a Premier foolish
enough to hope for a peaceful rapprochement with
the West. With Project Peter the Great and its
iceberg bomb spinoff, Nekrasov could become the
first absolute Soviet dictator since Stalin.

His thoughts were interrupted by the ringing of
his private telephone. Fewer than half a dozen
officials in the USSR had that combination.

"Excuse me," Nekrasov said, rising. He waved
toward the decanter on the table. "Help yourself."
He entered his office and closed the heavy, sound-
proofed door. "Yes?"

"Ryabkin speaking, Comrade Deputy Premier."
Nekrasov was instantly on his guard. Ryabkin spoke
in dry, official tones but there was tension in the
man's voice. "You wished to be informed if there
was significant news on the Estonian woman and
the man Taggart."

"Yes," Nekrasov said tightly.

"The Bulgarians tried last night, and they bun-
gled it."

"How?" To an outsider Nekrasov might as well
have been asking about a soccer match, but Ryabkin
knew the difference.

"The opportunity seemed perfect. Taggart,
Tammsalu, Ciano and another CIA operative, apparently assigned as Ciano's bodyguard, were observed leaving a party late on a rainy night with
isolated rural roads to cross in order to get home.
Perfect terrain and circumstances for an accident."

"And?"

"The Bulgarians had the accident instead. Three
of them, in two vehicles, ended up dead in the
bottom of a canyon, along with Taggart's automobile. The Americans have listed them as acciden-
tal deaths; late night, too much to drink, dangerous
roads; most unfortunate, but no overt suspicion of
foul play. . . of course."

"The fools!" Nekrasov barked. "They accomplished nothing and gave Taggart and Ciano a credibility they lacked before!"

"Possibly," Ryabkin soothed, "but there is so far no evidence that the Americans believe them as yet. The Americans really are invincible in their prejudice. Taggart is a man with many enemies. They may attribute this try to an old vendetta."

"How did the idiot Bulgars fail? As if being Bulgarian weren't sufficient cause."

"According to their radio contact," Ryabkin said, relieved not to be the primary target of Nekrasov's wrath, "they tried to drive Taggart off the road. They bawled to me about the American having some secret weapon, but I think he just outdrove them. Taggart is rated a first-class driver, and I am told that his personal auto, a very old Chevrolet, is still considered internationally to be one of the very best commercial vehicles ever put on the market."

"A superior man in a superior machine," Nekrasov said bitterly. "It was a mistake to send Bulgarians out on this. We must try again, and use one of our own."

"Comrade Deputy Premier," Ryabkin said, calmingly, "we tried once and that could be attributed to a vendetta. If we try again, it will be plain to everybody that we want to silence these three people in particular. It wouldn't do."

"You're correct, Ryabkin," Nekrasov admitted.

"I have an idea," Ryabkin said. "As far as anybody knows, it is only Taggart who is the target of this vendetta. He and the Estonian woman seem to have formed a liaison in recent weeks, so it would not seem odd if she were to absorb a few bullets sent his way, since they spend so much time together."

"Good, very good, Ryabkin. With those two out

of the way, we can probably ignore Ciano, since he carries so little weight with his colleagues."

"Just what I was thinking, sir. And we have a man on the spot; Major Borodin."

"An excellent choice," Nekrasov said. Borodin was a famous triggerman from the old days. The Americans would have considered him a cowboy. He had been groomed by Nekrasov's predecessor in the KGB, who had had a weakness for giving out codenames from Russian musical history. "Put him on it. By the way, who was the fourth person in Taggart's car? Anybody we know?"

"Decidedly. It was that eccentric Amazon, Schuster. You remember her, surely."

"Indeed I do. If there is a female equivalent of Taggart, she is it. So, the two of them were in the same car, eh? No wonder the Bulgarians bought it. And she is Ciano's bodyguard?"

"Not only that; they have become intimate."

Nekrasov shook his head. He remembered Schuster well, and he had seen the surveillance pictures of Ciano. The thought of the two of them together was mind-boggling. "Ryabkin?"

"Yes, Comrade Deputy Premier?"

"Do not disappoint me this time."

CHAPTER FOURTEEN

WASHINGTON, D.C.

The night was getting late, and they had an early flight in the morning to catch. Vandenberg was a continent away. They had left Ugo and Fred at Ugo's top-security apartment in the new VIP complex next to the Potomac. Ugo had taken a characteristic view of his new digs.

"You know, this place useta be part of a big complex of 'temporary government construction' built during World War One. It was finally demolished year before last so they could build these apartments. So I figure, they give this to me, I should be able to keep it for about eighty years before they knock it down again, if they keep going by their old schedule, right?" That seemed to make sense to Sam, too.

Now, he and Laine were in the parking garage of Sam's apartment building. He opened her door and helped her out of the still-unfamiliar little Japanese car, their hands staying together as they turned to head toward the elevator. He had to turn loose of her hand as they passed between a massive concrete pillar and a parked Cadillac. The space was barely wide enough for one person edging sideways.

Sam really didn't quite see the knife lancing toward his stomach. He was just stepping clear of the pillar and all his years of training and practice took over as he spun aside on the ball of one foot, letting knife and hand go past, catching the wrist with his forearm to improve the deflection. His left arm slipped over the man's right arm and then both his hands were gripping the wrist and he was yanking the assassin sideways viciously. It was a classic elbow-breaking *wakigatame*, but before the man's elbow could break, his head was shattered against a concrete pillar. Even as he fell, Sam's hand was snaking beneath his coat and he went into a forward roll and yelled: "Stay down!" to Laine. Such men never work alone.

In his peripheral vision he caught a hint of movement and Sam spun on his belly and came up in that direction, hearing the muffled pop of a silenced pistol and the ping of the slugs hitting the concrete nearby, feeling the sting of fragments kicked up by the slugs, feeling the adrenaline rush and thinking, absurdly, how good it felt to be in top form again. Two more shots pocked the concrete where he'd been. This was no bungling Bulgarian. The roar from Sam's unsilenced ten millimeter was deafening in the echoing confines of the parking garage and the reverberations were still dying away when Sam came up from behind a parked car and saw the Russian aiming in the wrong direction. This kind of mistake a pro only gets to make once and Sam wasn't about to let the chance slip by. His first shot caught the Russian's shoulder, spinning him to face Sam. He was badly hurt but still tried to bring his pistol around for another shot. Sam's next two shots hit him in the chest and the next one, just to be certain, was right through his forehead.

"Stay down!" Sam again cautioned Laine. His ears were ringing and he could barely hear his own voice. He did a quick sweep of the garage but there were no more gunmen. He stepped out through the garage door, gun still in his hand. The street was all but deserted this late, but a car was parked at the curb a few paces away and he could see the glowing coal of the wheelman's cigarette. Sam walked quietly alongside the car and rapped sharply on the door with the side of his automatic. "Hey, Boris."

The man behind the wheel looked up, startled and Sam leaned in, pressing the barrel of his pistol against the man's neck. "Don't even think about it. You know, you people sure aren't getting much mileage out of your diplomatic immunity these days. You might as well go home. Your friends won't be coming back, but you'll get their bodies in a delivery van or something. The papers will probably say there was a mob shootout here tonight."

"Crime in the streets," the Bulgarian said. "It's not safe any more."

Sam grinned tightly. "Beat it, Boris. It's past your bedtime." The Bulgarian shrugged, started the car and slipped it into gear and drove away. A rental car, Sam noted. They weren't yet brazen enough to use an embassy car on a hit.

In the garage, he found Laine leaning against a car with her hands in her coat pockets, looking wan. At least she wasn't as shattered as last time. Sam gave the knife man a brief glance, then went to the gunman. The gun was, as he had suspected, a thirty-two. Anything larger was too difficult to silence efficiently.

Laine came up to him. "KGB?" Her voice was quite steady.

"That's right. The knifer was a sacrifice; a distraction, just some Bulgarian thug. This one's a top Russian. He used to go by the codename Borodin. He was a major or colonel last I heard."

Laine would not look directly at the dead man but she did not seem horrified. "Is it always going to be like this? Dodging bullets in garages?"

Sam shook his head. "They won't try again. I'm surprised they tried a second time." He studied Borodin some more. "Jesus. I can't believe they're still wearing hats and trench coats. Why don't they just issue them uniforms?" There was nothing to be gained down here. "Come on. Let's go up to my apartment. I have to make a call to Langley. God, my landlord's going to be pissed about this."

In the elevator, Laine laid a hand on Sam's arm. "Sam, do you think they'll try for Fred and Ugo? We should notify them."

"In that fort? They'd have to send an ICBM. No, I think they were trying to get you and still hoping to make it look like a feud between me and the Bulgarians." He watched her closely, looking for a sign of delayed reaction. "You're taking it a lot better this time."

"I've had some time to think since last time. They were KGB killers and if it is them or us, I'd much rather we were the ones to survive. At first I was afraid that maybe you were like them, but now I know that you are not. I'm just glad that we are both alive."

In the apartment Sam made the necessary telephone calls while Laine sat silently on the corner of the couch. "Sam?" she said when he hung up. He looked at her as he sat on the couch. "Just because I'm not so upset this time doesn't mean I could not use some comforting." She even managed a smile as she came into his arms.

CHAPTER FIFTEEN

KREMLIN

The reception for the Bulgarian party chiefs was just wrapping up. The burly chief of the Soviet Army was leaving with the svelte secretary-hostess. Nekrasov had noticed the man eyeing her and he had passed word through a KGB agent to make the introductions and whisper a few words in her ear. She had played this role before, and Nekrasov was soon going to need all the leverage he could get with the armed forces. When his iceberg bombs struck he would need to gather the reins quickly, consolidating power in his own hands and putting Chekhov out to pasture. No, perhaps the Premier should be disposed of permanently. After all, some of the icebergs would be falling on Soviet soil, and the old man could just be standing under one of them. Nekrasov produced one of his rare smiles at the neat irony of it.

When the last guest had left Nekrasov went into his office and found Ryabkin waiting for him, pacing the room. It was a bad sign for the usually phlegmatic Ryabkin to be showing signs of nerves.

He motioned Ryabkin to sit and took a chair facing him.

"Comrade Deputy Premier, we have several problems. The second attempt to eliminate Taggart and the Estonian woman failed as well. Borodin is dead, along with his Bulgarian backup. We dare not try again."

"The damage is done," Nekrasov said. "You spoke of several problems. What are the others?"

"It seems that Tammsalu, Taggart and Ciano have pushed themselves far enough to address the National Security Council and they are being taken seriously. Ciano has been moved into high-security housing reserved for persons whose safety is crucial to the nation."

"How seriously are their charges being taken? After all, they have little evidence and they *know* nothing for sure."

"We come to the worst of my report. The National Security Council has made up an intelligence report concerning the charges made by these people. They have codenamed the iceberg plan Project Ivan the Terrible. Their present policy calls for massive nuclear retaliation against any such attack. The first fall of an ice or meteoric rock missile on American territory or in waters near enough to do damage to the American coast will be met by a nuclear counterstrike."

Nekrasov almost smiled again. "Project Ivan the Terrible. It's a good name. I should have thought of it myself." He regarded his former deputy with a look of pure stone. "Obviously you didn't come by this report through diplomatic channels or there would be an emergency session of the Politburo sitting right now. How did you get this information and how reliable is it?"

"We have a mole planted in the periphery of the CIA—"

"I know that," Nekrasov said impatiently. "I put him there."

"He saw the cover page of a highly classified document with the title Project Ivan the Terrible. The KGB chief in residence had passed word around to investigate any new programs directed at the Soviet Union and he managed to scan the report. He was of course mystified by references to ice bombs but he managed to report what he had learned to the local KGB chief who reported to me."

"Verbally? Nothing written or recorded?"

"Nothing."

"That's good. I want further confirmation of this. It could be that this massive nuclear retaliation is a contingency plan, not a settled government policy." He leaned back in his chair for just a moment.

"We have a double agent, a man who has been doing business with us and with the Americans for years. He is a Cuban who got into America years ago, during the Carter boatlift. Put him on it. When he reports results, have him thoroughly interrogated, using the new drugs, to make sure his report is accurate. Then get rid of him and destroy all evidence."

"It shall be done. Is the iceberg bomb project now cancelled?"

"Not at all. It shall go forward." He saw the dismay on Ryabkin's face. "It will be modified, of course. The Americans are not the only ones with backup plans. I foresaw this possibility from the first and drew up alternate strategies. Do you really believe they would use massive nuclear retaliation? It would be suicidal. Our new anti-missile defenses are now operational in all our most vital areas. They know we would shoot back with our own missiles and nuclear winter would probably kill whoever survived. I think that report was planted, which means our mole has been compromised. They're bluffing, Ryabkin. It's always the same with them: they talk tough but they back down rather than face a real threat. They're weak, Ryabkin. For years they've substituted money for strength and now they're too spineless to use what strength they have left. My Project Ivan the Terrible will bring them to their knees, have no fear."

"As you say, Comrade Deputy Premier." It was a remarkable tirade from the usually reticent Nekrasov. Ryabkin began to have serious doubts about Nekrasov's sanity.

CHAPTER SIXTEEN

PIONYER I

To viewers used to the spectacular launches of Space Shuttle or Space Truck, the launch of mankind's first deep-space mission would have been a disappointing sight. There was none of the shattering noise, clouds of smoke or gigantic vehicles lurching their way ponderously skyward. In fact, it was less dramatic than a typical launch of a small, unmanned interplanetary mission from a near-Earth orbit. In the launching of chemically-fueled rockets, most of the acceleration was accomplished during the initial few minutes, at which time the bulk of the fuel was ignited in spectacular fashion. After that, such a craft would coast along its ballistic path in accordance with the inexorable laws of Newtonian mechanics. Using such methods, a one-way trip to Mars, for instance, would take several years, making long-distance missions impractical for manned probes.

Pionyer I, witnessed only by the somewhat jaded crew of Space Station *Volga*, blasted off from orbit with little fuss. Ignition was signaled by a faint

191

glow from its thrusters and the ship began to move, quite slowly at first, from its position near the station. Unlike the conventional rockets, *Pionyer* was the first continuously accelerating spaceship, designed to bring interplanetary distances within the grasp of man. Hundreds of millions, even billions of kilometers, could now be crossed in time spans practicable for manned missions. If everything worked.

A shuttle, taking off from Earth, went from a dead standstill to several *G* forces within a few seconds. *Pionyer* initially accelerated at a rate of about 0.01 *G*. Such an acceleration is almost imperceptible. However, in interplanetary space, a *constant* boost of 0.01 *G* allows a ship to attain a speed of nearly 10 kilometers per second at the end of one day, and it is still accelerating.

Korsakov and his crew held their breaths for some time as the ship drew away from the station. Everything seemed to be working perfectly. Korsakov expelled his breath and grinned. The mission was in his hands now. *His*! Traditionally, Soviet space missions were controlled to the greatest extent possible from the ground, leaving the cosmonauts little autonomy. The distance involved in this mission did not allow such ground control. Korsakov would have unprecedented authority, aided, of course, by his computer.

Compared with a simple fly-by of a comet, as had been done with Halley's and others, this rendezvous-with-touchdown was an immensely complicated proposition. The fly-by involved a simple juxtaposition: the elliptical orbits of the comet and the probe had to cross at some point, and comet and probe had to arrive at the intersection at roughly the same time, at least close enough to allow study without a collision.

Pionyer had to match velocity, speed and direction with the comet *precisely* at the moment of encounter. Even the slightest difference in velocity could result in disaster. To complicate matters further, the ship's course had to account for the continuously changing mass of the ship as its reaction mass, the water in the storage tank, was depleted.

All this meant that the ship's course had to be continuously updated by a high capacity computer tied to a multiple-star sensor and inertial guidance system. A couple of decades before, that would have meant a linkup with a gigantic computer system on the ground. *Pionyer* I was equipped with the latest fifth-generation computer, providing onboard computing capabilities undreamed of only a few years before. Operating this computer and applying its recommended adjustments comprised Korsakov's main responsibility as captain and chief pilot until rendezvous, at which time he'd get to do some real piloting.

The comet chosen for this mission was a periodic comet whose orbit and return to the inner system could be precisely predicted. Its orbit was close to the ecliptic plane, the plane on which the Earth orbits the Sun. Its closest approach to the sun was little less than one astronomical unit, which is the mean distance of the Earth from the Sun. This reduced the danger of exposing the crew to excessive solar radiation during their mission. The comet's path also brought it fairly close to the Earth itself at its perihelion point.

Korsakov and the crew were immensely grateful for this last fact, since it made for a relatively short voyage. A good thing, since they were assigned no experiments or other scientific work and had very little to do except for the pilot on duty.

"Boredom could prove to be the greatest hazard of space travel," said Kaminsky, the Second Pilot.

He drifted on a short tether near the ship's tiny galley. "At least on the old sailing ships they had storms, sails to trim, things to break the monotony."

"Bigger crews, too," contributed Gurdin, the life-support systems engineer. "Not the same few ugly faces to look at all the time. Next time let's sneak in some of those computer games they're so fond of in the West. I played some in Switzerland once. They're a lot more fun than chess."

"They're decadent and designed to sap the will of the proletariat, hadn't you heard?" reproved Korsakov. "Put yourself on report for political laxity. I'm told that we'll soon have political education officers in space so we can all feel right at home." He checked his computer screen for the hundredth time since waking. They were getting close, as distances are calculated in space.

With a practiced flick of his wrist, Korsakov launched himself toward the tiny observation dome. Grasping the handholds, he stuck his head into the Neoquartz bubble, which was just large enough to accomodate a helmeted head. Korsakov scanned the stars briefly. "There it is," he announced. The others came crowding up and he abandoned the bubble to give them a chance to look. "Not much to see yet."

"It's just a fuzzy dot out there," said Kaminsky disappointedly.

"We're still days from rendezvous," Korsakov told them. "But at least we know that it's there. It would have been embarassing to arrive at the rendezvous point and sit there staring at our watches while it didn't show up."

"A woman once did that to me in Pskov," Gurdin said. "At least comets are more predictable."

"But comets are a thousand times more dangerous," Korsakov said. "We're going to be cutting pieces off that thing with a laser, something that's never been tried before. We'll all have plenty of opportunities to get our names on some monument to the heroic dead, so I want no mistakes when we get to work. Anybody who fails to follow orders exactly gets to walk home."

"It'll look much bigger tomorrow," Kaminsky said, drifting from the observation bubble. "Let's wake our relief. Let them be bored for a while."

By the time they were within a thousand kilometers of the comet, there was still ample water left in the ship's reaction mass tank. It was a tribute to Korsakov's skill. The onboard nuclear powerhouse had sufficient uranium fuel to last well beyond the anticipated return trip. The next generation of spaceships would harness hydrogen fusion, providing a literally inexhaustable quantity of fuel for space travel. That was many years in the future. Right now the crucial question was whether they could mine sufficient ice from the comet to replenish the ship's water tank, and whether the ice was pure enough for their separator to clean up for use. If those two factors worked out, even if they failed in detaching the two icebergs, they would have accomplished one of their major objectives: the first manned interplanetary flight.

The immense cometary coma, the nebulous envelope surrounding the mass which spread out into a long "tail" as the comet neared the sun, was little more than vacuum made visible. As *Pionyer* entered it days earlier, visibility did not change substantially for the expedition, despite the coma's hazy appearance from the Earth. As the ship came to within several hundred kilometers of the comet, the denser gas and dust particles began to obscure vision. The comet's nucleus, the solid core, was visible only on the ship's radar screen. This comet was icy, as opposed to some that were dusty, but there were dust particles in the coma, in particular near the nucleus, and moving at such speeds even dust could pose a hazard to a spaceship.

Making touchdown on a comet was not like landing on a planet or the Moon. It was not even like docking with an orbiting space station. It was more like harpooning a whale. The comet's gravity was detectable only by instruments, and since it rotated it would literally cast the ship away unless it were securely anchored.

For the last few hours Korsakov was in the pilot's seat without relief. None of the others could be trusted with these incredibly delicate maneuvers, perhaps the most difficult ever attempted in space. His eyes were glued to his screens with their television views of the nucleus and their continuously-changing readouts. It truly looked like a jagged snowball, with streams of gas streaking across its surface.

"Cast off grapples," Korsakov ordered.

There was a slight vibration through the ship. "Grapples away," reported Tamara Ulanova, the only woman aboard. The rocket-propelled grapples shot across the intervening space, trailing their thin but high-strength cables. Glowing red-hot, the grapples impacted the surface, burying themselves in the ice, then expanding explosively beneath the surface, extending their barbs to grip the ice firmly. The crew waited tensely for several minutes, letting the grapples cool and giving the ice a chance to refreeze over the metal.

"Check tension," Korsakov said.

Tamara started the ship's windlasses for a moment, putting a slight tension on the cables and reading the results on her screen. "Full tension on all four anchors!" she said exultantly.

"Reel us in." Korsakov ordered.

Slowly, *Pionyer I* inched down its anchor cables

toward the cometary surface. There was an imperceptible jolt. Nobody dared to say anything. Korsakov released himself from the pilot's harness and looked out through the observation bubble. He shuddered briefly from released tension.

Outside, it looked like a very foggy morning on Earth, with visibility limited to a few meters. The 'landscape', 'cometscape'? was surrealistic, eerie. Alien.

Korsakov looked down and saw that the landing struts had their feet firmly, solidly against the surface. Then he checked to make sure his microphone and recorder were operational. "Tsiolkovsky Center, this is *Pionyer* Base, on the comet. Mankind is now an interplanetary species." The crew broke into spontaneous cheering, their over-vigorous back-slapping sending them spinning about the cramped interior of the ship. Kaminsky pressed a vodka flask into his hand and Korsakov held it out toward the others. "To the future!" He took a long pull at it and passed it on.

After a lengthy instrument check and general stock-taking, they prepared for the first EVA. As captain and sovereign master, Korsakov had the honor of being first. The airlock hatch swung open to the foggy scene and Korsakov pushed himself along the rail of the spindly ramp. A shock of exhilaration shot through him as his feet touched the surface. So this was how Armstrong felt! It took a little hand-pressure on the ramp to hold himself against the surface. The comet's gravity, about one hundred thousandth of Earth's, was indistinguishable from free-fall. He only wished that this event was broadcast to the whole world like the American Lunar feats had been.

The work of the following weeks was the most difficult and arduous ever attempted in space. Clumsily, under conditions akin to those of deep-sea divers, the six-person crew worked continuously on eight-hour shifts, cutting ice. Hampered by their awkward pressure suits and the umbilical lines connecting them to the ship, they wrestled with the newly-developed laser saws to free the ice from its matrix.

The lasers had to be handled with utmost delicacy. The slightest slip could destroy their spacesuits, their umbilical lines, even their ship, and space is the most unforgiving of environments. All knew that a serious accident could have only one result: death. The only variable was the number of deaths.

They cut ice for the water tanks first. This they did in small chunks, getting practice for cutting loose two icebergs. First they melted smaller chunks to distill for the reaction mass tank, then they cut a somewhat larger chunk as reserve fuel. Even though the tank was now full, the return journey would consume far more reaction mass than the outward trip. Going back, they would have to accelerate and decelerate the mass of the two icebergs and the reserve ice in addition to the ship and its fuel tank.

Conditions were hampered further by the rotation of the cometary nucleus. When their site was facing sunward, they had a bright, dense fog. Visibility was limited, but the diffuse light made work fairly easy. With the sun on the opposite side, they were in twilight. The refracted light scattered by the water vapor and dust prevented total darkness but their environment was obscure and their floodlights proved to be of little use.

With much early frustration, they learned that the ice had to be separated quickly from its bed once cut with the laser. Even the minute gravitational attraction of the comet was sufficient to cause a new bonding to take place almost instantly. They improvised a tripod crane from the general-purpose strut material they had brought along, and with this and a grapple they kept their ice blocks under cable tension sufficient to lift it free as the final cuts were completed. The crane looked unthinkably spindly to support such massive objects, but the real problem was to keep its legs anchored down to keep both crane and ice from drifting off into space. At least the ship's nuclear generator provided all the power they needed for their tasks. That allowed for the repetition of jobs that failed on the first, second or third try.

At the end of three weeks, *Pionyer* I, with its cargo of dirty icebergs, was on its way. So far, the crew suffered from nothing but fatigue and one sprained ankle. They had been prepared, indeed had even expected, to absorb more casualties. Theoretically, the return journey could be made with a crew of three. That was the first major relief.

The second was that the ice was usable. The worst fear of the planners had been that the ice would contain too many large rocks. Testing suggested that there were some rocks near the core but the comet's surface was covered with dusty ice laced with trace molecules of such chemicals as ammonia and methane. These trace molecules were not sufficient to disrupt the operation of the propulsion system. The system worked most efficiently when the charge-to-mass ratio of ions used was the highest. Hydrogen ions extracted from water yielded the highest charge-to-mass ratio attainable. Hydrogen ions were separated from oxygen ions through a special device. Each ionic species was accelerated through separate ion-drive boosters for a maximum efficiency.

The ship, with no further use for its grapples, cast the cables loose. Slowly and deliberately, the ship began to accelerate away from the comet. Tired as they were, the trip back was not to be one of rest and relaxation for the crew. There remained the complicated task of equipping the two icebergs with auxiliary chemical thrusters for the final precision maneuvering at the time of the icebergs' entry into the atmosphere above arctic Siberia. Before doing so, however, they had to determine the exact center of inertia of each so that the thrust from the auxiliary booster would not throw the icebergs into a spin.

Difficult as it had been to free them from the comet, and terrible as their employment might be, they did not look very dangerous. Each iceberg was about the size of a small suburban house. The power released would be all out of proportion to their size. These were to be experimental bombs; there was technically no limit to the size of the icebergs that could be brought in except for the size of the comets themselves.

Korsakov had one more important task left after attaching the auxiliary thrusters. He had to steer his ship on such a trajectory that, when the icebergs were disconnected from *Pionyer I*, they would proceed on their way to their destination in Siberia. The icebergs would be released very near the end of their journey. The fine maneuvering at the time of the impact would be directed from one of the three new geosynchronous space stations: *Volga*, *Don* and *Dnepr*. Once the icebergs were cut loose, Korsakov's mission would be completed. He and his crew would have accomplished the greatest, most important feat so far in man's expansion into space. And if all went well the world would never know.

CHAPTER SEVENTEEN

VANDENBERG AFB, CALIFORNIA

The starscape in front of Sam was spectacular. Each star was a brilliant, steady pinpoint of light instead of the flickering display that most people see, filtered through a thick atmosphere. To his left was the immense blue bulge of the Earth. He could see a sizable hurricane developing to the south of Okinawa. Or did they call them typhoons in that part of the world? There was a knock on the door behind him. "Colonel Taggart?" called a young voice.

Sam got up and opened the door. Outside was a young Air Force buck sergeant with a message in his hand. Behind him Sam could see the huge hangar which at the moment was mostly full of trainees in the newly-designed Space Service uniforms. "Message for you, sir." The sergeant handed him the message and a clipboard and Sam signed for it. The sergeant stuck his head inside. "These simulators are unreal," he said. "This is better than Disneyland!"

"I wish they'd change the display," Sam groused.

"That storm's been hanging off Okinawa for six weeks. Were you ever on Okinawa, Sarge?"

"Yessir. Two years in Security at Kadena. Good duty there. Best sushi bars and massage parlors anywhere."

"Tell me something: Is it hurricanes or typhoons they have there?"

"Typhoons. I sat a couple out at Kadena. I think hurricanes are strictly Atlantic."

"Thanks. Where's the nearest phone?"

The sergeant pointed to a service hallway between a snack bar and classroom. "There's one over there, sir."

"Secure?"

"All the phones here are secure if you have the right code."

Sam glanced at the note again as he crossed the hangar to the phone. It said simply that Dr. Ciano had called from Denver and wanted Taggart to call back as soon as possible. Busy as Ciano was these days, he was as excitable as ever, and these calls were frequent. Sam punched the security code first, then the number Ciano had sent. A male voice answered: "General Spacecraft, Mr. McNaughton's office." General Spacecraft was the prime contractor for Bountyhunter-A. Ugo had been spending a lot of time there, and at other prominent aerospace-oriented companies. Sam had a suspicion that Ugo was buying up stock on the sly, getting outrageously favorable prices because of his government position, blissfully uncaring of probable future charges of corruption and conflict of interest. He'd probably get away with it, too, the arrogant little bastard.

"May I speak to Dr. Ciano, please?"

"One moment, sir." There was a brief delay, then: "Taggart, I need to talk to you."

"Ugo, what's the difference between a hurricane and a typhoon?"

There was a moment of silence. "You feeling all right, Taggart? They treating you okay? Have you maybe been for one too many spins in the centrifuge?"

"I'm fine. I've been looking at the same storm for the last six weeks in the flight simulator. I was wondering whether it was a typhoon or a hurricane. Since you're the world's greatest expert on everything, I just thought I'd ask."

"Well, just to set your mind at rest, they're the same thing. Both tropical cyclonic storms originating over water. Typhoon is what they call 'em in the Pacific; comes from Chinese. Hurricane is what they call 'em in the Atlantic and it's a Carib Indian word. Feel better now?"

"Thanks, Ugo. I knew you'd come through for me. Now, what's *your* problem?"

"I'm in a powwow with the head honcho of General Spacecraft right now. We need you here right away. How soon can you get here?"

"Just like that? Drop everything and fly to Denver?"

"Right. You got anything better to do?"

"You better believe it. I have a late lunch date with Laine in—" he glanced at his watch, "forty-five minutes, as soon as she's out of the acceleration chamber. Then we have plans for the evening. Is it that urgent?"

"Yep. Anyway, I don't know about this evening, but Laine ain't gonna have no appetite for lunch if she's spent the morning in the acceleration chamber. Just tell her it's a matter of national security, which it is. How quick can you get here?"

Sam fumed quietly. "If there's a spare F18 out there ready to go, I can be there in about two and a half hours."

"Try to make it two. I'll meet you at the airfield. Drive careful, now." Ugo hung up.

Sam left a message for Laine. The accelerated Shuttle training program had left them little time together during the last few months. This wasn't the first engagement they had had to cancel. On the airfield, he found the sergeant in charge of the flight line. "You have an F18 fueled up, Sarge?" Sam had taken care to ingratiate himself with the flight line personnel as soon as he had come here.

"Can you have it back tomorrow?" The Air Force staff sergeant looked absurdly young to be responsible for a whole line of high-performance aircraft. "I'll be needing it by 0900."

"Sure. If I can't bring it back myself, I can get someone to fly it."

"Just make sure and let me know who's bringing it back if it's not you. Sign here, Colonel." He handed Sam a clipboard.

After considerable arm-twisting, Sam had managed to get himself into the shuttle pilot program. To be flight-qualified involved accumulating sufficient pilot-hours on an F-18. He also needed to fly a specified number of hours each month to maintain his flight-ready status. To this end, the Air Force allowed astronauts to use F18s to run errands, on an aircraft-available basis.

As promised, Ugo was waiting for Sam at the hangar. He gave Sam a bearhug and a slap on the back, which his long arms permitted without needing a stool to stand on. "Lookit my newest toy!" Ugo gestured grandly at a low-slung sports car. It looked fast and expensive. Sam examined it, noting the special boosters on the gas and brake pedals. The clutch was a squeeze-lever mounted on the steering wheel.

"Is it as fast as it looks?" Sam asked. Immediately, he regretted the question.

"Hop in." Ugo said. Sam did, with trepidation. Unauthorized aerobatics in an F18 didn't scare him one tenth as much as the thought of Ciano at the controls of a bomb like this.

Sam's head slammed back against the headrest as Ugo hit the accelerator and the little car tore off in a screech of tires, trailing a plume of rubber smoke. He blithely drove out onto a runway and passed a taxiing airplane, whose pilot was yelling into a mike, probably asking the tower what the hell was going on.

They passed through a gate and Sam expected Ciano to show a little more circumspection out on the public highway, but such was not to be. "Ugo," he said, "you just went through a red light. There's nobody chasing us with guns this time."

"Uh-uh. If you'd've looked close, you'd've noticed it wasn't really red. When I get this thing going fast enough, the red lights violet-shift to green. You got to take into account the relativistic effects." With this concept firmly in mind, Ugo never stopped for a red light. They pulled up at their destination in a screech of brakes.

Sam read his watch unbelievingly. "We couldn't have covered twenty miles in that time."

"Relativistic effects again. This time it's time dilation. You have to brush up on your Einsteinian physics, Sam. I'll lend you some good texts."

"We got this problem, see," Ugo told him as they walked from the parking lot to the administration building. General Spacecraft was a sprawl of offices, shops and factories surrounded by a high chainlink fence. "The chairman of the board came to me with it, because they regard me as sorta the resident genius when I'm around, which is my cross to bear everywhere. The problem involves hardware, but I think the solution lies in people-engineering. And who's the best trouble-shooter in the people-engineering department but my old buddy Sam?"

"Ugo, I just don't know how to thank you."

"You'll think of something."

The administration building was an ultramodern piece of architecture designed for efficiency and security. There was a guard sitting at a console next to the private elevator which went to the chairman's suite, and he took Ugo's voiceprint.

"Do you really think someone might slip past you disguised as Dr. Ciano?" Sam asked the guard.

"Could happen," he said humorlessly.

The elevator opened onto an elegant lounge where they were greeted by an efficient young man whom Sam's practiced eye identified as the boss's bodyguard. He ushered them into a spacious office with a gigantic, floor-to-ceiling window providing a breathtaking view of the Rockies.

"Pretty nifty office, huh?" said Ugo. "I'm gonna get Uncle Sam to give me one just like it."

Ian McNaughton entered from a side room and greeted Sam warmly. He was chairman of what had become in recent years an immense aerospace conglomerate. In height, he fell into the sizable span between Ugo and Sam. He looked to be about fifty, which was not an advanced age for a top executive of one of the largest companies in the world. His hair and moustache were whitish-blond, making him seem a bit older. His clothes were conservative and expensive. He offered amenities but Sam and Ugo, both in training these days, settled for tea. When the tea was served, McNaughton came straight to the point.

"I trust Dr. Ciano outlined our problem to you on the way from the airport?"

Ugo tried to look innocent. "He did," Sam lied, "but Dr. Ciano tends to talk over my head. I'm pretty much a layman in these matters. I'd appreciate it if you'd go over it for me in simple terms."

"The work on Bountyhunter-A had been going rather well until this problem cropped up. The problem is with the system for zero-g separation of water from cosmic dust and other impurities in the comet's ice.

"To complicate the problem, we have only educated guesses as to the composition of comets. The Russians, on the other hand, have several successful cometary probes behind them, and may even have managed to retrieve physical samples. Automated returns are something of a Soviet specialty. You may recall that shortly after our initial Apollo landings, they got their own Lunar samples back using an automated return rocket.

"Since we have only guesswork to go on concerning the composition of comets, we're doing the 'worst case' design for the separation system, which makes our engineering task formidable indeed. In a manned mission, we can't afford to take too many risks, instructions from the Department of Space Defense notwithstanding. We think we can lick the problem in three years but probably not in two, no matter how many corners we cut. In order to keep to our schedule, we have to have this test completed within one year." He paused briefly to brush an imaginary speck of dust from the top of his spotless mahogany desk. He picked up his tea cup and Ciano seized the opportunity to leap in.

"Like I said, the problem ain't exactly insoluble. After all, the Russians have come up with an answer. And so have others—that's where you come in, Sam, my boy."

"I was wondering about that." Sam wandered over to the huge window and admired the spectacular view.

Ugo went on, "One of the maverick Japanese new-tech companies has recently succeeded in producing just the kind of separation system we need. They developed it for manufacturing work in space. But it's an industrial secret and they're holding it tight. We've gleaned just enough info to be pretty sure it'll do the job for us."

Sam scanned the multitude of buildings below. "So buy it. This outfit doesn't look short on capital."

"Now you've come to the soul of the problem," Ugo said. "They won't sell us that sucker at any price."

Sam smiled. "So you want me to steal it for you? Or bribe somebody?"

McNaughton maintained a poker face and said nothing.

"Hell, we're among friends here," Ugo said. "Sam, we already tried to bribe them. We struck out clean. Luckily it didn't turn into a public scandal."

"So now you need an expert on breaking and entering?"

"Sam!" Ugo's hand clapped dramatically over his heart, the picture of wounded innocence. "Would I ask you to do such a thing? Look, you're a persuader, Sam, you got contacts all over the world. Admittedly, I'm a genius, but I can't twist arms like you can. Surely you know somebody in the Japanese government you can talk to, maybe blackmail a little. Nothing really illegal. Of course," he shrugged and spread his hands helplessly, "if you gotta shoot somebody, that's okay, but don't get caught—and get us that separator."

"I'm not hearing this," McNaughton said.

"What's the name of the Japanese company?" Sam asked.

"Uchu Kogyo K.K., which translates as Space Industries, Incorporated," McNaughton said. "The president is one—" he consulted a file on his desk,

"—Goro Kuroda, if I have the pronunciation correct." He didn't catch Sam's quick smile.

Sam continued to study the sprawling facility below. "How come the Japanese got this thing first? Your company must be nearly as big as NASA. Weren't your R&D people working on it?"

"Not our line of work." McNaughton shrugged. "It wasn't a priority project with us until now. General Spacecraft does very little generalized research. Our contracts usually involve weather and communications satellites as well as defense and intelligence contracting. You're well aware that that means mostly orbital technology. Our investors don't like to see their money spent on non income-generating projects. Why should they?"

"Japan, on the other hand," Ciano said, maliciously, "is different. Lots of entrepreneur spirit there, and lots of government cooperation. They ain't afraid of a little risk." McNaughton said nothing, but his left eyebrow went up a fraction of an inch at the word, "little."

"All right," Sam said. "I'll take care of it. Mr. McNaughton, I need to make a transpacific call under Utmost Secret code. Is there a phone here that can handle it?"

"Well," McNaughton said uneasily, "despite all our government work, I've never heard of Utmost Secret, but my desk phone is supposed to have all the latest security gadgets."

"It'll have to do. Mr. McNaughton, I'm going to have to ask you to leave the room while I make this call. I won't take long."

"Uh, Sam," Ugo said queasily, "maybe I should go with Ian, I mean, I don't—"

"You stay here, Dr. Ciano," Sam said, sternly. "As Deputy Director of Project Bounty Hunter, you are going to have to be in on this."

McNaughton exited hastily and shut the door.

Ciano ran a finger under the collar of his shirt, as if it had suddenly grown smaller. "Uh, I don't know, Sam, maybe—" Taggart silenced him with a glare as he punched a seemingly endless number code.

A delightful female voice came through the desktop speaker: "*Uchu Kogyo Shacho-shitsu desu* - Space Industries, President's office."

"May I speak to Mr. Kuroda, please."

"Yes, sir!" the woman said, briskly. Anyone calling the president of the firm on his private line was a VIP and she had standing orders to put any such call through at once.

A pleasant baritone answered in English: "Good morning, Goro Kuroda speaking."

Sam glanced at his watch. It would be about 10:00 AM in Japan. "Good morning, Kuroda-san. I trust I'm not interrupting anything?"

Kuroda recognized the voice immediately. "Taggart-san! It's been years. Where are you, Sam?"

"Colorado. Goro, sorry to give you such short notice, but would you have time to see me tomorrow afternoon?"

"You have no need to ask. Any time you want to see me, I will make room. It will be a pleasure. I'll meet you at Narita Airport. What flight will you be on?"

"I don't know yet, but I'll let your secretary know as soon as I have my reservations. I look forward to seeing you tomorrow at the airport."

"Have a good flight." Sam depressed the shutoff button and looked up to see Ugo glaring at him.

"You sadistic sonofabitch. You just love to make people squirm, don't you? You knew the guy all the time!"

Sam smiled ferociously. "I said I'd repay you for this. Now, if you're all through disposing of my time and talents, I'll be on my way."

"Say, Sam," Ciano's fury melted away and he grew crafty. "I got an idea. My buddy McNaughton here has given me free access to his corporate jet. I bet he'd send you to Japan on it gratis. I'd be happy to fly your cute little jet back to Vandenberg for you. See, as Deputy Director for Bountyhunter, I don't get a whole lot of time to devote to my astronaut training, but I'm qualified for solo flight, and I'd just love to take up one of them F18s."

"Sorry, Ugo. I missed my lunch date with Laine, but if I step on the gas I might make it back in time for a late dinner. Now, if you'll promise to stop for the red lights, I'll let you drive me back to the airfield."

Ciano grumbled the whole way, but Sam was unmoved. Ugo behind the wheel of a sports car was terrifying. At the controls of a jet he would be a menace to Western civilization.

CHAPTER EIGHTEEN

TOKYO

Sam left the enormous jetliner feeling relaxed. He had stretched his legs and allowed himself two inflight bourbons in celebration at the beginning of the flight. He wanted to be in top form when he met Goro at the airport. On the flight over, he had wondered whether there really might be a typhoon down there somewhere. However, they had made a typhoonless landing at Narita and he went through the quick, efficient customs process which was much more agreeable than the one that greeted returning Americans. Kuroda was waiting for him outside customs.

"Welcome to Japan, Sam." Kuroda looked Sam up and down. "You don't look a day older than when I last saw you."

"I can say the same for you." It was perfectly true. Goro Kuroda looked exactly the same. He was somewhere in his mid-forties and impeccably dressed. He was of median height, a bit on the tall side for a Japanese, with handsome, rugged, nail-hard features. Despite his western suits and brush-cut hair he always gave Sam the impression of wearing the Samurai's *hakama* and swords and a topknot. Kiroda's chauffeur took Sam's suitcase.

Kuroda's limousine was a late-model car with a dashboard that looked more complicated than the controls of the shuttle simulator Sam had been training on. As he sat back into the luxurious seat, Sam said, 'Tell your driver that I'm staying at the Hilton."

"No, you aren't," Kuroda said, grinning. "I was afraid you might book yourself into one of those dreadful, western-style hostelries, so I took the liberty of putting you into the Japanese Inn. It's a much better place, you'll love it."

"Sounds good to me." Sam rapped the bullet-proof glass of the side window. "Problems?"

Kuroda's grin disappeared. "Terrorists are everywhere these days. This is a precaution we take for all our top executives and their families, especially for our representatives abroad, but here, too. My own younger brother handles our corporation's affairs in France. Two years ago a kidnap attempt was tried. He was saved by his bodyguards and his armored limousine, but one bodyguard was killed. We never even found out which group it was, but there are so many that nobody can keep track of them all."

The drive from Narita to downtown Tokyo took over an hour. Kuroda, however, was far too polite to press Sam about his reasons for coming to Japan until he was rested. Mostly, they reminisced about their earlier times together. Sam had told Ugo a hair-raising story about how he had once saved Kuroda's life in Singapore during a joint U.S.-Japanese operation involving cutthroat industrial espionage, Chinese Triads, Japanese *yakuza*, Mafiosi and all manner of other dramatic trappings. It had been a fine story but it was an utter fabrication.

Actually, the two had met a dozen years previously in Dusseldorf, and what had brought them together was not espionage, but judo, which Sam was practicing passionately in those days. He had taken up the sport as a boy, and in his early days with the Agency it had served as a fine cover, since there were judo meets going on all over the world all the time. Sam had been stationed in Dusseldorf, and Kuroda's business had taken him there for several years, as Uchu Kogyo had their European headquarters in that city. They had met in a local judo club.

Kuroda, in his early thirties then, was a *yondan* or fourth degree black belt. Sam, in his midtwenties, was preparing to take the promotional test for his *nidan*, the second-degree black belt. They took an immediate liking to each other and became fast friends, practicing judo almost daily, when their schedules permitted. Kuroda was amazed at Sam's athletic abilities and his most un-occidental capacity to internalize the subtle principles of judo. Sam found Kuroda to be a great teacher who made even the most difficult principles easy to learn and enjoyable to practice.

When Sam took the *nidan* promotional, Goro sat as one of the judges. Although Sam passed with flying colors Goro did not consider him to be anywhere near fully accomplished yet. Now it was time to put the polish on his training. First, he taught Sam the Tomiki system of aikido, developed by the late Professor Tomiki of Waseda University, who had studied under both Professor Kano and Master Uyeshiba. Tomiki had developed a system of aikido which was both realistic and scientific in its training method and elegantly simple in its principles. Sam made his first black belt in record time. Then Goro decided that he was ready for some really serious training. He taught Sam a truly devastating combat version of judo which, in later years, saved his life on more than one occasion. One of those techniques was used on the Bulgarian in the Washington parking garage.

Between throw-and-bruise sessions, they had partied all over Europe on weekends. At that time Sam was posing as a clerical employee of the American consulate. Kuroda, who was nothing if not astute, had quickly divined Sam's real profession. He said nothing about it at the time, but years later he had occasion to call on his friend's peculiar expertise, and Sam had risen to the occasion.

It was nearly dusk when the limousine pulled up at the exclusive Japanese Inn. The entrance looked rather modest, but Kuroda led him into a world that left noisy, flashy Tokyo far behind. Inside, he found himself in a Japan of an earlier, more gracious time. Leave it to Goro to know about something like this in the middle of Tokyo. Kuroda was firing some rapid-fire Japanese at the staff, then he turned to Sam. "I'll leave you in the capable hands of these people, Taggart-san. I'll return in a couple of hours after you've had a chance to relax and refresh a bit. Then, if you feel up to it, we might have an informal dinner here. The Inn is famed for its classic cuisine."

"I am looking forward to it."

Sam removed his shoes at the entrance hall as custom dictated, and stepped onto an elevated floor of highly polished wood where a pair of slippers were laid out for him. He was led past several turns of passageway and was shown to a room detached from the main part of the Inn but connected to it by a corridor of polished wood. Except for such amenities as glass, electricity and plumbing, the Inn might have been lifted unchanged from eighteenth-century Japan.

The room was tatami-matted in traditional style. Two sides of the room had large, paper-screened sliding doors opening onto several feet of wooden floor, at the edge of the which were glass-paneled sliding doors. Intrigued, Sam slid back the glass doors. He found that the detached room was an island in an exquisitely designed Japanese garden. Pebbles covered the ground next to the elevated wooden floor of the building and stepping stones led to a pond full of large, rainbow-hued carp. A miniature bridge crossed the pond and the path disappeared into a small mound. Trees and shrubs had been carefully planted to give an impression of naturalness. The entire garden was delicately crafted to give the illusion of a self-contained cosmos. As the sky darkened, Sam heard the chirping of crickets. It seemed impossible that he was in the middle of downtown Tokyo.

For the first time in years, Sam felt like dropping his perpetual guard. He only wished that Laine were here to share this meditative tranquility. He made a vow to return with her when this was all over.

As he came back into the room, a girl in her early twenties entered carrying a tray. On the tray were steaming Japanese tea and a small, porcelain plate containing two pieces of a jello-like Japanese cake called *yokan*. Sam thanked her, setting off a gale of giggles that would have seemed immature in a young Western woman, but which here sounded good-humored and polite. She bowed and left the room.

There was a private bath adjacent to the room, its oversized tub already filled with steaming water. Sam was familiar with Japanese baths, in which the tub was strictly for soaking. He soaped up and rinsed off with hot water in the tiled area outside the tub. Only after the suds were thoroughly rinsed off did he lower himself into the tub, which was large enough to accomodate him and a couple of girls without any forced intimacy. He sighed deeply. Where had Western culture gone wrong?

For the first time in months, Sam checked out his latest set of battle scars. They were fading in among the others, now, and the wounds no longer pained him. At least, no worse than other, earlier wounds. This, he knew, would have to be his last field job. Luck had saved him too many times lately, and you couldn't count on luck. But what would he do? Leave the agency, for one thing. Damned if he'd take a desk job. But what then? Then he remembered that he and the rest of humanity might not have a whole lot of future to worry about anyway. He decided to postpone midlife crisis for the duration of the emergency. That felt much better.

Shaved, cologned, powdered and thoroughly refreshed, Sam put on a cotton after-bath kimono which he remembered was called a *yukata* and returned to his room. He sat on a large, silk-covered cushion equipped with a recliner back on which he leaned comfortably. He found that he was in perfect proximity to a low service table on which was centered a tall, cold glass of Kirin beer. He could not have sworn to it, but it looked as if the beads of condensation on the glass had been placed there with exquisite care by the same artisan who had designed the garden. It almost seemed an act of vandalism to drink it, but he did anyway. Perfectly on cue, the giggly girl arrived just as he set down the empty glass. She announced the arrival of his dinner guest.

Kuroda stepped in with his familiar wide grin. He declined to sit in the place of honor in front of the alcove. Sam pressed politely. Eventually, they compromised by sitting with the alcove between them. This had been the intention all along, but the formalities had to be observed.

The informal dinner turned out to be an eighteen-course banquet. "Goro, explain something that's been bothering me for years: How did a nation with such warlike tradition make an art form out of relaxation?"

Kuroda picked up a shallow, saucer-like cup of sake. "We have had many centuries to study both fighting and relaxation, and to refine each, particularly the latter. You people have been too busy being frontiersmen." He put down the cup. "Now, of course, we may all be frontiersmen again. I mean the United States and Japan and Western Europe. The next few centuries may see the greatest mass exodus of humanity since the opening of the New World, and the expansion into Siberia and southern Africa."

This was getting a little too close to Sam's actual business here, and he didn't want to discuss it just yet. "How's the family doing, Goro? Is Miyoko all right?" Sam knew that Kuroda's wife had died shortly after bearing him two children, and that he had never remarried. Sam had more reason than most to know just how devoted Kuroda was to his children.

"She is perfectly recovered. She graduated from Ochanomizu and is now doing graduate work in geophysics at the University of Tokyo." He grinned again. "I sent her to stay with her grandparents for a year. In the States, you turn your children over to a psychiatrist after a traumatic experience. We send them back to the family."

"I can't imagine that she needed much recovery time. That girl is pure samurai. And your son?"

"He took his degree from Tokyo Institute of Technology and is now an engineer with Toshiba's Space Division." They spent the rest of the long, leisurely dinner in casual talk. When the plates were cleared away and the waitresses gone Goro got up and opened all the paper-screened doors. He left them ajar, which Sam knew to be a security precaution. Kuroda was following his ancestor's practice for a secret conference.

Goro reseated himself. "And now, Sam, I think it is time we spoke of your reason for coming here. Much as we enjoy each other's company, this is not a casual visit. I believe we can talk freely now. I have used this place for confidential meetings in the past."

"Goro, recently you or somebody in your company were approached concerning a zero-gravity separation system for water. I believe a bribe was mentioned."

Kuroda's expression did not change, but his eyes narrowed slightly. "That is so. The bribe was, of course, refused."

"I just learned about it. That attempt was made by a colleague of mine who is renowned for his tactlessness even in the States."

"Like most people in the space program, I know Dr. Ciano by reputation. He exceeds all expectations. How did you come to be involved with him?"

Sam poured sake for both of them. "Get comfortable, Goro, I have a long story for you." As soon as he had heard Goro's name mentioned in connection with the crucial separator, Sam had resolved to tell him the whole story with perfect honesty. It was a course his superiors never would have understood.

At the end of the recitation Goro sat stone sober despite several empty sake bottles. "Much trouble and embarrassment might have been spared if I had known that you were involved in this, Sam."

"Likewise. I'm afraid that the people I work for would never think of full truth and honest action when they see a chance for bribery or coercion."

"Then it remains for men of honor to correct their mistakes." Goro thought for a moment. "Your story does not sound as far-fetched to me as it might to those unacquainted with the possibilities for exploitation of the solar system. And, too, I have a certain Japanese bias. I can easily believe this of the Soviets. There have been whole decades when you Americans have persuaded yourselves that they were your friends. We have never confused a wartime alliance or a temporary relaxation with goodwill. They have threatened us since the days of the Tsars and I do not see that changing. If this Project Ivan the Terrible is aimed at you, it is aimed at us as well. I need hardly point out that this nation is enormously vulnerable to an ocean strike."

"I'm no scientist, Goro, but people I trust assure me that we can build our first interplanetary ship in about a year *if* we can have your water separation system. To do it on our own would take at least two years, but more likely three. That may be too late. We have to stop them now. We know that you're not interested in money for the system. Would you let us have it as a personal favor to me?"

Kuroda did not hesitate. "No, I cannot do you this favor or any other favor, as you well know." He saw Sam's bewildered look and rushed on. "Favors are not possible between us. I am in debt to you for the rest of my life. Quite aside from the mutual danger to our nations, I owe you this. Since you ask for it, it is yours."

CHAPTER NINETEEN

DENVER

"Come *on*, Taggart! What kinda leverage did you have on this guy? I don't buy that story about the Mafia and Singapore." Ciano looked as if he were about to burst or collapse with apoplexy, but since he looked like that most of the time, nobody paid much notice.

"Mafia?" said Fred. "Singapore? I must not have been involved in that one." They were enjoying a rare moment of relaxation in a ski-type lodge near Denver. The snow was falling heavily outside but a fire crackled on the hearth. The little cluster of cottages had better security than Camp David. Fred lay in a lanky sprawl near the fire, and Laine sat crosslegged on a cushion with Sam lying back in her lap. Idly, she stroked his hair, which she noted was beginning to get thin on top. He seemed totally relaxed, so different from the violent, tautwired man she had met—how long ago had it been? It seemed like ages.

"Yeah, tell us, Sam," Fred urged. "You know how I love to talk shop."

"Just a minute," Laine said. "Is this going to be another of your cowboy stories, all full of shooting and dead people?"

" 'Fraid so," Sam told her. "Not as bad as some, but it got a little rough."

"Then I have some work to catch up on." She got up and Sam's head dropped to the floor with a thunk. "I'll be in my room. Call me when dinner is ready."

"I don't think Laine's going to reconcile herself with your profession, Sam," said Ugo when she was gone.

"She won't need to," Sam said. He sat up and picked up his wine glass. "All right, since you insist. Remember, you never heard this. I had no business taking part, I just let my better nature get the best of me."

"You think I can't keep a secret?" Ugo demanded, hurt. Sam didn't answer him.

"Well, it was about three, no, closer to four years ago, just before that operation that got me shot up. . . ."

It had been a nasty business all the way around; not the kind of well-planned and executed mission Sam liked, but instead a spontaneous, vicious piece of work that, by a miracle, had ended well. Sam had been in Rome on a rather routine investigation in cooperation with Italian authorities, trying to find a link between certain Central American guerrillas and the Italian Red Brigades. In the middle of the night, he received a phone call from Goro. His friend sounded close to panic. The two had met briefly during a judo tournament in Graz the month before, and Sam had given him his Rome address and phone number.

Goro's desperate story was drearily familiar in Italy, where kidnapping was still the major growth industry. This time, it was Goro's daughter, Miyoko.

She was then a junior at Japan's exclusive girl's school, Ochanomizu University. Taking advantage of her two-month vacation, she had attended summer school at the Sorbonne to improve her French. There she met an intense young woman from Milan, who invited Miyoko to visit her there on her way back to Japan. She accepted, and Goro's next word from her came in the form of a ransom demand. Having no faith in the Italian police, his first thought had been to contact Sam.

One look at the wording of the ransom demand told Sam which group they were dealing with: It was a faction that had split from the Red Brigades as being too moderate, working in conjunction with an extreme fringe of Al Fatah and a splinter band from the JDL. Ugo broke into the narration at this point. "This is another one of your silly spook stories, isn't it? I mean, I didn't buy the Triad-Mafia-Yakuza story, so you want to see if I'll swallow this?"

"I heard of that bunch," Fred said. "Hell, I've seen weirder combinations than that. I know an old-timer in FBI who worked back in the sixties. He once busted an arms-smuggling ring that turned out to be run jointly by the KKK and the Black Panthers. Terrorists don't let little ideological quibbles keep them from having their fun."

It was not Sam's assignment, and he had no authority to take action on behalf of the Agency. What he did instead was call in a lot of outstanding IOUs from colleagues in Italy. Meanwhile, they stalled the kidnappers by demanding proof that Miyoko was alive. The accepted practice was for the kidnappers to send a photograph of the victim holding a copy of that day's newspaper with the date plainly shown. Within a few days Sam had good news: his agents had located the terrorists at a remote mountain hut in Calabria. The bad news was that this bunch had a reputation for killing their victims as soon as the ransom was paid. There was also the matter of the mountain hideout, which was too well-guarded to be taken by assault without giving the kidnappers plenty of time to kill Miyoko.

The security setup consisted mainly of guards instead of a lot of technological gimmickry, and Sam knew that it was a relatively simple matter for a small group to penetrate such a system, as long as they were willing to kill a few people to do it. After a brief consultation, Sam and Goro decided that they owed these people no favors at all. On the evening of the day they received the photo, Sam and Goro were at the bottom of the mountain, dressed in black, with blackened faces. Both were heavily armed and the night, fortuitously, was moonless. They took out the first guard just after midnight and within ten minutes were on their way back down the mountain with Miyoko. The girl was badly shaken but relatively undamaged.

The next morning Italian authorities found five bodies on the premises; one with a broken neck, one dead from a stab wound, and three perforated by small-arms fire. They picked up thirty shell casings but Sam had used only Czech-made ammunition. Goro had wanted to leave a Japanese dagger in one of the bodies, but Sam advised against any grandstanding. Terrorists were incapable of learning from their mistakes. Officially, the affair was written off as a vendetta between rival gangs, but Sam found himself swiftly booted out of Italy. Once again, he was in the doghouse. It seemed he could not be sent on a simple investigation without getting involved in a shootout. Worse, he had let himself be influenced by things like friendship, morality and personal honor, for which there was scant room in Agency operations. He was packed off to Central America where, he was told, he could pick a direction at random and open fire without anybody paying much attention.

That Christmas, he was spending a few weeks in Washington when a package was delivered to his apartment. After taking his usual precautions with the oblong box, he opened it. Inside was a Japanese sword in a perfectly plain black-laquered sheath. Its handle was bound with white rayskin and wrapped with black silk tape. Its form was elegant but simple as a Zen ink drawing. Sam called a friend whose hobby was Japanese swords and the man arrived with an armload of books and a tiny brass hammer. With the hammer and a wooden dowel, he drove out the retaining peg that bound handle to blade and slipped the handle off, revealing an age-blackened tang deeply cut with Japanese characters. Sam's friend refused to make any pronouncements, since forgery of Japanese swords was such a big business, but he made a rubbing of the handle with charcoal and thin paper and took several pictures of the sword, along with closeups of the inscription, and promised to have them authenticated. He also recommended that Sam keep the sword in a bank vault.

Weeks later, in a tiny Indian village in the tropics, he received a letter from something called the Japanese Sword Society of America. It identified his sword as an ancient masterpiece by the swordsmith Munemitsu. It was known to have been a treasure of the Kuroda family for generations. Valuation: "priceless."

"That was a better story than the last one," Ugo said, up and pacing as usual. "Sam, I wanna meet your friend Kurodo."

"Kuroda," Sam corrected. "Why? He'll probably wring your neck for that bribery attempt."

"Fred'll protect me. Just give me ten minutes with him and I'll have him eating out of my hand. I got a proposition for him I think he'll like. I been talking with my man McNaughton and some other people. We're making plans."

"What kind of plans?" Sam asked, suspiciously.

"You think when we've settled this Project Ivan thing the salad days'll be over for old Ugo Ciano? Not a chance! I got plans, Taggart, and this guy Kurodo—"

"Kuroda!"

"—sounds like my kind of man. You'll want in on it, too. Since you and Laine will be getting married—"

"Hold it! Who said anything about marriage?"

Ugo shook his head pityingly. "Come on. I got eyes, and God knows I got brains. You're gonna have to grow up, Taggart, settle down, stop being a kid. You don't get to play cowboy forever. Besides, your guy with his bulletproof car and his kidnapped kid and his almost-kidnapped brother knows the kind of world we live in. I don't like living in a world where things like that happen, either. Once I get things rolling, we can leave worries like that behind."

"Wait a minute," Sam protested. "Somewhere in there I lost the thread of this conversation. You're going to fix the world?"

Ugo stared upward and raised his arms in a dramatic appeal to heaven. "They don't listen to me, God! Why did you make me so smart and the rest of them so dumb?" Receiving no answer, he went on. "Sam, everywhere we look in this project there's golden opportunities, ideas, paths opening up. No, I ain't gonna fix the world. Barring divine intervention, nothing's gonna keep the world from going straight to hell. What I'm gonna do—what *we're* gonna do, is shape the course of history!"

"Ambitious, isn't he?" Fred commented.

Ugo shrugged. "You was wondering what to do with your life after this little caper's over anyway, Sam. You might as well stick with me."

Once again, eerily, Ciano was reading his mind with some accuracy. He was at loose ends about his life after leaving the Agency, true, but did he want to stake his future on a mind-reading maniac like Ugo Ciano?

Washington

McNaughton and Chambers studied the agreement Sam had worked out with Kuroda as the most acceptable to all parties involved. It would meet the emergency security needs of the U.S., protect the possible stake of Japan in the matter and safeguard the financial interest of Uchu Kogyo. The details were left to be hashed out at the working level, but in essence Uchu Kogyo was to manufacture, at cost plus modest fixed fees, two or more separation units for Project Bountyhunter according to the specifications provided by General Spacecraft.

McNaughton raised a question at this point. "Is their security adequate?"

Chambers shrugged. "We tried hard enough to crack it."

Kuroda would not reveal to anyone, not even to his executive vice-president, the nature of Project Bountyhunter. It was given a different project name at Kogyo. A mutually agreed upon American agent would be free to inspect security measures at the Japanese plant upon request.

After completion, the engineers of Uchu Kogyo would travel to the U.S. for the integration of the separation system with the rest of the interplanetary spaceship. During the integration, no photographs would be taken. This was to protect any secrets concerning the interplanetary ship that the Americans might want to maintain. Since all the basic technology for ion-drive and nuclear engines was well known to the engineering community, there was really no secret to be stolen just by looking at the hardware. To forestall future legal problems, Uchu Kogyo would immediately file a patent claim for their separation system throughout the world. Sam had guaranteed that their patent application in the U.S. would go through in record time.

Chambers raised an eyebrow at the final condition. It stipulated that Kuroda and two assistants of his choice were to be present for in-orbit testing of the separation system. Japan had a growing manned space program employing their mini-shuttles, but it was limited in scope compared to U.S. and Soviet programs. Only a few technically trained personnel could go into space. Goro, for all his wealth and power, had virtually no chance of going into space in the Japanese space program.

"This project is filling up with frustrated zoomies," Chambers commented. "Two assistants, huh? Did you tell me Kuroda has two grown kids, Sam?"

"That's correct, sir," Sam said, correctly and innocently.

"What do you want to bet that's who these 'assistants' are going to be?" Nobody took the bet.

CHAPTER TWENTY

DEPARTMENT OF SPACE DEFENSE

WASHINGTON, D.C.

There were fifty men or women in the room, some in uniform, most in civilian clothes. One entire wall of the room consisted of a high-resolution TV screen. It was the latest system and provided far cleaner detail than had ever been achieved by photographic film and projection. In the key seat of the long table sat the President. Far down to one end sat Sam Taggart, still in his uneasy position as astronaut-Agency liaison-observer.

Colonel Chambers stood. "Gentlemen, ladies, you have been called to this emergency meeting because of events within the Soviet Union which have the utmost significance for us all. Dr. Ciano, will you brief the members on our latest reports?"

Ugo stood before the screen. "Sam, would you dim the lights?" As a Lieutenant Colonel Sam was the lowest-ranking person in the room. "This is a sequence shot by one of our spy satellites early this morning, D.C. time." The picture showed a greenish, flat, nondescript landscape of frozen tundra. It looked much like the view from an airplane's window at about ten thousand feet. "What we're looking at here is a piece of the Western Siberian Lowland. It's just about the most desolate, empty piece of landscape God ever put together. It's north of the Ob River, south of the Pur and the Taz. The nearest cities are Surgut and Kargasok and they're way the *hell* far from this spot. Death Valley is Manhattan compared to this place."

"We get the picture, Dr. Ciano," said the President. "Just what happened in this garden spot?"

"Coming right up. At *exactly* one A.M. Washington time, which is ten A.M. in this part of Siberia, this is what happened."

In the upper left hand corner of the screen a digital insert marked off the minutes, seconds, and tenths of seconds. Precisely on the turn of the hour, the center of the screen was bisected by a brilliant fireball trailing a fiery tail. Then there was an immense flash which blinded the camera for a few moments. Gradually, the picture resolved itself once more. A huge, circular section of tundra was glowing a dull red through a haze of smoke and steam. The room was dead silent.

"Exactly two minutes later, about three hundred miles to the east of that blast, there was another." The sequence was repeated. It might have been a rerun of the first display.

"Each blast was about 10 kilotons, and there was no radiation. Our satellite surveillance of the Russian space stations confirms that a Soviet spacecraft returned a few weeks ago from beyond circumterra space to a docking orbit with Space Station Volga. That's one of the clinchers: those were ice bombs, folks."

"Have the Russians made any statement yet concerning these blasts?" asked the Chairman of the Joint Chiefs.

"Almost immediately," Chambers answered. "The noon Moscow broadcast reported the falls and claimed they were meteorites. They praised Soviet scientists who have been predicting a rash of meteorite activity for some time. Some European astronomers have already made requests to be allowed to visit the fall sites. It was midafternoon in Europe when the official broadcast went out, remember. They were turned down on grounds of national security."

"Dr. Ciano," the President said, "you said the report about Space Station Volga was 'one of the clinchers.' I'd be interested to hear what the other ones might have been."

"Ah, Dr. Ciano has some theories that the rest of us don't necessarily—" Chambers' attempt to waffle was immediately interrupted by Ciano's steamroller delivery.

"It was the timing, Mr. President! You all saw the clock on that first blast. It struck at *precisely* the turn of the hour, on the second, almost on the millisecond. Now my esteemed colleague on the other side, Pyotr Tarkovsky, does not concern himself with niggling details like this. It would make no difference to him what time the damned thing came down because it's scientifically irrelevant. Tarkovsky is a genius of wide-ranging and generous mentality; a man much like me.

"But," he waved a finger in the air, "everything I've read about Sergei Nekrasov says that he's just the kind of man who'd demand such precision, and he has Tarkovsky under his thumb." Ciano pounded on the table for emphasis and said, triumphantly, "We are dealing here with a classic anal retentive!"

There was a long moment of silence following this outburst, then the National Security Advisor cleared his throat. "I take it this means that the

Russians are ready to play for real when the next target of opportunity comes this way?"

"Unless they're stupid," Ciano went on in a more subdued tone, "and let me clue you that they are not, they won't miss the next comet with a favorable orbit."

"When will that be?" asked the President.

"Slightly less than two years from now."

"I hate to mess up your little scenario," said the chairman of the Senate National Security Committee, "but isn't it possible that what we just saw was a *real* meteor fall?" The Senator was an old-fashioned supporter of bigger land armies and notoriously hostile to the whole idea of space defense.

Ugo started to go purple but this time Chambers managed to forestall him. "Not a chance, Senator. You saw the recording. That was an aerial burst at approximately five thousand feet. The dust was negligible, there was no significant cratering. That was ice, Senator Lardner." The Senator settled back, grumbling. He saw the funding for his pet computerized tanks and missile submarines and aircraft carriers being poured into space.

"So we have less than two years," the President said. "Does that give us time to get our birds into space?"

"Into space, yes," Chambers said, "but not fully tested. Under normal circumstances, we'd want five more years at the least, just for testing in space."

"Normal times be damned," said General Moore. "We're now, for all practical purposes, on wartime status. In times like this, you don't wait until everything is proven safe. We've sent our people up in planes and down in subs when we didn't have the first goddamned idea what their limits were. In wartime you take risks."

"As a matter of fact," Ciano said, "in that little

time we'll be damned lucky to have any of this show on the road at all, tested or not. However, it's times like this that bring out the best, and we have no shortage of volunteers. We've got a second and third team in training." He did not bother to suppress a gleeful grin. He had wangled himself a place on the crew selection board, claiming his indispensable expertise on interplanetary science and cometary environment.

As the meeting broke up, Senator Lardner ambled his considerable bulk over to Ciano. "I guess you're pretty relieved, Dr. Ciano," Lardner said with a politician's ability to sound vicious and bland at the same time.

"Why?" Ugo asked.

"Well, you must've been sweating blood for months. This," he waved an arm at the screen, "is the first real evidence that Project Ivan the Terrible was anything more than another of your crackpot theories."

"Nah. I had it all figured out: timing, the most probable locations for the icefall, all of it. It was no coincidence that our sky spies were looking so close at just that part of Siberia. It's the same kind of terrain as where the Tunguska blast took place, but a hell of a lot more accessible to Russian observers."

"Pretty sure of yourself, aren't you?" Lardner said, nastily.

Ciano seemed honestly puzzled. "Any reason why I shouldn't be?"

"Jesus!" Lardner spun around and stalked out of the room.

Ciano shook his head and turned to Chambers and Taggert, who were standing nearby. "You know, they elect some real wackos to public office these days."

CHAPTER TWENTY-ONE

TSIOLKOVSKY SPACE CENTER

KAZAKH REPUBLIC, U.S.S.R.

Tarkovsky lit his fiftieth cigarette of the day. He had spent most of the afternoon bullying the Project Engineer for the new road system which was necessary for transporting the heavy vehicles now coming in from the immense heavy-equipment plants at Minsk and the Likatschov works near Moscow. The Project Engineer tore at his thinning hair and gestured dramatically, scattering maps and blueprints all over his office. "Comrade Tarkovsky, you demand the impossible! It isn't the task that is daunting, it's the laborers I must work with! Where in the world did they find Goldi tribesmen?"

"Northern Siberia," Tarkovsky grunted.

"I never even heard of them before they arrived here. Not one of them can speak Russian. I have Kipchaks, Kalmucks, Uighurs, Polovtsi and God knows what else. None of them can understand us or each other. It's like feeding time at the United Nations out there, but without the translators. If it weren't for this moronic emphasis on secrecy, if we only had Russian workers instead of these Tartars, we'd be months ahead of schedule on the road construction, instead of more than a year behind!

"At least find me foremen who are bilingual and literate. We have to direct them with sign language!"

"You must make do with what you have," Tarkovsky went on relentlessly, "and you must catch up with the schedule. You realize," he grew uncharacteristically confidential, "that we're not just playing catch-up games with the West here. None of this is for prestige any more. With the man we now have in charge, it's like the old days of Stalin again. You're too young to remember; I was just a boy myself back then, but he had a very short way with anyone who failed him. This one is just like him." Like everybody else, Tarkovsky was reluctant to use Nekrasov's name, but everybody knew by this time who was really running the Project Peter the Great.

Gorshkov grew subdued. "I'll do my best, Comrade Tarkovsky."

Tarkovsky clapped him on the shoulder. "That's all I ask, Gorshkov. I know you can accomplish it." He went outside and got into his "staff car," an antiquated East German Barkas, a small military truck very much like the American Jeep of WWII. He wondered if the head of NASA had to oversee this kind of piddling detail.

As they drew up to the Administration building his driver said: "Visitors, Comrade Tarkovsky."

"Oh, no." Two men were getting out of a Lada in front of the building. It was Ryabkin, followed by one of the faceless KGB men. He wondered what Nekrasov's pet hound wanted this time. It had to be bad news. Tarkovsky hadn't seen Nekrasov himself in months, but Ryabkin or Baratynsky arrived, unannounced, on an almost weekly basis.

As Tarkovsky entered the building the girl behind the desk pointed at his office and mouthed, elaborately and silently, "K—G—B". Tarkovsky nodded curtly.

"Good afternoon, Comrade," Tarkovsky said as he opened the door. "What brings you to our facility this time? Care for some vodka?" Ryabkin was standing, instead of making himself at home, as usual. The faceless man was hanging up his coat and hat on the wall rack. Ryabkin looked decidedly uncomfortable and said nothing.

Then the faceless man turned around and said: "A little vodka sounds like a good idea." Dmitri Chekhov, General Secretary of the Communist Party and Premier of the Soviet Union was a small man, with a face as commonplace as his name. He smiled as he sat. "We do not get to see one another often enough, Comrade Tarkovsky." He took the glass Tarkovsky offered.

"It was not my doing that we have seen so little of each other of late, Comrade Chekhov." Tarkovsky said.

Chekhov glanced at Ryabkin. "So I have heard. Well, first let me congratulate you on the ongoing success of Project Peter the Great."

"Thank you, Comrade," Tarkovsky said, bursting to talk but not knowing how far he dared to go with Ryabkin present.

"Excellent vodka. Now, Pyotr, you must tell me all about your progress. Especially," he smiled, "I would like to hear about something called Project Ivan the Terrible."

CHAPTER TWENTY-TWO

SPACE STATION MIDWAY, *USSF*

Sam was in the "shower" when the intercom paged him. Even in space, some things never change. The shower was a watertight closet which erupted with a short burst of needle-jet warm water when the door was shut. A suction pump removed the free-floating droplets for reprocessing, followed by a blast of hot air to dry the inhabitant. As baths go, it was Spartan in the extreme, but it was a luxury unknown to the inhabitants of earlier stations such as Skylab.

"Lt. Colonel Taggart, please report to General Penrod's office immediately," the speaker said again. "Acknowledge, please."

"Taggart here. I'll be there right away." He was cutting it close, but he wouldn't be getting a shower for several hundred million kilometers. From here on, it would be a sponge bath maybe once or twice a week. He pulled on his dark green coverall, newly chosen as the fatigue uniform for the Space Marines. The service was so new that it had no insignia yet. At its founding months before, Sam had found himself at loggerheads with the President and General Moore.

"*Space Marines?*" Sam had said, incredulous. "Are you kidding? In the first place, the word 'marine' comes from the Latin word for ocean and there's no ocean up there. Second, and far more troublesome, the Marine Corp's going to be mad as hell that you've taken their name. They've never had to explain what *kind* of marines they were before."

"Sorry, Sam," Moore had said. "The new Space Service is expanding and it's going to have big, long-range ships. Naval traditions have developed over the centuries and it's inevitable that they'll be transferred to a new, shipborne service. Space Marines it is."

Thus it was that Lt. Colonel Sam Taggart, Space Marines, pulled himself along the handholds towards the General's office. There he found the crews of *Bountyhunter* 1 and 2 already assembled, with the exception of Ciano. Present were: For Ship 1, Col. Hoerter, chief pilot and captain; Major DaSilva, copilot; Lt. Col. Kita, engineer; Lt. Col Taggart, senior space marine; Col. Ciano, astrophysicist and Captain Flower, space marine and assistant engineer. For Ship 2: Col. McDonald, chief pilot and captain; Major Schaeffer, copilot; Lt. Col. ("Just don't call me Buck") Rogers, senior engineer; Captain Tammsalu, astrophysicist (and recently naturalized citizen); Lt. Col. Hansen, space marine and stand-by engineer and Major Schuster, space marine.

Colonel Ciano came floating in a few minutes after Sam. The little group clustered at one end of the room, leaving General Penrod to float at the other end. It occurred to the General that it had been some time since an American officer had been in this position; sending out his best officers on a desperate, long-range mission from which it was likely they would not return. They had no backup, no cover, no hope of rescue should there be a disaster. And disaster was exactly what they were facing.

Originally, they were to depart as soon as the Russians were beyond the point of recall so the Soviets could not arm themselves against possible interdiction by the Americans. There had been technical difficulties, hangups, delays, glitches: now they were to depart ten whole days after the Russians. The delay put the American expedition at a severe disadvantage since they must now expend more reaction mass than planned, making their water reserve rather precarious by the time they made rendezvous with the comet. There would be little or no room for navigational errors. Because of the necessary differences in trajectories caused by the delay, the ten-day advantage translated to at least two weeks of head start for the Russians. They hoped that the Soviet expedition would require at least three weeks to finish their tasks at the comet. That was the best educated guess anyone could make. The fact was, nobody knew how many icebergs the Russians planned to bring back, or how long it would take them. All this went through Penrod's mind before he began his premission briefing. The crews already knew the odds.

"Friends, your ships are now fully commissioned for the first American interplanetary voyage. I wish the mission were less desperate. You're all aware of the risks of taking these untested ships on this hazardous journey; yet you all volunteered. On behalf of the Space Service, the President and the nation, I wish to thank you. There is one more hard fact to face: even if your mission succeeds, your deeds may remain unknown to the public at large, at least for a long, long time. When you return, there will probably be no bands, no ticker-tape parade, no reception on the White House lawn. Your only satisfaction will have to be in the knowledge that you just may have kept World War III from happening.

"Although this is a military mission, you are only to take hostile action to keep the Russians from dropping those icebergs on us. You will at all times remain alert for further instructions from the base. Your mission could be altered at any time if there are new developments on the international front."

He looked at them, going from one face to another. "At this time, I am required to ask you for the last time: If there is any one of you who wishes to withdraw from this mission, you may do so with complete honor. The circumstances have changed the odds against you considerably. There are two astronauts standing by for each of you who can take your places on an instant's notice." As he expected, nobody even blinked. "Very well. There's an old formula they used to give to sub commanders that seems to me to fit this situation: Ladies, gentlemen, godspeed and good hunting!"

In the big bay near the major airlock, Sam, Laine, Ugo and Fred floated in a four-pointed star, holding hands like skydivers. "You see, Sam," Ugo said, "this is what it's all about. This is why we're in space."

"Why?" Sam asked.

"You dumb jerk, because here I'm as tall as the rest of you!" He grinned at Fred, who for once was at eye level with him. "You see, in space nobody's tall or short, there's only relative *length*, and that don't matter."

"Ugo," Laine said, "I knew there had to be some great reason why you were so determined to push humanity into space."

There was a great deal they might have said, a

great deal they wanted to say, but Sam and Laine absolutely refused to talk about their future plans until the mission was behind them. They had been silent about it for months. Ugo was keeping his own plans secret until the mission was over as well. Fred wasn't particularly reticent, but the fact was that just now, there was no reality for any of them except the mission. They said no more until the airlock hatch cycled open.

Ugo grinned tightly at the only real friends he had ever known. "Let's go get 'em," he said.

INTERPLANETARY SPACE

The initial excitement of being on the first American interplanetary ships soon gave way to day-to-day routine. Just now, the only people aboard with exacting jobs were the pilots and copilots. They had to monitor the position and direction of the ship continuously, using the integrating inertial guidance systems and multi-directional star sensors. The data from these devices were digested by the onboard sixth generation computer which determined the ship's velocity vector. The pilot would then choose the optimum acceleration vector for that instant. Ugo tried to obtain authorization to use the immense capacity of the multi-million dollar computer for his pet astrophysical research. He wanted to relieve the tedium of the voyage. He was turned down as his astrophysical research was not essential to the mission. As a consolation prize, he was told he could use the computer for his analysis of the interplanetary and cometary environment, both of which were germane to the task at hand.

Although the mission was primarily military, they were to bring back samples from the comet for analysis. If time permitted, they were also to perform experiments to learn the structure of the comet. This was Ugo and Laine's department. Perhaps their most important responsibility was to perform an *in-situ* analysis of the cometary environment, as so little was known about the physical conditions close to the nucleus and on the surface. In this, the Russians had an immense head start.

The space marines had another task, one which would begin at the comet. They were to inspect the Russian craft and to verify whether they were in violation of the recently concluded Geneva accord banning all non-defensive weapons from space. The treaty provided for on-site inspections, although none of the signatories had ever anticipated such a site for an inspection. If the marines were unable to attain the first objective, they were to destroy the icebergs or incapacitate the Russian spaceships. This was a last-ditch option, as it could precipitate a war.

The American ships were assemblages of spheres and boxes, tubes and struts. They were ugly, functional and looked as if they had been designed by a committee, which was precisely the case.

"Y'know," Ciano said on the second day out, "if I was in charge of design on these things, I'd say to hell with functional logic. I'd design these things to look like real spaceships."

"They are real spaceships," said Kita. "What are they supposed to look like?"

"You mean make 'em to look like the covers from science fiction magazines back in the fifties?" Hoerter raised his eyebrows, a gesture which lost much of its significance as he was hanging upside-down in relation to Ugo.

"Naw, I was thinking more of those Art Deco ships from Alex Raymond's old Flash Gordon strip. Now those was ships that looked like spaceships.

See, I'd fit a shaped neoquartz cowling over the whole ship, fake portholes and everything, with a spiky nose that has a blinking red light on its tip."

"He always like this?" DaSilva asked Sam.

"Since I've known him," Sam said. "He's been on his best behavior to get on this mission, though. Now you're seeing his true colors."

"I'm serious," Ugo insisted, gesturing wildly and sending himself into a spin, from which Kita retrieved him. "I mean, these ships work, but a buncha orange crates and pipes tied up with baling wire ain't calculated to inspire people with enthusiasm for the future of man in space!"

"Let's hope this expedition doesn't inspire anything," said Hoerter.

Ciano plowed right on. "And these uniforms!" He glared accusingly at his coverall. "This is what garage mechanics wear. Now I'd design real slick-looking uniforms with double fronts and rows of buttons and boots and the whole works."

"I used to have a uniform like that," Flower said reflectively. "Back in my high school marching band."

"It's all PR, man," Ciano insisted. "You want to whip up enthusiasm for space exploration, it's like anything else; you gotta have heroes and classy hardware and good-looking clothes." Ugo folded his arms across his chest and glowered, rotating slowly. "Those morons back at the base wouldn't even let me and Fred try The Experiment. *That* woulda put the U.S. space program back in the headlines!"

For weeks, the favorite topic of conversation in *Midway* had been The Experiment. At an open meeting of all personnel, Ugo had suggested that he and Fred have the honor of being the first couple to attempt freefall sex. There had always been rumors that astronauts had tried it, but the ever-present tv monitors made it unlikely. Somebody would have seen. It was rumored that Fred was game, but the chief scientist had come up with all manner of scientific and medical reasons why it shouldn't be permitted.

"Penrod told me," Sam said, "the real reason they wouldn't let you do it was they couldn't figure out where the President should pin the medal."

"I heard," Kita contributed, "that the Russians've already tried it. It was Bunchinsky and what's-her-name, Gribkova."

"What did they have to say about it" Sam asked.

Kita put in a broad Russian accent. "Yust another docking maneuver."

With such weighty matters they passed the days while closing the distance. They watched with awe as the comet grew closer. They would have to be very close before they would know whether the Soviet mission was still there. There was always the possibility the Soviets had not reached their destination at all. What should they do if they got there and there was no sign of the other expedition? Should they wait and see if anybody showed up, or should they fuel up as fast as possible and pursue an enemy that might not exist any more? Chances of catching up were minimal at best, and action would probably be best left to orbiting defenses. As the comet loomed ahead, filling more and more of their vision port, there was a general holding of breath and gnawing of fingernails, at least among those who were not nerveless career astronauts.

"They're here," reported McDonald from Ship 2. Through the heavy mist, the ships' radar systems identified two metallic objects on one hemisphere.

"We got 'em!" Ugo said, tensely.

"Not necessarily," Hoerter said. "That could be

stuff they left behind. They might jettison a landing system, like we did on the early Moon shots."

"Man, don't say things like that." Ugo stared through the port with sweat standing out on his massive forehead. In the gravity-free environment, the sweat would not run down his face, but once in a while a drop would break loose, form a perfect sphere, and hang around his head for a moment like a minuscule moonlet before being sucked toward an air intake.

"Plan A is still in effect," Hoerter announced. "Ugo, pick us a spot to land." One of Ciano's duties was to find a suitable landing site. Ideally, it should be far enough from the Soviet base that they would not be detected, but near enough that a trek by the marines from the U.S. base to the Soviet site would be possible.

"Damn," Ugo said, "it all looks the same. Can't tell much about terrain features through that fog." Finally, he settled on a spot that looked at least as good as anywhere else. "Okay, Captain Ahab, there's your whale. Fire away."

"Commence landing sequence," Hoerter ordered.

Kita armed the pilot harpoon and fired it. Harpoon and trailing cable disappeared into the mist. "Anchor in contact." He studied his instruments for a few minutes. "It's solid."

"Continue landing sequence," Hoerter said. Da Silva began to reel the ship down the cable while Ship 2 fired its own pilot harpoon. They went down into the mist and soon they could see the surface, which seemed mercifully smooth.

"Touchdown," DaSilva reported, as a clunk-shudder made the ship vibrate.

"Ship 2 down," said the radio.

"We're the first Americans to land on an interplanetary body," Flower said.

"Hip hooray," said Hoerter. "We'll celebrate on

the way home. Make her fast." From the "top" of the vessel, six more anchors were fired into the surface, giving the ship a tentlike web of guy cables and the stability that would be needed for the ice-mining operations. "All right, gyrenes," Hoerter said, "suit up and go out on patrol."

Flower and Sam helped one another into what were probably the world's first combat spacesuits. Dull gray in color, they were lined with Kevlar, a fabric that was almost bulletproof but vulnerable to high-velocity armor-piercing projectiles. They were compartmentalized so that a bullet or other projectile piercing some non-critical part of the body would not destroy the suit's integrity. It wasn't much, but it was the best the engineers could come up with. They had special traction boots, backpack rockets, an integrating gyro compass and direction sensors for the ships' radio beacons. If a marine stepped too lively and catapulted himself into space, he could use the rocket pack to fly back to the ship.

Potentially more dangerous to them than enemy action was a solar flare during the outdoor activity. High-energy particles in the solar wind could be deadlier than bullets. The Earth Base could signal dangerous solar activity, but that would do little good when they were several hours from the nearest shelter.

The ship extruded a landing ramp and Sam and Flower pulled themselves down to the surface. Within a few minutes, Fred and Hansen joined them from the other ship. The crews were already getting ready to start feeding the water separation system. This was the priority mission for the crews and they would be at it around the clock until they had plenty of reaction mass for the return trip. Ugo and Laine would have to conduct their experiments, collect their samples and study the cometary environment when they were not busy feeding the hungry water machine, if ever.

"Who touched the ground first?" Fred asked when the marines were assembled.

"Flower and I came down the ramp about the same time," Sam said. "Flower, did you touch down first or did I?"

"I didn't notice."

"Well I was the first one down from Ship 2," Fred said. "But which of us touched the surface first? This is a historic moment, dammit!"

"We have more important things to worry about," Sam said. "If everything works out, none of this ever happened anyway. Everybody checked out?" All answered affirmatively. There was always the possibility of close combat, and the question of weapons had been a difficult one. Conventional firearms were no good, as the recoil would knock the shooter right off the comet. Lasers would have been ideal, but a manageable handheld laser had yet to be developed. Sam had a minituarized, low-power rocket launcher that looked like a cross between a mini-bazooka and a shot gun. The payload was a sticky miniature grenade that just might attach itself to an enemy's spacesuit and explode. Each of the remaining three marines carried a modified recoilless rifle. It was decided that, in space, the idea was not to attack the enemy's body but to attack his *suit*. Impact weapons like clubs and axes were useless in free-fall; a combatant would have to take a firm grip of an opponent in order to shove a knife into him. For that contingency, however, each marine carried a sharp, double-edged dagger.

"Good luck," said Hoerter. Sam and Laine had agreed to dispense with parting words. They would resume their lives after the mission. "I'd say something historical and inspiring," Hoerter went on, "but I'm plumb out of inspiration. We can always lie about what we said. Get going."

"We have four klicks to cover," Sam told his team. "Me first, followed by Fred, then Flower, then Hansen. Keep close, it'll be easy to lose each other in this fog. If anyone gets separated don't try to go on to the Russian base. Return to the ships. Now let's move out."

On Earth, a four-kilometer jaunt would be a pleasant walk, in good weather. An experienced jogger would scarcely have worked up a sweat in four kilometers. To an old-fashioned American, it would be a bit under two and one-half miles. On the surface of the comet, it was an endless nightmare. None of the marines had ever walked on a low-gravity body before, not even the moon. The minuscule gravity of the comet made even moon-type walking impossible. They had no leisure to learn and practice. It was on-the-job training with a vengeance.

They found that they could cover distance faster by not using their feet at all. Instead, they pulled themselves along the surface with their hands, always careful not to push away from the surface and lose such little traction as they had. The rocket packs were for emergency use only. There was too much danger of their becoming separated should they use them. They had practiced with the rocket packs at *Midway*, but *Midway* had no obscuring fog. So, like crustaceans scuttling along a murky ocean bottom, they made their way toward the Russian base.

The surface was not as smooth as it had looked at first. It was broken by innumerable fissures and jagged prominences, all of them impeding progress. The fog was thicker in some places than others, forcing them to maintain close contact. Sometimes the surface was slippery, other times crumbly, and at no time was it easy to traverse.

"We must be getting close by now," Sam said. Then he was staring over a straight lip into a deep hole. The fog made it impossible to determine how far the hole extended, but its straight lines looked decidedly artificial. The others lined up with him, staring into the hole.

"We've found their quarrying operation," Flowers said.

"Let's go find the ships," Sam said.

Carefully, they skirted the lip of the hole. It seemed to be about fifteen meters across. "There're the ships," Fred said.

Looming ahead of them in the mist were two squat, boxy Russian ships, both of them just as formless as the American craft. Hansen started taking pictures with his helmet-mounted camera. There was nobody visible outside the ships, and no activity was to be seen. There were no cranes or other equipment lying about. "Keep clear of the rocket nozzles," Sam cautioned. "They look ready to go."

Gingerly, they skirted the ships. The hulking apparitions looked as if they had been abandoned there, but when Sam touched his helmet to the side of one, he thought he could sense movements inside. What to do now? The original plan had called for him to approach the Russian party peacefully, invoke the clause in the new Geneva accord and claim their right for on-site inspection of the Russian ships for possible violation of the accord. Sam had pictured himself walking up to the gaping, spacesuited Russians, his hands out, showing empty palms and saying something like: "White man come in peace." Things just never worked out the way you'd planned.

"Flower, try to establish radio contact." Flower

was the one who had studied Russian in college. Should his Russian prove inadequate to the task, they could always call on Laine. If all else failed, Sam had his explosives.

"What's that over there?" Hansen said. They looked where he was pointing.

"Let's go take a look," Sam said. "Flower, you stay here and keep trying radio contact." They made their way to a pair of tremendous frames, cradles each containing six icebergs. Each cradle was tethered to the surface by thin anchor lines to prevent the centrifugal effect of the comet's rotation from casting cradle and icebergs into space. A much more substantial cable connected each cradle to one of the ships.

"That's what they came for," Sam said.

"If nothing else works," Hansen said, "we could always cut these suckers loose. We have enough C-4 to make saddle charges for both of these cables. I'd feel better using the ship's lasers, though."

"It'd be a violation of international law," Sam mused. "Better than touching off a full-scale atomic war. We could always say I went nuts and did it in a fit of anti-communist sentiment." They went back to the first ship.

"Still no answer," Flower said. "Either they aren't listening on any of the frequencies I've tried, which isn't likely, or they're ignoring us, which is."

"What the hell," Fred said, "why don't we just knock?"

"Might as well," Sam said. "We are about to pay mankind's first trans-lunar neighborly call." He pulled himself up to the airlock hatch and pounded on the door. At the first impact, the Russian craft began to vibrate.

"Shit!" Hansen called. "They just cast their anchors loose!"

"Into the hole!" Sam ordered. He clambered

down a landing strut and they frantically scrambled to the first hole they had come across. In near-panic, they were making a slow job of it. The Soviet ships activated their boosters and began an almost imperceptible movement forward. Hansen and Flower hauled themselves over the lip first and disappeared inside. Fred made an ill-judged step and went sailing over the hole, floundering helplessly. "My Buck Rogers won't cut in!" she yelled.

"Oh, Christ!" Sam swore. This was what came of inadequate testing and preparation. He launched himself at her and managed to grab her by what passed, in a spacesuit, for the scruff of her neck. With both feet, he shoved her down into the hole, propelling himself away from it at the same rate. He managed to get himself pointed in the right direction, prayed, and hit the power switch of his rocket pack. It cut in just as it was supposed to and he accelerated toward the hole. Now, if he could just keep from squashing himself against the side or bottom—He flipped end-for-end and fired a short burst from the pack to decelerate. His feet contacted the floor of the hole with no great impact and he was safe. For the moment.

"That was a slick move, Sam," said Hansen, admiringly.

"Yeah. Let's not celebrate just yet. If one of those ships passes right over us we'll fry like shrimps in a wok."

They held their breath and stared up, picturing zillions of high-energy ions sizzling from the nozzles of the Russian ships. Once, they caught sight of the upper framework of one of the ships as it passed the rim of the hole in perfect silence. Then, for several minutes, nothing.

"Let's go on up," Sam said.

The ships were gone, along with the cradles and

the icebergs. Nothing was left on the site but the cast-off anchor lines. After they had rounded the curvature of the cometscape, Hoerter's voice came across their helmet radios: "Taggart! What the hell's going on?"

"The Russkies have flown the coop. Either they knew we were coming or they were ready to go home anyway. They have a dozen big icebergs."

"Hell, I know they left! We got 'em on our instruments as soon as they pulled away. Why the hell didn't you answer when I tried to call you?"

"Because we were hiding in a hole, goddammit!" Sam said. He was in no mood for a dressing-down from somebody who had been safe all this time. Relatively safe, anyway.

"All right, just come on back while you have air to travel on. Don't lose anybody on the way. Out."

"Out," Sam said. Then, to the others, "Remind me to kick his butt sometime."

"So much for the first interplanetary raid," said Flower, disappointedly.

"None of our great firsts is working out," Fred complained.

"Let's be the first interplanetary raiding party to get home alive. Move out, people." They made their way back to the ships with a little less difficulty. They were learning.

When they returned, the water-mining was proceeding at maximum speed. The Americans had come prepared for a short stay, and they had brought heavy ice-diggers with conveyer tubes. When they were inside Ugo helped Sam get his helmet off. "The separation system works like a charm," Ugo reported. "Your buddy Goro turns out a good product. Luckily, the job ain't been all that demanding so far, just dust and a few pebbles to sort out. We oughta have the tanks full in about forty-eight hours."

Hoerter pulled himself back to the airlock. "Good job, Sam, just bad timing, I guess. Get some sack time. As soon as you're awake, I want you to take Ugo and Laine back to the Russian site. Measure those holes and bring back samples from the surrounding matrix of each. I want to know to the kilogram how much mass they're heading out with."

"Hey!" Ugo complained. "What about my experiments?"

"Do them on the way," Hoerter said, "or do them at the site, or do them coming back, or don't do them at all, but get me those figures."

"Once again," Ugo said when Hoerter was gone, "science takes a back seat to the military. He's turning into a real hardass, ain't he?"

"So am I," Sam said. "It's looking more and more like a war, Ugo."

"Yeah. Space War One. Who woulda thunk it?" He scratched in his beard. All the men had beards these days, and nobody smelled very good, either. Space travel could put a severe strain on interpersonal relationships. "We'll catch 'em, though."

"You're sure about that?" Sam sounded dubious.

"Positive. Each of them ships is carrying back six great big hunks of ice. That's a lot of mass to accelerate. All we're taking back is the reaction mass for our return trip. We got rockets and long-range lasers and they're probly unarmed, since they never thought they'd have to fight in space. We'll blow their ass away if they don't listen to reason."

"If we can find them," Sam said.

"No sweat. Between me and that fancy computer, we'll locate them."

During the next two "days," the water was loaded and two large chunks of ice were cut away with lasers for spare reaction mass. Ugo and Laine measured the Russian excavations and managed to collect surface samples and core samples as well as take measurements of the cometary environment. Neither slept during their time on the comet. Among his other souvenirs, Ugo collected a large bump on his forehead. He had forgotten that Newton's law of inertia still works perfectly well in free fall.

"Ah, Sam—" Ugo said during the measuring expedition on the second day, "Fred told me about how you saved her butt here yesterday. I want you to know—"

Sam broke in hastily. "I didn't even know which one of them it was," he lied. "I wasn't going to lose *any* of my people."

"Yeah, sure," Ugo said, knowing better. "But, tell me, weren't you a little disappointed there wasn't any trouble? You came over here all primed for a fight and they just waltzed away."

"I was never so relieved in my life," Sam protested. Then, after some consideration: "Well, maybe I was a *little* disappointed."

Ugo cackled. "Once a cowboy, always a cowboy."

Three days after the Russians' departure, *Bountyhunter* I and 2 cast off their anchor lines and boosted away from the comet. The chase was on. Nobody else shared Ugo's sanguine confidence. They did not know the vector of acceleration of the Soviet ships. A variety of combinations was conceivable for continuously boosting ships. They had to depend on Ugo's intuitive ability to bridge the gaps in logic and radar data.

"Who's their best pilot?" Ugo asked on the fifth day out from the comet. He was glued to his instruments constantly now.

Hoerter thought for a moment. "Korsakov."

"Then that's who we're up against. The guy's brilliant! He's varying the magnitude and direction of acceleration, which makes it hard as hell to predict his course just from radar ranging. He must have a damn good computer, because that's his only hope of making it to Earth at the right time and the right terminal velocity, unless he's got reaction mass to spare for really profligate deceleration."

"They have plenty of reaction mass," Kita said. "All those icebergs, remember?"

"I don't think they want to use them," Ugo said. "I been looking at those pictures of the cradles. I think they were supposed to pick up eight icebergs for each ship, not six. They musta had to break off operations when they saw us coming in. So already they're four icebergs short. They don't want to use up any for reaction mass, because that could disappoint old Nekrasov real bad. I wouldn't want to disappoint that man."

Once they were free of the relatively dense, inner region of the cometary coma, they were able to locate the Russian ships using their diffraction-limited telescopes with computer assisted image-intensifiers.

CHAPTER TWENTY-THREE

ABOARD PIONYER I

Korsakov still could scarcely believe that the Americans were pursuing him. When they had detected the approach of the American ships, it had been the shock of his life. He had ordered mining operations broken off immediately and he quickly had everybody back aboard and the ships buttoned up. None too soon, either, as mere hours after the first alarm he had gaped unbelieving at his television screen to see the sinister, spacesuited figures come creeping out of the mist. It was like a dream.

Now he was facing the toughest decision of his life. He could still get away from the American ships. His head start would make that easy. But, it would mean jettisoning his cargo of ice. That would be the end of Project Ivan the Terrible, at least the opening phase. If he did not cut the ice loose, the Americans were almost sure to catch up. They were then sure to do one of two things: They would destroy both Russian ships, or they would invoke their right to an on-site inspection and board, at gunpoint if necessary. And he was perfectly sure that the American ships were armed, heavily. Else why bother to pursue the Russian ships? For a while he futilely cursed the fact that his ships were unarmed. He had been a fighter pilot for years; and he knew that, with adequate armament, he could blow both American ships to bits.

"We could let them board," said Kaminsky, breaking into his thoughts. "After all, what is there for them to see? The ships are unarmed. Are they going to raise a fuss about some ice? We just say it's for perfectly peaceful purposes. After all, if they protest bringing back bulk cargoes such as raw ice or rock, how can they ever hope to exploit the mineral wealth of space themselves?"

Korsakov nodded. "I've been thinking of that myself. We could brazen it out, but then they'd get pictures of the inside of this ship. I don't want to be known as the captain who gave away the tightest-kept secrets of the Soviet Union to the Americans."

"When our negotiators signed the accord," Kaminsky pointed out, "they must have known what an on-site inspection would entail."

Korsakov pounded a noncritical portion of the console with his fist. "Nobody ever expected them to pull an inspection unexpectedly, in deep space! We've had no time to get ready, and we have no way to dismount and hide the sensitive equipment."

"Korsakov," Kaminsky said, pitching his voice low so the others could not hear, "I don't really know what this Ivan the Terrible business entails. None of us do. But it's something big and military. We all know old man Tarkovsky's theory about comet ice and the Tunguska blast. And we all know Nekrasov's pulling the strings here. They aren't chasing us because they want the exercise. Those Americans are armed and if we get too close to our destination I don't think they'll hesitate to shoot. Let them board. A few pictures of some gear that's outdated to them anyway and a little embarrassment—why bother? I think it's all up anyway. They're armed and we aren't."

"We have our heavy-duty lasers," Korsakov said, stubbornly. "Once they're close enough to board, the lasers will be just as effective as their long-range weapons."

Kaminsky was shaking his head. "That's the fighter pilot talking, not the cosmonaut. They have two ships. Do you really think that they'll bring both of them so close? Not a chance. One will stand off with its lasers sighted and its rockets locked on and the first hostile move on our part will end everything. If there was something to be gained from fighting, I'd say do it. But there isn't. It's just a setback, not the end. We've had plenty of those. And if it's the end for Nekrasov—" Kaminsky performed a weightless shrug, "well, we've seen a lot of them come and go too, haven't we?"

"I've sent an utmost priority directly to Nekrasov himself," Korsakov said. "I'm asking for instructions. No answer yet."

"When did you send it?"

"Three hours ago."

"No more than a half-hour delay each way at this point. What's taking him so long to answer?"

Korsakov had nothing to say.

CHAPTER TWENTY-FOUR

KREMLIN

Nekrasov was preparing to leave for dinner with Marshal of the Soviet Union Petrovich when the message from *Pionyer* I was brought to him. The telecommunications director at Tsiolkovsky Space Center had standing orders from the Deputy Premier to deliver any message from either vessel to him immediately, regardless of the time of day or night.

The news about the arrival of the Americans did not alarm him much. He already knew from orbiting surveillance reports that the Americans had sent out two ships, probably interplanetary in nature, ten days after the *Pionyers* had left parking orbit. It took little imagination to figure out where those ships were headed. In war, you could never have things all your own way, it was necessary only to have a decisive advantage. He knew that his time advantage was adequate. The Americans would need around two weeks to refill their water tanks, he had been told.

He was somewhat disappointed to find that each

crew had been able to bring back only six icebergs instead of the planned eight. Still, twelve bombs were marginally enough to accomplish Plan B of Project Ivan the Terrible. It was always wise to have backup plans and a sizable built-in redundancy factor.

He glanced at his watch. There was still plenty of time to meet with Petrovich. He went to his super-secure telephone and punched the code for Baratynsky's corresponding instrument.

"Comrade Deputy Premier?" Baratynsky answered. Nobody else had that particular code. Nekrasov read out the report he had just received.

"Is there anything whatever to concern us?" Nekrasov asked. "I truly dislike unpleasant surprises."

"Nothing," Baratynsky assured him. "It sounds as if the Americans have sent out a suicide mission. Water separation alone will cost them a great deal of turnaround time. Their devices aren't up to it. Two weeks minumum, and if they take longer than that—" Nekrasov could picture Baratynsky feeding the figures into his computer: velocities, the comet's orbit, consumables, other things. A minute later he continued: "If it takes them any longer than that, then they aren't coming back at all."

"That is good to know, Baratynsky. I will see you at the extraordinary meeting of the Politburo in three days."

The dinner with Petrovich went as planned. It was really no more than a confirmation of the plans he had been laying down for years. Petrovich was a bulky man with the bearish, jovial disposition stereotypical of high Russian officers. Nekrasov did not trust stereotypes and he knew the cold-eyed Petrovich to be a scheming, ambitious climber who had reached the top of his profession and was looking for new worlds to conquer. Such men were easily manipulated by men like Nekrasov. To this end, Nekrasov had certain files in his possession on Petrovich's more questionable activities over the years. Early in his life, Nekrasov had taken to heart Stalin's maxim: "Trust is good, but control is better."

They had agreed that the time to spring their trap was at the extraordinary Politburo meeting which was being held, ostensibly, to discuss the astounding success of the latest comet mission and its impact on future Soviet policies toward the non-communist world. Nekrasov had proposed the meeting and Chekhov, a fool if ever there was one, had agreed to it.

There came a time when, after all one's planning and plotting, one had to make the decisive move. This meeting would be Nekrasov's moment. He had in his pocket the only two men besides himself who were of real consequence: the head of KGB and the Marshal of the Soviet Union. Most important, he had early on seized control of the most momentous scientific and technological breakthrough of the age. Such an opportunity fell to a man of power only once in a generation, if that often. Roosevelt had had his atomic bomb, without really knowing what he had. Nekrasov had Project Ivan the Terrible, and with it he would make the Soviet Union the only unquestioned superpower on Earth. With himself at its head. At the meeting he would announce his objectives, make a few arrests, and install himself as General Secretary of the Party, Chairman of the Presidium of the Supreme Soviet and Chairman of the Council of Ministers. Since the Revolution only Stalin and, briefly, Brezhnev, had held such power. And neither had wielded such power *outside* the Soviet Union. Petrovich he would reward with the post of

Defense Minister, edging into retirement the aging Marshal who now held the post. Ryabkin would then occupy his own position, Deputy Premier, and would be allowed to name one of his own protegés as KGB chief.

It was not, after all, as if he had been doing anything for which there wasn't plenty of precedent. The coup by fait accompli was as old as the system itself. Sometimes it was accomplished peacefully, sometimes there was bloodshed, but in the end it consisted of a brutal power play which was, if at all possible, restricted to the Politburo. Then, next May Day, the observers would see a slightly different lineup of dignitaries on the reviewing stand. The Western press would speculate about what had happened, the Soviet press would take no notice. There was a time when all such power plays had been accompanied by a rash of executions. Things had calmed a bit since those days. Forced retirement was the preferred tactic now. The ousted man went to his dacha to tend his rose bushes and he was watched and he never, never had a chance to wield power again. Nekrasov saw no reason to have Chekhov shot. He was a nonentity who had come to power in a period of relatively easy relations with the West and who had been content to share power and prestige with other high Party officials. Not the kind of man needed for the hard decisions which would be made now.

The members of the Politburo took their seats around the long conference table, pitchers of water and ashtrays arranged neatly before them. There was none of the usual paper-shuffling, low conversation or other signs that this was a typical meeting. That suited Nekrasov perfectly. Events like this did not occur often, and it was just as well that everyone was in a proper frame of mind.

To Nekrasov's left sat Baratynsky. He was not, of course, a member of the Politburo, but was here by special permission as Nekrasov's scientific advisor. He had promised Baratynsky a seat on the Politburo in a newly-created office: Minister for Science and Technology. Ryabkin was in his seat as Minister for State Security and Petrovich was, as usual, sitting in for the absent Defense Minister.

"Comrades," said Chekhov, opening the session, "Deputy Premier Nekrasov has called for this meeting in his capacity as holder of the portfolio for our space program. He has announcements to make which are of the highest importance to the future and to our national security. Please give him your fullest attention." He nodded to Nekrasov.

Nekrasov stood, savoring the moment. "Comrades, it gives me great pleasure to announce that the dreams and prophecies of these men—" he gestured at the group portrait of Marx, Lenin and Engels, "—shall soon be fulfilled. Within a few days, the Soviet Union shall be the unchallenged leader in space, and therefore on Earth. For the first time since the Revolution, we shall be in a position to utterly dominate Western Europe, Japan, the U.S.A., in brief, the world. We shall be able to dictate a Pax Sovietica!"

This extraordinary statement was received with absolute silence. Not a muscle twitched in a single face. He had expected nothing else. The British Parliament would have been shouting chilly demands for resignation at this point; the American Congress would have been babbling to one another and drawing lines of alliance; members of the Israeli Knesset would have been jumping up and demanding heads. Russians understood the principle of utter silence and noncommitment. They were waiting to hear what came next. He gave it to them.

"First, Comrades, let me explain about something which the Americans have codenamed Project Ivan the Terrible." He described, in far greater detail than at the last meeting, the destructive potential of the ice bombs. He also outlined the unauthorized steps he had taken to set the stage for their use.

"Nuclear retaliation?" said one member, in a perfectly expressionless tone.

"There will be none," Nekrasov assured him. "They haven't the will to carry out such an attack, nor the courage to face the consequences. This project will cripple their potential for expansion into space so severely that we will have a clean lead in deep space for at least a decade. The centers of spacecraft production worldwide are few, and easily eliminated with the initial icebomb strikes. Once we establish dominance in deep space, with a fleet of 10 *Pionyer* class spaceships fetching icebergs from suitable periodic comets we can take our time to destroy their other vital industrial and commercial capabilities over the next several years, while never permitting the reconstruction of their spacecraft industries. Selected military targets will also be included in the second phase of Project Ivan the Terrible."

He looked around the room significantly. "We will of course be dropping some icebergs in the Soviet Union and our satellite states to make the destruction appear non-selective; I have already selected such targets that will not be harmful to our Marxist cause. In Poland, for examples, the destruction of Gdansk will be salubrious. I need scarcely point out that Japan, for one, is particularly vulnerable because of her heavy concentrations of industries. If she insists on pursuing her capitalistic ways, we can finally settle our scores with them for the events of 1904 and 1905."

The Deputy Premier raised a finger and gestured like a fussy schoolmaster. "Best of all, this offensive gives the Americans what they want most of all: an excuse *not* to strike back with their nuclear arsenal! They will know where the strike originates from, at least their highest security people will, but they can still pass it off as a natural disaster. Ice from space. Their newspapers and television programming, with my encouragement, have been full of nothing else for months. They are expecting such a disaster; they have been hoping for one. Yes, comrades, never underestimate the power of bourgeois guilt. They have been plundering the world for so long that now they long for punishment. Since World War Two they have been obsessed with disaster. They eagerly await their state of California sliding off into the ocean, despite an absence of geological likelihood. They lust for Apocalypse, and embrace hysterical religious cults promising such things. They wallow in their postwar humiliations. Believe me, they will thank us for putting them out of their misery.

"Once they see which way the wind is blowing, Western Europe will fall to us without a fight. The Middle East likewise. We will dominate the Mediterranean and Atlantic. The Americans will make noises and do nothing. They have had it soft for too long, they are not prepared to make sacrifices. They have not had a war on their own soil for nearly a century and a half. Since World War Two, a war to them has meant sending their surplus Negroes and other minorities to die in squalid tropical nations while the rest of them take no notice and go on with life as usual. No American political party will make a move which means asking the voters to give up their automobiles and television sets. They are hopelessly weak and decadent, they are finished on the stage of history and it is time we let them know it." He looked around the table from face to face and blank masks looked back at him.

"To that end," he continued, "the ice bombs are on their way. They shall be in their proper positions within a few weeks. Their targets have been chosen and I have given orders to commence operations for affixing their booster rockets. Comrades, you have the rare privilege of being present at one of the great watersheds of history. Until now we have not succeeded in fully dominating one continent. Soon, we shall dominate this entire planet and our solar system!"

Once again the silence was deafening. This wholly extraordinary harangue was quite unlike anything that had ever been heard within the confines of the Politburo, and nobody seemed to want to make the first comment. Finally, it was Chekhov himself who spoke.

"Comrades, as you can see, Deputy Premier Nekrasov is quite mad. Overwork, no doubt." He stared at Nekrasov with glittering, ice-chip eyes. "He has certainly been undertaking labors outside the already quite demanding duties of his office. This is not the first time politico-military adventurism and neo-Stalinism have arisen among us, but it is certainly the first time that it has taken such virulent, indeed maniacal form. This man is about to plunge us into what is, despite his protestations, a nuclear holocaust which can have no winner. Let us put an end to this fantasy. I demand an immediate vote to strip Comrade Nekrasov of all official positions, including his Party membership."

Once again, there was silence. The real powers had not yet been heard from. Nekrasov looked at

Marshal Petrovich and nodded. Petrovich raised a big, meaty fist and every eye followed it and saw the thick thumb and middle finger come together. The sound of his finger-snap was as loud as a pistol-shot in the closed room.

Nekrasov smiled frostily at Chekhov as uniformed men burst into the room. "Comrade Chekhov, your letter of resignation will be sufficient to—" then he noticed that the uniforms were not KGB. His brain refused to function for a moment. Was this a foreign invasion? Western commandos staging a raid on the Kremlin? Then the fog in his mind cleared and he recognized the black uniforms of the Army's new, elite special forces.

Chekhov pointed at Nekrasov. "Arrest that man for high treason!"

Stunned, speechless, Nekrasov stood looking very old as a captain's hand clapped him on the shoulder, the gesture that cuts a Russian off from all human contact, makes him an unperson. Right now, Korsakov, millions of miles out in space was closer to his fellow Russians than was Sergei Nekrasov. He was taken from the room. Chekhov looked around the table.

"I take it that the vote against former comrade Nekrasov is unanimous?" There were no dissenting votes. He turned to stare at Baratynsky, who sat with his fingers laced across his large belly, impassive but very pale. "I shall require a full report from you concerning this incident. Leave out nothing, especially your own instigation."

"I merely obeyed my superior. Am I to be punished for that?"

"It is a good thing you have the habit of obeying your superior, Comrade Baratynsky. Your new superior, who runs the Bakunin power station in Okhotsk, is said to be an exacting man. You may leave." Baratynsky walked out, glad the orders weren't for execution, but with his grandiose dreams crumbling. Now Chekhov turned to Ryabkin.

"Comrade, you have done well, but you understand that your bureau is now under something of a cloud, since it was formerly the charge of Nekrasov. Your headquarters and principal offices are now being occupied by units of Marshal Petrovich's new elite guard. You and all your officers are to consider yourselves under temporary arrest until a thorough investigation can sort out the traitors. See to it." Ryabkin, who had not said a word during the meeting, nodded and left, well aware of how thin was the thread from which his life dangled.

After a few comments and a brief discussion, Chekhov dismissed the rest. "This matter will occupy us for some time to come, but the crisis is past. Be ready to be summoned to another extraordinary session at any time, though." They all left except for Petrovich and his aide. The two men sat back in their chairs and lit cigarettes.

"How many would-be Stalins does this make, Petrovich?" Chekhov asked.

The massive general shrugged. "Five or six since I made brigadier. This one came closest, though. He was the most dangerous."

"Very true. He might have pulled it off. I hate to think of the consequences. The man is utterly mad." He knocked an ash into the tray before him. "Not that his plan was all bad, mind you. It was a good one. But he refused to admit that the West would retaliate. His grasp of reality ended there."

Petrovich nodded. "He was right about space, too. That's where we must beat them."

"That sounds odd coming from an old foot-slogger like you."

"I recognize military reality. We are simply not going to do it with men and tanks and artillery. Not with ICBMs either. But out there, we can grasp the lead. They are rich, but this is costing them too much and they are too corrupt. It's our one chance." The Marshal lit a second cigarette from the coal of the first.

"I'm inclined to agree," Chekhov said. "I like his idea of a Minister of Science and Technology right here on the Politburo, to coordinate all our efforts in that area and keep the rest of us informed. Not that swine Baratynsky, though. I think I'll put Tarkovsky in the post, if I can pry him away from his rockets and get him here to Moscow."

They were interrupted by the arrival of a messenger. The young man saluted, clearly awed by the power of the men before him. "Highest priority message for Deputy Premier Nekrasov from Tsiolkovsky Space Center. His orders were to bring these to him no matter where he might be." The boy's voice trailed off on a note of uncertainty.

Petrovich smiled sourly. "Well, he won't be accepting any messages where he is now, son. Give it to the Premier."

Chekhov scanned the message. "A good thing this arrived now and not two hours ago. I must go to my office." He got up and left, trailed by two of the black-uniformed men. Until the KGB investigation was finished, he would go nowhere without a guard of these men.

In the office, the communications specialist on duty looked up as Chekhov entered. "Get me Tsiolkovsky Center," he ordered. When he had the Center on the line he dictated his orders, then he dismissed the communications man. When he was alone, Chekhov crossed to the Red Phone which was, on this side of the Atlantic, indeed red. He flipped it on and waited for the President of the United States to answer.

CHAPTER TWENTY-FIVE

PIONYER I, INTERPLANETARY SPACE

Korsakov decoded the message and stared at it in disbelief. It said: "Project Ivan the Terrible cancelled. Do not, repeat do not jettison icebergs. Allow on-site inspection by Americans. Further instructions will follow shortly. Signed: Premier Chekhov."

Kaminsky read the decoded message over Korsakov's shoulder. "Chekhov?" he said, a lifetime of political changes encapsulated in his upraised eyebrows.

"They want me to let the Americans aboard *my ship*!" Korsakov fumed.

"It isn't your choice, though," Kaminsky said. "Better signal them. They'll be in shooting range soon." Korsakov notified *Pionyer 2* and began calculating a course that would bring the four ships together without disaster. Then they received a signal from the Americans, on their own frequency. "Where did they get our frequency?" snarled Korsakov.

"From Moscow, obviously," Kaminsky said.

"While we've been up here playing hound-and-hares with the Americans, there must have been some high-level conversations going on down there."

Then a delightful female voice, devoid of accent, spoke in Russian from one of the American craft. "This is U.S. Interplanetary Probe 2. Request permission to board your ships in accordance with the provisions of the Geneva convention on mutual inspection of space vessels suspected of carrying mass destruction weapons. You are also invited to inspect our ships, should you wish to do so."

Korsakov turned to face Kaminsky. "I wonder if she's as pretty as her voice."

"I heard that," said the voice.

"Stand by to receive course-matching data," Korsakov said.

Another voice came across the radio, this time speaking terribly accented Russian. "This is U.S. Ship 1, and I already have the figures we need. Just stand by to be boarded."

"What kind of barbarous accent was that?" Kaminsky asked.

"Brooklyn," said the woman's voice.

Several hours later, the airlock hatch of *Pionyer I* swung open and the Americans entered the Russian ship. Korsakov saw Hoerter, whom he recognized, turn to a wild-bearded, wild-eyed man next to him. "Told you it was Korsakov," Hoerter said. The Russian crew came forward and shook hands with the American party, then they all had to listen while Korsakov made the pro forma protest that the Americans should ever even suspect a Soviet space vessel of carrying weapons, and what about all those rockets and heavy-duty lasers on the American ships, anyway?

"Perfectly legal," said Hoerter. "The convention bans weapons of *mass* destruction. Now, we all know that the real weapons out here are those icebergs you're towing."

"I know nothing of the sort," said Korsakov, whose English was excellent. "And you will have a difficult time convincing an international court that ice is a weapon. Especially—" he smiled, "if you intend to do any real deep-space work. You'll be transporting a lot of ice, you know."

Hoerter smiled back frostily. "As long as everybody knows what's going on, there's no problem." The Americans conducted their inspection of both Russian ships and then, according to agreement, invited the Russians to do the same. Korsakov longed mightily to get a look inside the American ships, but his instructions said he was not to. "We trust you," he said with heavy, Slavic irony.

Korsakov and Kaminsky escorted the Americans into the airlock separating the two vessels when the inspection was over. He nodded to Kaminksy and the Second Pilot shut the door on the Russian side. "This is the one place on my ship where there are no microphones," Korsakov said. The lean-faced American who had been introduced as Colonel Taggart closed the American hatch and they all shut down their recording systems. For the first time in mankind's history, people would speak together as sensible space dwellers, wondering what the maniac Earth people have been up to.

"What has been going on down there?" Korsakov said.

"We don't have the whole story either," Sam said, "but it seems that the lunatics were in charge for a while. We came within an inch of a space bombardment followed by a nuclear exchange. It looks as if a lid has been clamped on the situation for the moment."

"The nutcases were on your team," said Hoerter.

"*This* time," said the peculiar man named Ciano.

"*This* time," Korsakov repeated. They reopened the doors and went back into their ships. The marines Taggart and Flower were to ride back the rest of the way aboard *Pionyer 1* in accordance with instructions received from both governments. An American Shuttle would pick them up at Space Station *Volga*. They were to be kept isolated and not allowed to see the rest of the station.

CHAPTER TWENTY-SIX

TOKYO

Sam Taggart, now a full colonel, sat on the wooden porch and listened to the rain falling on the beautiful Japanese garden. He felt completely at peace—nobody seemed to want to kill him. He was a bit of a national hero these days, having taken part in the celebrated joint U.S.-Russian deep-space mission to a comet. He was even allowed, in fact encouraged to talk about it, as long as he stuck to the official version. For one thing, there had never been any Project Ivan the Terrible, nor any Project Bountyhunter. What he had taken part in, it seemed, was Project Argonaut. He had even gotten off a quip to the press about returning with the "golden fleece," waving at a huge pressroom-screen picture of the beautiful, gleaming icebergs parked in their cradles at *Volga*.

The project, according to the official version, had been the brainchild of those two architects of East-West accord, the President of the United States and the Premier of the U.S.S.R., and had been kept secret because of the Soviet Union's well-known policy of keeping space projects under wraps until successful completion.

Laine broke into his thoughts as she put a fresh pot of tea on the tray next to him and sat by his side. She smelled fresh from the bath and her hair was pinned up. She wore an after-bath kimono that was part of an elaborate wedding present from Goro Kuroda. They were ending their two-month honeymoon in Japan. "What have you been thinking?" she asked.

"About how things change. When we met, I was about to join the ranks of the unemployed and you were a hopeless refugee. We looked like life's prize losers. Now—" he waved a hand toward the garden and the future, "all sorts of things opening up for us; offers of jobs and positions everywhere."

"Which will you pick?" she asked, although she was sure which he would choose.

Shortly after their wedding, Sam and Laine had been asked to come to the office of General Hart, Secretary of Space Defense. Chambers, now also a general, was there. "Sam," Hart said, "your temporary assignment from CIA to this department expires at the end of this month." Sam said nothing, but waited for him to continue. "Take all the time you need to think about this, but the Space Marine Corps is now a permanent part of the service. General Chambers has agreed to serve as the first Commandant. There's a hell of a lot of work to be done, Sam, and quite frankly, you've demonstrated a rare ability for leadership under very difficult, even unprecedented conditions."

"I'd like you to be my number two man, Sam," said Chambers.

Sam knew better than to jump. "You probably know that I've been offered a Deputy Directorship in the Agency."

"You'll never get back into space that way,"

Chambers said. He knew which of Sam's buttons to push.

"On that subject," Sam pressed on, "would my duties be in space, at least for a large part of the time? I might as well tell you now that I'm not interested in a job on the ground while the rest of the Service is in space." Damn, it felt good to have people courting him for his services.

"We're asking you because of your proven abilities in space," Chambers said. "If we wanted a desk-bound bureaucrat we sure as hell could've found one with better qualifications than you."

"Point well taken," Sam said. "My duties?"

"The marines have to be trained where they'll be working. There'll be preliminary training and sorting on the ground, of course, but the rest will be in orbit, on the lunar base and on interplanetary ships."

Hart broke in. "We would also like to invite Dr. Tammsalu, ah, Major Tammsalu-Taggart, to accept a permanent appointment with this Department as a staff scientist in the Astrophysics Branch. Dr. Ciano has already agreed to serve as my senior science adviser with a reserve rank of brigadier, although his main interests these days seem to be in the private sector. If you accept, Dr. Taggart, you'll be named his deputy with the option of remaining on active duty or going on reserve status."

Laine smiled very slightly. "Let me think about it. My husband and I must, of course, talk this over."

"Of course," Chambers took up the baton, "it's no longer practical to regard space as merely a place for a tour of duty. It's going to be a place to live. That means provisions for married personnel such as living quarters, family allowances—hell, we're already planning schools for people raising families up there."

"In case you were wondering," Hart said, "the other marine vets have already signed up. After all, how often does anyone get a chance for instant seniority in a new service?"

Sam and Laine had laughed about it all the way to the airport. "I was expecting them to force us to sign at gunpoint!"

"They might try it yet. Let's play hard-to-get for a while."

Now, in the garden of the Japanese Inn, it was time to decide. "I know you want to take the Department position," Sam said.

"And I know you don't want to work at a desk for any salary. Shall we take them up on it?"

Sam reached into his kimono and drew out a piece of hotel stationery. "I've already written up a message. We can send it from the hotel desk."

She took another slip of paper from her own kimono. "Let's see how close your wording is to mine." They scanned the two papers.

"Almost identical," Sam said. They sat and sipped tea for a long time, then they went to send their message.

Elsewhere on the same island, Goro Kuroda was emerging from the entrance hallway of the Prime Minister's residence at Nagata-cho. He climbed into his bulletproof limousine and settled himself comfortably. The conference had gone much more smoothly than he had expected.

He had disliked holding back from the Prime Minister, a man whose candor was legendary, but Goro had given his word. If a man was not as good as his word, he was nothing. Besides, it wasn't as though he was holding back something vital to Japan's national interest in space.

What he did tell Prime Minister Isaka was sufficient. It was enough to convince him that he must fight fiercely to invigorate Japan's space program, especially the manned program. The Prime Minister had been completely in agreement that resource-poor Japan vitally needed access to the virtually unlimited resources of the solar system. They were claimed, as yet, by no other nation and all that was needed to gain access to them was technological knowhow, the financial means to apply the technology and, of course, the national will.

Kuroda informed the Prime Minister that the leaders of the Association of Industries for Space Exploration, which he had headed for the last year, were prepared to make major commitments if the government would take the necessary lead role. There was some mention of a new agency to coordinate the industrialization of space, an excellent place to start. It was this kind of business-government cooperation, almost unknown in the West, which gave Japan a great advantage in such an ambitious venture.

Now relaxing in his limousine, Kuroda reflected upon his brief trip to Space Station *Midway* for the *in situ* testing of the water separation system for *Bountyhunter* 1 and 2. Or, rather, *Argo* 1 and 2. It had been enjoyable, but in the future he would have little time to indulge himself. His son and daughter had gone with him into space; they would be going back.

MOSCOW

The immense ballroom glittered as it had in the days of the Tsars. Premier Chekhov was throwing a Kremlin party for the crews of *Pionyer* 1 and 2. Most of the Politburo members were present, along with the ranking members of the Ministry for Science and Technology. Just about everybody who really counted in the U.S.S.R. was there. That made it a small party by Western standards. Korsakov got the Lenin medal first, along with a bearhug from the Premier. The rest of the crew followed. The Premier proposed a toast in honor of the daring crew who had paved the way to the rest of the Solar System. He said nothing about any American involvement. Tarkovsky, the new Minister for Science and Technology, possibly soon to occupy a place on the Politburo, was handed the microphone.

Tarkovsky spoke glowingly if somewhat inebriatedly of the U.S.S.R.'s future in space. He spoke of the construction of permanent Lunar settlements, of the building of a catapult system utilizing solar energy on the Moon to fling material to yet another project, the L-5 colony program. He spoke of industrial solar power satellites and a series of manned flights to Mars. He even spoke of terraforming Venus by first seeding its extremely dense atmosphere with microrganisms for the dissociation of carbon dioxide. Most of these projects were incredibly ambitious for the limited resources of the financially-distressed Soviet Union, but just now they enjoyed a lead over the rest of the world in a propulsion system for interplanetary travel and they fully intended to take advantage of that lead. They would fully realize the dream of Constantin Tsiolkovsky. This was one race they could not afford to lose.

PARIS

The second extraordinary session of the European Space Agency (ESA) was convened, like the first, at its headquarters in Paris. It was to last for two days. This was the third day and no end in sight. It might last weeks. Everybody complained, but there are far worse things than extra days spent in Paris.

The first executive session had been held two weeks earlier, and it had been decided that the program was in need of a dramatic shoring up. The secret U.S.-U.S.S.R. mission had stunned everybody. Well, if the Americans wanted to play games like that, so could the Europeans.

The real fun began at the second meeting. Each of the contributing nations wanted a maximum share of the benefits with a minimum participation in the financing. The countries that had been contributing the lion's share to the budget wanted to see their generosity reflected in the awarding of contracts. The countries making smaller contributions wanted a more equitable distribution of contracts and benefits.

Over everything hung the specter of ELDO, the European Launcher Development Organization of the sixties, which after several years of expensive efforts had failed to make a successful launch of their giant rocket. It was said that the sections of the rocket, made in different countries, did not even fit together.

By the end of the second week of the proposed two-day meeting, it was decided that contracts would not be awarded in proportion to budgetary contributions but in kind, according to national technological capabilities. The Germans would contribute and build the ion engine, the French would contribute the nuclear powerhouse, etc. Thus, cranking and puffing, but determined not to let the upstart nations gain ascendency and prestige over them, the Europeans lurched into the race.

DENVER

Ugo was gesturing wildly, spilling wine in the process. "I'm telling you, folks, this is just the beginning! I'll hold down this job for a while, sure. But that's just to make sure that the U.S. gets off to a good start. After that, I'm going into business for myself. Me and Fred, that is."

Sam and Laine were settled into the conversation pit of the little chalet, Fred was sprawled in front of the fire, and Ugo was pacing as usual. "This is the big plan you've been dropping heavy hints about for months?" Sam asked.

"That's right. Me and Ian McNaughton are planning to form a big space exploitation operation. That is, I'll join as senior partner as soon as I resign from the Department in a few years."

"You mean after you've had most of your expensive R and D work paid for by the taxpayers?" Sam demanded.

"Hey!" Ugo said innocently, "I never thought of that. Not a bad idea, though. Thanks, Sam."

"And did you get Mr. Kuroda to go along with you?" Laine asked.

"He's playing cagey, but I'm pretty sure he'll play ball." Ugo had lost none of his sublime confidence.

"I've got our housing assignments arranged," Fred contributed. "Ugo and I are going to have quarters in the VIP section not far from yours. Just think of it: you'll never lack for his company."

Ugo walked over to the picture window that went from floor to ceiling and stared up into the clear Rocky Mountain sky. He flung his arms wide with exuberance, splashing wine over several paintings. "Hey out there!" he shouted happily, "Here we come!"

**For
Fiction with Real Science In It,
and Fantasy That Touches
The Heart of The Human Soul ...**

Baen Books bring you Poul Anderson, Marion Zimmer Bradley, C.J. Cherryh, Gordon R. Dickson, David Drake, Robert L. Forward, Janet Morris, Jerry Pournelle, Fred Saberhagen, Michael Reaves, Jack Vance ... all top names in science fiction and fantasy, plus new writers destined to reach the top of their fields. For a free catalog of all Baen Books, send three 22-cent stamps, plus your name and address, to

*Baen Books
260 Fifth Avenue, Suite 3S
New York, N.Y. 10001*

HAVE YOU FOUND YOURSELF ENJOYING A LOT OF BAEN BOOKS LATELY?

We at Baen Books like science fiction with real science in it and fantasy that reaches to the heart of the human soul — and we think a lot of you do, too. Why not let us know? We'll award $25 and a dozen Baen paperbacks of your choice to the reader who best tells us what he or she likes about Baen Books. We reserve the right to quote any or all of you...and we'll feature the best quote in an advertisement in <u>American Bookseller</u> and other magazines! Contest closes March 15, 1986. All letters should be addressed to Baen Books, 8 W. 36th St., New York, N.Y. 10018.

VERNOR VINGE
THE PEACE WAR

55965-6 • 400 pp. • $3.50

BAEN BOOKS